PAIN IS
THE BEST PERSUADER

Someone groaned and I looked around. When I turned back to Georgie he had a small gun in his hand.

"Georgie, that's just stupid," I said, and keeping my eyes on his face, I suddenly went low and threw a roll block at him, hoping I would be able to come in beneath his gun. He fired as my shoulder slammed into him. I felt the heat as the bullet passed just above my back. The second time I bounced into him he dropped the gun.

I kicked it across the room. Georgie was looking as though nothing had just happened. I studied his face. All that showed was viciousness, and the only way to get the truth out of him was pain.

"WHO'S DOMINGO?" I shouted into his ear and at the same time reached up between his legs and squeezed.

Other Avon Books by
L. A. Morse

THE OLD DICK

THE BIG ENCHILADA

A Sam Hunter Mystery

L.A. MORSE

▲ AVON
PUBLISHERS OF BARD, CAMELOT, DISCUS AND FLARE BOOKS

THE BIG ENCHILADA is an original publication of Avon
Books. This work has never before appeared in book form.

AVON BOOKS
A division of
The Hearst Corporation
959 Eighth Avenue
New York, New York 10019

Copyright © 1982 by L. A. Morse, Inc.
Published by arrangement with the author
Library of Congress Catalog Card Number: 81-66475
ISBN: 0-380-77602-2

First Avon Printing, February, 1982

AVON TRADEMARK REG. U. S. PAT. OFF. AND IN
OTHER COUNTRIES, MARCA REGISTRADA, HECHO EN
U. S. A.

Printed in the U. S. A.

WFH 10 9 8 7 6 5 4 3 2 1

ONE

It was another stifling hot summer day. A sulphurous yellow haze hung over most of Los Angeles. From my window I could see the cars backed up about two miles at one of the freeway interchanges. Down below the winos were shuffling around looking for some patch of shade where they could escape the sun. Even the packs of kids that would usually be breaking windshields or ripping antennas off of parked cars were not on the streets today. It was that hot.

As I watched my old fan rotate and attempt to push the hot air from one corner to another, I thought it would be a good idea to take a vacation from all of this for a while. A couple of weeks on a beach in Mexico, and the worst of the hot spell would probably be over, and I would be able to get some work done. If it got a little bit cooler, I might also have some work to do.

The lettering on the door said SAM HUNTER, INVESTI-GATIONS, but there had not been much to investigate lately. The law about no-fault divorces had cut into my business, and the same with all the computers they were using for credit checks. But it could have been worse. There were still nasty people who wanted dirty jobs done. They wanted the goods in order to get an especially juicy alimony settlement or to do a little civilized blackmail. And that was fine with me. The nastier and the dirtier they were, the more I would charge them, and they didn't have any choice because I usually turned up just as much dirt on them. So I was working less, but my income was just about the same. It wasn't one of your noble callings, but most of the time it suited me all right, and best of all I was on my own, I didn't have to account to any son of a bitch for what I was doing, and if I wanted to tell someone to fuck off, I did just that.

I had a few cases going on, but they were strictly back burner stuff for a while. If I took off for a couple of weeks, that would probably be just enough time for them to come to a boil, and I could finish them off quick. I don't care how messy an assignment is, it's the waiting around for something to happen that gets to me.

So I had pretty well decided that I would go somewhere south of Mazatlán and was considering if I should take Maria with me. She'd been with me about eight months as my secretary, and so far I didn't mind having her around. She was dynamite to look at, and she had the good sense to keep her distance until I wanted her for something. What she had to do, she did right, and she didn't try to do any more. She didn't try to dig herself in and get a stranglehold on me and the office. There were women who had tried to do that to me, who thought they could improve upon the way I did things, but they didn't stay around long. So far Maria was okay. She also spoke Spanish and was not a bad lay, so I thought I might as well take her with me.

I was about to call Maria in to tell her we were going to Mexico when I heard her say something like, "You can't go in there."

Whatever she had said was obscured by the door to my office flying open and slamming against the wall. Even though the door was unlocked, my visitor had not bothered to use the doorknob but had pushed it open with such force that the jamb had splintered and the door itself had nearly been ripped off its hinges.

It happened so quickly that I had no time to react when the doorway filled with the biggest, ugliest man I had ever seen. He must have been more than six-eight and weighed nearly five hundred pounds. His shoulders touched either side of the door, and he must have been sixty inches around the chest and seventy-five around the waist. All of his features were grotesquely over-sized except for his eyes, which were little black slits nearly lost in the masses of flesh of his overhanging forehead and puffy cheeks. His forehead and jowls were covered with dozens of ugly red warts, as were the backs of the largest hands I have ever seen. They looked like giant yellow sponges on the ends of his arms. They were so large that at first I didn't even notice that he was carrying a gun in his right hand. It was a police .38, which is a fairly large weapon, but it looked like a child's water pistol in his giant fist.

He moved into the center of the room, his vast bulk dwarfing everything in it.

I had stood up by this time, angry at the way he had entered my office, angry as hell at him pointing a gun at me, and getting madder every second looking at his ugly hog's face.

Before I could say anything, a kind of gurgling sound came from somewhere in his face, and I heard, "Stay away from Domingo."

"Who are you and what do you want?" Not the best line, but it was all I came up with.

His expression remained unchanged, but that same gurgling voice coming from far away, deep inside all that flesh, said, "You heard me. I had a message to give. I gave it. Stay away from Domingo."

I was really angry then. As others have learned to their misfortune, I do not take kindly to orders, no matter who gives them. This time, however, the size of my visitor, and the size of his gun, suggested that some caution was in order. Especially if I was going to find out what the hell was going on. I had never heard of any Domingo, but obviously Domingo had heard of me. Figuring that subtlety would be lost on the ape in my office, I was very straight.

"I don't know what you're talking about. I don't know any Domingo. Who sent you with the message?"

He had not moved an inch from where he had settled in the center of the room, but he seemed to be tensing his muscles for the effort of turning his body around. I noticed that his lips hardly moved when he spoke.

"Last time. If you want to stay healthy, stay away from Domingo."

He slowly turned and started to move toward the door.

I moved quickly around my desk and started to grab his arm.

"Listen, you ugly son of a bitch—"

Before I could finish my sentence he had whirled around with a speed I thought impossible for him. With the thumb and first two fingers of his left hand, he grabbed me at the base of my jaw. With seemingly no effort he lifted me about a foot off the ground so that I was slightly over his head. He

looked up at me with the small black slits in his face, and a
sound came from inside him that I suppose was meant to be a
laugh. Then, as though he was tired of the sport, he threw me
through the air for about ten feet, where I crashed into the
wall. I hit with the back of my shoulder, and it felt like I'd
been slammed with a sledgehammer. I went momentarily
numb, and then my back started throbbing.

Now, I'm more than six foot three and weigh more than
two hundred pounds, but he handled me with no trouble at
all. In fact I don't think he was even straining. As if to make
that point, he put two fingers under the edge of my desk.
With about as much exertion as you would use to brush away
a fly, he raised his hand. The desk flew three feet in the air,
flipped, and crashed upside down with a splintering sound.
The desk was a large one, of solid oak, but he treated it like it
was cardboard.

With that display he turned and left the office.

I was standing up, still a bit dazed from being thrown
against the wall, when Maria rushed in and threw her arms
around me with a sob.

She was shaking and badly frightened, but that only served
to make her more attractive. She had some Indian blood in
her which gave her a light olive complexion, and she had
shiny black hair which she wore long. She had a full, rich
body which she displayed to good advantage. That day she
wore a very short skirt that showed almost all of her long,
well-shaped legs. She had on a thin blouse that was open
except where it was tied beneath her large firm breasts. She
was wearing no bra—she never did—and her dark nipples
were easily visible beneath the semi-transparent material.

Holding her close, I felt the musky scent of her hair begin
to have its effect. She was still crying, and I could see she was
badly frightened, but that was all right. I've found that
nothing makes a woman readier for sex than a good scare.

I turned her head up so that she was looking at me.

"Sam, are you hurt?" she said between sobs.

I didn't answer her. Instead I kissed her hard on the mouth.
After a second she responded, and my hands went to the knot
in her blouse, untying it. I covered her magnificent melon
breasts, feeling the nipples grow hard in the palms of my
hands.

I felt her hand slide up my leg. She quickly unzipped my fly and put her hand around me.

I put my hand under her skirt and felt the heat rising off her. I put my hand under the flimsy material of her panties and tore them from her.

I entered her quickly and took her standing up against the wall. I bounced her roughly into the wall, my hands squeezing, digging into her breasts.

Soon the nature of her sobs changed. She was no longer frightened. Her fear turned into mindless ecstacy as I slammed her again and again.

When I was through I let her down slowly. She slid down the wall until she was sitting on the floor, skirt above her waist, legs spread wide, totally spent.

I zipped up my pants and left the office.

I wanted to get something to eat.

I also wanted some information. About Domingo. Whoever or whatever that was.

My vacation would have to wait. Until after I found Domingo.

At the very least, Domingo owed me a new desk.

TWO

Sitting in the back booth of Luis's burrito place, I was feeling a bit better. I had eaten a couple of one-pound chile relleno burritos that were so hot they drained my sinuses, scalded my throat, and temporarily turned the tendons in my elbows and knees to water. But they filled up my belly and helped to clear my head. A couple of Dos Equis beers, and the fire in my mouth had died down, and my initial anger had also cooled.

I gave it some thought. Did I really care about what had happened? My office and my dignity had been messed up, but neither of those were worth a hell of a lot. At least my office sure wasn't, and my dignity wasn't such a precious commodity either, but—shit—there was something at stake.

When I was a young kid my father once sat me down for a serious talk, probably the only one we ever had. He looked at me for a long time, and I remember thinking he seemed kind of sad. "Don't let them fuck you over," he said, "don't ever let them fuck you over. There are a lot of assholes out there who, because they've got more money or more muscle or more fire power, think they can make everybody play their game. And mostly they're right, and everybody does play their game, but there's no way that they can deal with the man who doesn't give a shit about their game—who plays his own game in his own way. They're so used to getting their own way that when someone doesn't jump when they say jump, they don't know what to do. If he doesn't drool when they shake the carrot, they can't run him. The man that won't jump is a dangerous man because he's his own man. It's not a question of manhood or pride or any of that shit; it's a matter of survival. If you let them stick it to you once, then you're theirs, and you're playing their game. But the man who won't take any shit—and who doesn't give a shit—is a free man, no matter what happens."

12

My father was a straight man in a crooked town. A week after he talked to me he was killed. I don't know if he died a free man or not, but I do know he died. Besides his last advice, his legacy to me consisted of a dog-eared copy of *Moby Dick* and a book on how to win at poker. I wasn't sure what happened to the books, but I always remembered what he said. For a long time I never really understood it—what kid would?—but then I went to Viet Nam.

Somehow or other I found myself in military intelligence. Some people say those two words are contradictory, and they may be right, but I had a pretty good time learning how to conduct an investigation and assess information. I had a better time, though, when I wasn't working. I was living with a Vietnamese girl. She was the only woman I ever lived with, and the only one I ever wanted to live with. She was delicately beautiful, serenely composed, and genuinely tender. While physically very different, Maria reminded me of her in a lot of ways, but I tried not to think about that too much.

I had planned to take the girl back stateside with me when my tour was up. At least I had planned that until four army punks got drunk and decided they wanted a woman and she happened to be nearby. She never regained consciousness.

It hit me harder than anything in my life, but I was still playing by the book in those days. I conducted the investigation myself and built an air-tight case against the four punks, but it turned out that one of them belonged to a congressman and another to a general. So, in spite of my protests, the matter was allowed to drop quietly because there was "insufficient evidence," because nobody needed a scandal, and because, anyway, who cared what happened to a slope? I finally got my father's message. The four who did it thought the whole thing was pretty funny . . . right up to the time I got to them and made sure they wouldn't ever again think anything was funny.

Then the army started to pay attention to me. They wanted to put it to me but decided it might backfire, and so they sent me home with nothing but an education in the way things were in the world and a cold, hard, empty space inside me. They also made sure I'd have a lot of trouble ever getting a job, and so I decided to make use of all the things they had taught me. It had worked out all right, I guess.

I shook my head. Christ, I thought, being thrown against

the wall must have jarred something loose to send me on that trip down memory lane. Fuck it. Whatever the reasons, I knew I couldn't let the episode in my office pass.

I thought about it. Domingo meant nothing to me. I kind of had the nagging feeling I had seen the word somewhere recently, but as hard as I tried to place it, it kept eluding me. I knew there was no point in pressing it. If it was there, it would have to surface by itself.

When Luis brought me another beer, for no particular reason I asked him if he had ever heard of anyone called Domingo.

"Domingo? I do not think so, Señor Hunter. The only Domingo I know is Sunday. That is the Spanish word for Sunday."

"Yeah, Luis, I know. You've never heard of a club or a gang or anything like that called Domingo?"

Luis screwed up his face as though he was thinking real hard, but I knew that all his brains were in his fat belly. "No, Señor Hunter, I do not know anything like that. All I know is cooking, and I do not get into trouble."

"Who said anything about trouble?"

"I know you, Señor Hunter, and if you are looking for someone, there is trouble." He picked up the empty bottles and waddled back to his stove.

I kind of liked Luis. He wasn't very bright, but he sure could cook. And this time he was right, there was going to be trouble. I just didn't know who was involved or what it was about. But I began to think it must be pretty important to go to all that trouble to tell me to stay away from something I didn't even know about. That felt like it meant big money, and that began to look like it might be worth my while.

The more I thought about it, the stupider this whole thing seemed to be. If that gorilla had not come to warn me off, I would have been on my way to Mexico for a few weeks of fishing and screwing. Now, because of that warning, I was determined to find out what the hell it was all about.

Of course, that might be the point of it. A setup of some kind. Get me involved in something that's going to mean trouble for me. Set me up as a fall guy to cover up for someone else or to get revenge for something I had done. It was possible, but I didn't like it. To set me up this way as a fall guy seemed too uncertain. If someone wanted to do that, there must be a dozen surer ways.

Revenge was a better possibility. From Viet Nam onwards I had made more than a few enemies. I didn't keep track, but there were a lot of them. And a lot of them hated me enough to kill me—the ones I had sent to prison, the ones I had smashed up, the ones whose sweet deals I had soured. There were a lot of them, all right, but they'd probably want to get me in a more direct way. A shotgun blast in the stomach, maybe. Or they would have had that ape finish me off. The way things had gone, he could have done it easily, but he obviously had instructions to be gentle. No, it didn't look like revenge was the reason.

That meant one thing, though I sure didn't see what it could be. In something that I was doing I must be getting close to someone or something that was supposed to stay hidden. It had to be something like that, but the cases I was working on seemed to be straightforward.

Clarissa Acker wanted to find out what was going on with her husband, Simon Acker. She wasn't exactly sure what use she would make of the information—divorce, blackmail, power, revenge—but she first wanted to satisfy her curiosity. As she had said, "I know that son of a bitch is up to something, and I want to know what." Obviously, theirs was not a storybook relationship, unless your storybooks are by Strindberg.

Simon Acker was the president of a small pharmaceutical supply house, and apparently fairly well off. It looked like his wife had a pretty good time of it, with a huge house in Bel Air, servants, exclusive country clubs, and nearly all the money she could spend. Acker made few demands on her, and she could do just about whatever she wanted. To me it didn't seem like such a bad deal, but after fifteen years of marriage, I guess it didn't look that way to Clarissa Acker.

She really didn't seem to care about the money and all that other shit, but she did care about the fact that she hated her husband and that he hated her. The reasons no longer made any difference, but the hatred did, and it was the kind of hatred that can be a much stronger bond than any amount of affection. She and her husband were locked in a struggle, each clawing and scratching at the other, each determined to

have the final scratch. It was a crazy, no-win situation, and
Clarissa Acker had finally had enough. She wanted to get out,
but she also wanted to get even. Not a nice picture, but it was
one that I was used to.

The surprising thing was that I quite liked Clarissa Acker.
This was a little unusual, as my clients are generally not very
likeable; if they were, they probably wouldn't hire me. But
she had a kind of rough honesty that I didn't see very often
and that I found attractive. Her attitude to her situation
didn't bother me; if anything, her openness about her motives
made her more attractive. Most people who wanted me to do
something dirty tried to hide behind some self-serving bullshit that maybe fooled them but didn't fool me. Not Clarissa
Acker: "Let's bury the bastard," she had said. Nice clear
instructions.

She was a good-looking woman, and was also pretty
intelligent, but she had a volatile personality. She liked her
pleasure and was open about it, and she was equally open
about her displeasure and anger. It was not in her nature to
hide her feelings—whatever they were—beneath the surface.
I thought she probably would be a good friend, a better lover,
and an enemy to reckon with. I don't have to like my clients
to do my job—and I usually don't—but I liked her, and I
wanted to do what I could for her.

I didn't know if it was what she wanted, but so far my
investigation had turned up only one interesting thing. However, it was very interesting. Up front, Simon Acker appeared to be a dry, reserved, priggish sort of man. Very cool,
very efficient, very meticulous—the exact opposite of his
wife. A couple of years back he had taken over Medco
Pharmaceutical Supplies, a small company that manufactured
and processed chemicals to be used in products put out by the
big drug companies. I didn't know much about it, but Medco
probably wasn't a very big operation, even though it was big
enough to give Acker a giant-sized salary that he spent pretty
freely.

All that was on the surface, and on the surface Simon
Acker was a dull man. However, after I had been following
him around for a while, I discovered that he kept a little
apartment in West L.A. that no one knew about. One day
when he was at Medco, I used a skeleton key to get in, and
another side of dull Mr. Acker was revealed. The apartment

was your typical furnished place, if you happened to rent in a Gothic castle. The walls and ceiling were painted black. Heavy velvet drapes covered the windows. Decoration was provided by a collection of whips and copies of medieval weapons that were mounted on the walls. The closets contained several robes and cloaks that were also in keeping with the medieval motif. Acker was quite a history buff.

Under surveillance, I saw several tall blondes go into the apartment at various times of the day and night. They were obviously prostitutes, and they always came out looking somewhat the worse for wear. Fifty dollars to one of them bought me the info that Simon Acker was a peculiar man. He would dress up in one of his robes, continually mutter and rave something about "The Power," and beat the girls until he climaxed. Even though he paid high for their services, very few girls returned for a second engagement.

I hadn't told my client about this yet. It was good stuff, but I'd thought I would stay with it a little longer to see what else developed. Nothing developed. Acker stopped going to his apartment, and his life again became exactly what it appeared to be on the surface. He had gotten so careful, in fact, that I suspected he knew he was being watched.

I was pretty sure I hadn't tipped him, but I thought his wife might have. Clarissa Acker was by no means a stupid woman—except maybe where her husband was concerned— but she did have a temper, and her husband, after fifteen years of practice, would know just the way to make her explode. I figured that during an explosion she told Acker about me. That would account for his recent caution; if I was right, it meant I wouldn't get anything more on him, and that was why I had decided to let it go for a while, to see if his confidence would return and he'd get careless again. But if I was right, it also meant that he knew about me and could have sent the warning. I decided I'd have to look into it.

I had another domestic case that was even more charming than the Acker one—a case of suspected patricide-to-be. George Lansing owned record stores, a chain of fast-service restaurants, and bits of a dozen small companies in the entertainment field. He was loaded, and his only son, George II, had been heavily indulged. Not surprisingly, like most spoiled brats of Hollywood families, he was a disaster. Not content with an Alfa Romeo, unlimited credit at the best

stores, and an allowance that was larger than what I earn in a
good month, two years ago he decided he wanted it all and
made plans to kill his father. The attempt was pure fantasy,
involving a phony kidnapping and hired gunmen, and it might
have worked if the kid had not read too many comic books.
As it was, it failed completely, and the father ended up paying
off the hit men. If Lansing had any sense, he would have
broken the kid's neck or thrown him in the slammer. But he
wouldn't press charges and all was forgiven. Shit, he didn't
even reduce the punk's allowance.

Everything was fine for a while, and then, surprising only
his father, the kid got heavily into dope and started hanging
around with other rich kids who were involved in some kind
of black magic thing. A couple of months ago Lansing started
to receive vaguely threatening letters and packages containing gutted cats, goats' heads, and things like that. He was
worried that maybe all of this was leading up to another
assassination attempt, and he wanted me to head it off. I told
him the best way to do that was to take the kid out into the
ocean and drown him, but he wouldn't hear of it and still
thought he could win Junior over. I was just supposed to find
out what was going on.

I started to make some inquiries among George II's
friends, but they closed up pretty quick and got hostile. They
all seemed to be like the kid—too much money, with brains
rotted from dope—and I would have enjoyed smashing them
around a bit, but a good opportunity had never presented
itself.

I had even spent about five days staking out the Lansings'
Beverly Hills house, to see if I could get a line on what was
going on, but nothing seemed to be working, and I had to
think of something else. There didn't seem to be much
urgency since the father was leaving the country for a few
weeks and I doubted anything more would happen until he
came back.

Still, George II's friends knew who I was, and that strange
warning about Domingo could fit in with the comic book
black magic that they practiced. But why bother? I wasn't any
threat to them. It didn't make any sense, but nothing those
degenerate brats did made any sense, so I'd probably have to
check it out. Maybe this time I could give them a bit of my
magic, two hands-full.

My last case wasn't even a case. I ordinarily wouldn't have bothered about it, but it was a favor for a friend of mine, Mel Perdue, who lived up in Oregon. About two and a half years ago his daughter, Linda, who was not quite fourteen at the time, had run away from home and come to L.A. This is so common as to be a cliché, but it's never common for the families involved, and it shattered the Perdues. At first they occasionally heard from her, but then nothing. They became more and more worried, and they tried everything—police, social agencies, advertising—but there was no trace of her. Mel made several trips down here to look for her, and on the last one we happened to run into each other. He told me the story and asked me to help. I didn't see what I could do, and told him so, but he kept begging me. He even wanted to hire me, and I finally agreed to look into it, even though I thought there was no chance that I'd come up with anything. Two years is a long time in a town that can gobble people up and never spit them out. Perdue wanted to pay me, but I told him there'd be no charge unless I found something that would take a lot of time to follow up.

I usually don't give freebies, but it seemed to be such a lost cause, and I wasn't very busy anyway—and, hell, he was kind of a friend—that there I was going around with a snapshot of a pretty, blond, innocent-looking thirteen-year-old girl, who, if she was still around, probably looked like some sci-fi mutant.

Surprisingly enough, I managed to get a line on her. It seemed to lead to a porno filmmaker named Starr Monroe. I had a couple of sessions with him, but he didn't seem to know anything. As far as I could tell, he had no reason to lie to me since I only wanted information and I didn't care how he made his living, and I let it drop. Only recently did I meet a girl who had known Linda and who thought that she had been in some movies for Monroe, but I hadn't followed it up. There seemed to be no point. The girl also thought that Linda had gone to work at a place called the Black Knight—some kind of club. Linda had said she was onto a good thing there, and seemed happy about the chance. Her friend had left town soon after that, and they had lost touch.

I had never heard of the Black Knight and started asking around. Most people didn't know anything about it, but the few that did got very evasive and nervous, and looked at me in a funny way. I gathered that it was a private club that maybe dealt in kinky sex, but I couldn't get much beyond that, no matter where I asked, and I had pretty well decided to forget about it.

So, even though there seemed to be nothing to connect Linda Perdue with the warning I received, people knew I was asking about her and Monroe and that club, and it didn't seem like I could write off that angle either. Shit.

My review had gotten me nowhere. It didn't look very likely, but Domingo could be tied in with any of my cases— Acker, Lansing, or Perdue. Or it could have nothing to do with any of them. It was time to find out. Anything was better than going around in circles. If you want answers, you have to ask questions. You have to push if you want to find out if there's any substance there.

I was ready to start pushing.

I paid Luis and bought a pack of Gitanes, which he carried especially for me.

I put one of the fat cigarettes in my mouth and inhaled deeply, the smoke of the black tobacco filling my lungs.

I stepped out into the shimmering afternoon heat. The pavement felt soft as I went to my car.

I felt pretty good.

I was moving again.

THREE

I had decided I would pay a visit to Clarissa Acker to make sure that my suspicions about her letting her husband know about my investigation were correct. I didn't call before I left. I usually don't, having found that it's often better to arrive unannounced.

Driving through the winding, tree-lined streets up into the hills of Bel Air, the temperature seemed to get a little cooler. The suffocating heat that sat on the rest of Los Angeles was not as severe here, seemingly fanned down by the flap of hundred dollar bills. But the sky was the same dirty yellow, and the air smelled just as foul. Even in L.A. money could buy only so much.

My old heap was really out of place among the seven- and eight-hundred-thousand-dollar mansions with their Continentals and Rolls-Royces and thirty-thousand-dollar sports cars. Even the servants drove better cars than mine. But I wasn't going to play the Detroit sucker game of a new car every two years—each new car more expensive and of poorer quality than the old one. I'd drive my car as long as it ran. When it stopped, I'd buy something that did run. Nothing more.

The Acker house was located on one of the dead-end streets near the top of the hill. From the street the house didn't look very large or very impressive. I had an idea about what it must have cost, though, and I'd have trouble making even the tax payments on the place.

I parked on the street in front of the house and walked up the long circular driveway. The house looked quiet, and I didn't hear any response inside when I rang the bell. I tried a couple of more times, but nothing happened. This was looking like one time I should have called first.

I was just turning to leave when I heard footsteps through

the thick door. It was opened by Clarissa Acker herself. It took her a few seconds to recognize me.

"Mr. Hunter, I didn't expect you. You should have called first. Come in. All the help is gone. My husband thinks we should have lots of servants, but I can't get used to the idea, and I always let them go early, before they can get any work done. Isn't that something? So I was lying by the pool, wondering what the fuck I was doing lying by the pool just like every other Bel Air rich bitch. Am I a Bel Air rich bitch? God, I hope not." She smiled.

"I don't know," I said. "Bel Air rich bitches usually hump their gardeners while they're lying by the pool. Is that what you were doing?"

"Oh, shit! I was thinking about it. We've got this beautiful little Mexican—just a kid—and I've been wondering if I could seduce him. Hunter, I'm doomed!"

I smiled and followed her inside. As I said, I found her a very likeable woman, likeable and a little surprising. She was good-looking, in her late thirties, and well-taken-care-of in the way that a lot of money can do, but I didn't think she cared anything at all about the money. She was small, but her body was nicely fleshed and rounded. She was wearing a kaftan that was cut very low in front, and she didn't seem to have anything on under it. Her hair was a soft brown, and it set off a smooth dark tan that betrayed a lot of hours by the pool. Her features were a little too strong for her to be considered pretty, but her eyes displayed a humor and self-honesty that gave her an odd kind of beauty. As far as I could tell, the only thing wrong with Clarissa Acker was her self-destructive relationship with her husband, and maybe I could help her there.

Following her down the two steps that led from the foyer to the living room, any idea of the house being small vanished. The living room was large enough for a tennis court with probably a putting green on the side. One whole wall was glass and looked out on a swimming pool that was nearly large enough for Olympic trials. Beyond that was the edge of the hill, and spread out below was a large piece of Los Angeles.

The furnishings were mostly leather, fur, and stainless steel. They revealed nothing except a lot of money and the taste of some faggotty decorator. The room was not intended to be comfortable, only impressive.

She caught my expression and laughed. "Yeah. It's really a dump, isn't it? My husband's idea."

She motioned me to sit down on the couch. She sat two cushions away and faced me, curling one leg beneath the other. I thought there was a shadow of uneasiness behind her eyes.

"Well, Mr. Hunter, did you find something? Did you find out what my husband is doing?"

"Yes and no, Mrs. Acker. I've been having some trouble lately."

"Trouble? I thought you were supposed to be such a hot-shit detective." She seemed to be unusually uncomfortable.

"I'm pretty good. Except sometimes I need some cooperation from my client At a minimum, a little secrecy is required. If a client wants me to catch someone red-handed, it generally helps if the target doesn't know I'm watching him."

"What do you mean?" There was a small frown.

"My investigation started off pretty well. I found that your husband keeps an apartment in West L.A."

"He what?"

"It's decorated in a most unusual way—all black satin and whips and chains. He uses it to entertain highly specialized professional ladies. I imagine this is just the kind of thing you wanted me to find out. I was just waiting to see if there was anything else, but then all of a sudden, he gets very cautious. No more visits to the apartment. It was as though he knew he was being watched."

She kept looking at me very steadily, trying to keep her face blank. I used my punch line.

"I think he did know he was being watched. You told him."

Her face turned red momentarily under her dark tan, but she kept her voice level. "Why would I do that? You must think I'm awfully stupid."

"I don't think you're at all stupid. I don't think you intended to tell him. I think that it probably just came out—maybe during an argument. You don't hide things very well, and whether you admit it or not, your reactions now have told me that I'm right."

She looked at me for a long minute. "Shit!" she said, shaking her head, disgusted with herself. She smiled sadly. "You *are* a hot-shit detective, and I apologize for playing games with you. You're right, of course. Everything you said was right. I made a mistake, and then I made it worse by not telling you, because I was embarrassed. I'm usually not so dumb. But I was afraid you'd stop working for me. It happened just the way you said. Another argument. Or rather I was arguing, and he was just sitting there, not saying anything as usual, just being his cold, courteous self. Shit, that man really knows how to drive me up the wall. I had to get some reaction out of him, so I told him I was having him investigated. At first he didn't believe me. I hadn't told him your name, but I finally had to, to prove I was telling the truth. Dumb, huh? I know. I knew it as soon as I said it, but it just came out, and I did manage to get him to react. It didn't last long, but that dead fish of a son of a bitch of a husband of mine actually looked scared. Real bright, right? I get the satisfaction of scaring him for thirty seconds, and I tell him everything I'm doing. Jesus! How can I let him get to me like that? But I do, and he does. All the time. I'm sorry I gave you problems." She stood up. "I'm going to have a drink. What would you like?"

"Gin and a couple of ice cubes."

"No mixer?"

I shook my head.

"Macho, macho," she said, and went to fix the drinks.

I lit up a cigarette, drawing the strong smoke deep into my lungs. So I was right that Simon Acker knew about me, so what? If anything, I was further away from finding out what was going on because one more possibility was now confirmed. I should have been pissed off at Clarissa Acker, but somehow I couldn't manage it. The reason she screwed things up was the same reason she hired me.

She came back with the drinks and bent over as she handed mine to me. The front of her kaftan ballooned out, giving me a good view of her small, well-shaped breasts and a lot of her belly. She stayed bent over a good while, making sure I got a long look. I obliged, and then moved my eyes up to her face. Her expression was absolutely blank, and then one eyelid dropped in a tremendous wink. I laughed, and she sat down, this time closer to me, with both her legs under her and the kaftan pulled up over her knees.

My drink was a large one, and I took a big pull at it. Not surprisingly, it was good gin, smooth as satin but with just enough of an afterburn to let you know you're drinking something.

She took a sip of her drink and said, "Am I forgiven?"

"There's nothing to forgive. Just pay the bills and be straight with me."

"'Just pay the bills and be straight with me,'" she mimicked. "Jesus, Hunter! Don't be such a creep."

I laughed. "You're right. I'm sorry. Look, don't worry about it. Your telling him probably won't make any difference, and maybe it'll turn out to be a help."

"Does that mean you'll keep on working?"

"Yeah, sure."

"Thank you." Her smile was warm and genuine, and it made her look pretty good.

Shit! This was a woman who could really get to me. With no trouble at all, and without trying. Just by being the way she was. Careful, Hunter, I thought, and quickly got back to the issue.

"You said your husband looked scared when he finally believed that you had hired me?"

"Maybe not scared exactly. More sort of worried. But it didn't last long. My husband has a lot of self-control. It's one of the things I hate about him. He's so mechanical. He—" She cut herself off with a shake of her head. "No, I won't get started on that. Besides, you already know what I think of him."

"Why do you suppose he was worried?"

"I don't know. Because of what you found out? Because I was going to win the battle once and for all? Because I was going to get information that would expose him for what he was? Because he was afraid of exposure? Because he thought it would ruin him? I don't know."

It might be possible, but somehow I doubted that that was the reason. What I'd turned up could be embarrassing for Simon Acker, and it could probably get his wife a pretty good divorce settlement, but not much more. Oh, there might be a small scandal, but this was Los Angeles, not some small town, and whatever scandal was created would be forgotten by the time the afternoon papers were out. Surely Acker realized that, and that wouldn't scare him. But maybe he was worried I'd find out about something else?

"Tell me about your husband's business."

"I don't think I can. I don't really know anything. Nothing concerning my husband has been of any interest to me for years. Anyway, it's been mutual, and he hasn't confided in me for a long time. He's become a very closed man."

"He wasn't always like that?"

"No, that started about four years ago. . . . No, maybe it even started a couple of years before that. Up until then we'd had an open relationship, always discussing whatever was going on. Actually, it wasn't bad. Not great, but not bad. But then he began acting strange—saying things I didn't understand. I thought he was having a breakdown. He was never a very warm man, but he got even colder. I wanted to help, because I still cared for him and for our relationship, but he wouldn't let me, wouldn't let me near him. And it just kept getting worse, until three or four years ago he closed up completely. Never said a word, just looked at me with cold contempt. I've thought about it a lot since, and I honestly don't think it was my fault. I guess that was when I really started to hate him, the bastard. And I'm sure he hated me as well."

"Then why didn't you get a divorce? You asked, didn't you?"

"Of course I asked. He would just stare at me for a long time and then say things like 'It is forbidden'—like he was making a pronouncement. Shit, he isn't even Catholic. At those times I felt like shooting the son of a bitch. It scared me, Hunter."

"So why didn't you leave? Just leave. You could've."

"What, and give him that satisfaction? No way."

I looked at her and she shrugged.

"Hey, Hunter, I didn't say it was smart. Just that that's the way I felt—feel. You want rationality, talk to a computer. But I want out now. I want to go, but I want him to know it. I want him to hurt." She gave me a crooked smile and shrugged her shoulders again. "So I'm a vindictive bitch? I admit it. But he owes me."

"There's not necessarily anything wrong with revenge," I said, thinking of things she couldn't know about. "But it can be hard. You can hurt yourself almost as much."

She looked at me for a long time, her face serious. "Yeah, I guess you'd know about that, wouldn't you? I think I hired the right investigator."

That was a tough lady. Maybe a little crazy, but that was okay, too.

"Let's go on," I said. "Three or four years ago he closed up. What caused it? What was he doing?"

"I don't know, but whatever it was, it took a lot of money."

"What do you mean?"

"I mean, we never had all that much, but we were fairly comfortable. Not Bel Air comfortable, if this is comfortable," she said, waving her arm at the expanse of living room, "but okay. And then for a while there seemed to be no money. His job was good, but he was spending it somewhere, and spending a lot of it. I never found out where it went."

"Weren't you curious?"

"Maybe I should have been more curious. Maybe it would have made a difference, but I couldn't get anything out of him about anything, and I got tired of trying after a while. And besides, money was never that big a thing with me, not like it is with my husband. He gets off on all this Bel Air shit, like he was some feudal lord."

"Okay. What happened next?"

"Well, a couple of years ago, Medco was going to be taken over by some big corporation—Megaplex, I think it was. One of the few things my husband said to me was that he didn't know what would happen when the company was sold. He thought he'd probably lose his job. He was only managing director, and he figured he wouldn't be kept on. He seemed very concerned about this, and then his mood changed. He got very happy—almost elated—like he'd had some great experience, only he wouldn't tell me what, just got that sly, mysterious look of his, the shit. And then one day he comes in and tells me he bought Medco—that he's the new owner."

"Weren't you surprised at this?"

"I guess I should have been, but, again, I wouldn't give him the satisfaction of showing it."

"Where'd he get the money?"

"I have no idea, but we soon had a lot of it, and I became your typical Bel Air matron, dreaming of balling her gardener . . . and maybe her private eye."

She winked again with that deadpan expression of hers. The invitation couldn't be clearer, but I wasn't quite ready to accept. Did she look just a little bit annoyed as I went on?

"So your husband starts acting strange. He spends a lot of money somewhere. He acts stranger. He's going to lose his job. Something happens and suddenly he owns Medco Pharmaceuticals. He makes a go of it, and there's a lot of money and a house in Bel Air and everything else. Interesting sequence."

"What do you mean?"

"Just that. Interesting."

"You think there's something fishy going on with the factory?"

"I don't know yet," I said. I noticed she was getting a speculative look in her eyes, and I quickly continued, "Look, it's probably nothing—just coincidence. Forget it." Maybe there was nothing there, but it felt funny to me, and I didn't want her slipping again and talking to Acker before I could do some checking. I changed the subject.

"Have you ever heard your husband mention Domingo?"

"No. Who is it?"

I told her what had happened earlier in the day, and how I thought it must be connected with one of the cases I was working on. She had never seen the big ugly that threw me around, and she was not liable to have forgotten him if she had.

She was concerned about what I told her, but it was clear that she had some trouble paying attention. Her mind was occupied elsewhere. Not surprisingly, the elsewhere was Acker's secret apartment, about which she wanted to hear more.

I described the place to her in some detail, but she impatiently asked me about the women that went there. I passed on what the pro had told me—the kinds of things that Acker liked to do, the way the girl had to act to turn him on, the way his personality changed when he got into costume and held a whip in his hand. There was nothing very unusual in any of this, but it was like a brand new world opening up for Clarissa Acker.

I took another big pull on my drink and watched the changing expressions on her face as she considered my report. At first she looked surprised and bewildered at this totally unexpected revelation, and then she considered whether this was the information she needed to do whatever it was she wanted to do to her husband. Her expression grew hard as she thought about Acker's activities.

". . . so that's what he likes . . . that's what it takes, the bastard . . ." she said to herself, but she was clearly puzzled, and she tried to imagine what it was like. Her imagination must have been pretty good. Her eyes closed and her breathing got deeper. Drops of perspiration appeared above her upper lip. Almost unconsciously her hand started to caress her body, running over her thighs, her belly, up to her breasts, and then inside the kaftan to rub her nipples.

Suddenly she opened her eyes, surprised to see me. "Oh, shit, Hunter!" she said, and then threw herself on me, her mouth greedily attacking mine, her tongue moving fast, surging deep into my mouth. There was a kind of desperate urgency to her—almost violent—as though all the frustration and anger and hatred of the last few years had suddenly found an outlet. It was exciting, but also a little frightening—and a little sad.

Her hands were at my waistband, hurrying to get my pants open, frantically grabbing to get me exposed. When she succeeded, she quickly got between my knees, taking me whole into her mouth. As her lips and tongue did their dance, a low growl escaped from deep inside her throat.

She stood up and pulled the kaftan over her head. I was right about her sunbathing. Her tan was dark and continuous. She had not worn a bathing suit in a long time. Her breasts were rapidly rising and falling, the nipples vibrating. The downy hair that covered her mound glistened with the moisture of her juices. She was pretty spectacular.

An audible sigh passed her lips, and she was trembling. She was clearly impatient, almost unbearably so, but she controlled it. She was not selfish. She wanted it to last, and she wanted it to be good for me as well. She came over to me, and slowly, slowly removed my clothes, her mouth and hands lingering over me. Her sighing deepened, her trembling increased, and still she delayed, intent on giving me pleasure before she took hers.

I picked her up and laid her on the fur rug. I entered her in one quick thrust that made her gasp. Her body folded to meet mine and I felt her breasts beneath my chest and her buttocks in my hands as each of us struggled and fought to completely drain the other.

It was all right.

Exhausted, we lay next to each other. After a minute, I got up and went over to get my drink. Most of the ice had melted, and I finished it in one swallow. I lit a Gitane and let it hang on my lip. I looked down at Clarissa Acker, who was starting to stir on the rug. She was something, all right, but I forced my thoughts away from her and back to my problem. I was not any further along, but at least I had a new angle to look into.

She rolled over and looked up at me. She had the smug, happy look of a kitten glutted with heavy cream.

"Oh, Hunter, I needed that. Thanks."

"Just part of the service, lady."

She laughed, a rich, throaty sound. "Hunter, you really are a creep."

I decided that she was a dangerous woman. At least for me. I got into my clothes.

"You have to go?" she said.

"Yeah."

"Okay."

Dangerous.

As I left the house, I got the feeling that it was very precariously placed. It wouldn't take much to push it off the hill, down to the hot, dirty, common level of the rest of the city.

And I wondered if Clarissa Acker would go over with it.

FOUR

I had some time to kill before I could pay my next visit, and there were a couple of phone calls I wanted to make, so I drove back downtown to my office.

The sun was starting to get low. This was always the hottest time, when the accumulated sweat of the day seemed to hang in the air and form an almost visible haze. I didn't understand it. It used to be desert here, but it seemed to be getting increasingly humid. Probably due to all of the swimming pools. Put together, all the pools must add up to more inland water than the largest lake in the world, and the evaporated moisture couldn't get past the constant level of smog that hung at 2000 feet. This was getting to be a shitty place to live, and I'd go somewhere else if I thought there was any place better.

After inching through the perpetual traffic jam, I finally arrived at the old brick building where my office was located. It had never been a very classy place. In the last twenty years the area had gone badly downhill and was now a slippery step above skid row. The owners of the building had only made whatever repairs were necessary to keep the place from falling down, but the rent was cheap and the location suited my purposes. At one time I had considered getting a better office, but I couldn't think why I should. I didn't need to impress anybody. If my clients needed me, they needed me, and if they didn't like my office, they could go to some fancy ass in Beverly Hills who wouldn't touch a job that clashed with his pretty decor. Fuck 'em. I was selling my guts and my brains, not my office.

The elevator only worked part of the time, and I walked up the three flights of stairs. I shared the floor with the Elegante School of Modeling, which promised dreams of high-fashion glory to starry eyed girls fresh off buses from the midwest and Chiquitas who couldn't speak any English, and gave them the chance to staff a cheap call-girl service, twenty-five dollars a trick, they keep half. The other office on the floor was the Jiffy Music Publishing Company. In four years I had never seen anyone go in or out, though occasionally a light showed in the crack between the bottom of the door and the floor.

My name was on the door, so I guessed that I was still in business. The door was locked. Maria must have gone home, or wherever it was she went when she left the office. I went in and turned on the lights. I walked through the coat closet where Maria had her desk and that served as a waiting room, into my office. There was my desk upside down and cracked in the center of the room.

I didn't keep anything of importance in my desk except for a couple boxes of bullets, and I pulled these out of the wreckage. The telephone had been flipped off the desk, but it was still working.

I got my bottle of gin out of the filing cabinet. It was next to my .357 magnum in its holster, and I thought it might be a good idea to start wearing it. If I met the brother of Godzilla again—and I fully intended to—it would serve as an equalizer. Even that monster would find it tough to function with a hole in him the size of a baseball. The gun could probably take out an elephant, but I figured if I had to shoot, I didn't want to be lobbing marshmallows.

I found a glass that didn't look too dirty, and filled it halfway with the gin. I took a big swallow, felt it burn as it went down, and poured some more in the glass to replace what I had drunk.

I sat in my chair, put my feet up on the windowsill, lit a cigarette, and leaned back. I grabbed the telephone cord and pulled the phone over to me. I dialed the number for Ellis Maycroft of Spode, Maycroft and Burbary, Stock Brokerage, not really expecting to find him there since it was after working hours. I was surprised when Maycroft himself answered.

"Maycroft, this is Sam Hunter. What are you doing there so late, doctoring accounts again?"

He gave an uneasy laugh.

"Just finishing some work that had to be done. I haven't heard from you in a long time."

He didn't sound especially pleased to be hearing from me now. I had cleared up a mess an absconding junior partner had made, and I kept it so quiet that no one ever knew about it. But in the process I had turned up some stuff on Maycroft that wouldn't do him any good. As a result, he was a useful source when I needed some information about the world of high finance.

"Maycroft, I need some info on Medco Pharmaceutical Supplies. Go back a couple of years. Especially what was going on around the time of the attempted merger. Also, the status of the company now. Also, anything you've got on the president, Simon Acker."

"Now, Hunter." He was starting to whine. "That's not my field. I can't—"

"Your firm has files on everything. Get one of your juniors to put together the complete story. I'll come over about eleven o'clock tomorrow."

"But that's not enough time. I need—"

"I'll see you at eleven. . . . Oh, Maycroft, I promise I won't smash up your office or do anything that would embarrass you." I emphasized "embarrass" and heard him swallow hard before I hung up the receiver.

I drank some more gin and smoked another cigarette before I made my next call. It was to Detective Charles Watkins of the Los Angeles Police Department, Narco Squad.

He wasn't a very good cop, but he was one of the few who would still talk to me. We went back a long way together, and he would always owe me a favor since I had twice saved his life when we were in Viet Nam together.

After being placed on hold and transferred about four times, I was finally connected with the right department and got him on the line.

"Charlie, Sam Hunter here."

"Sam! It's good to hear from you. How've you been? Staying out of trouble?"

"If I'm out of trouble, I'm out of business. You know that."

"I guess I do. What can I do for you?"

"You can get me whatever there is on the Black Knight Club in Hollywood."

"Never heard of it. What is it?"

"A private club of some kind. Might be a sex place. Vice

should know something about it. You probably won't get too much, but ask around."

"Sure thing. What's this about? Important?"

"I don't know yet. Should I come over tomorrow to see you?"

"Uh, I don't think that's a good idea. You know, you're not exactly welcome around here after that Lafferty business."

I knew. I had created a lot of paper work for the boys in blue and made them look pretty bad in the bargain. There had been a lot of screaming up and down the line over that one. They tried to make me the patsy and lift my licence, and all they accomplished was to make themselves look worse than before. They didn't have much use for me, and the feeling was mutual. Not that there aren't good cops. I just hadn't met many.

"Look, Sam, why don't I ask around tonight, and I'll stop by your apartment tomorrow morning before I come in."

"Okay, see you then. It might be a good idea if you didn't mention my name."

"I know that better than you, old buddy. When you started the shit flying, more than enough hit me. See you tomorrow."

I replaced the receiver and thought that it was cops like my friend Charlie that made the crime rate rise. Still, he'd get me what I wanted.

It was starting to get dark, or rather the sky was turning the brown-green color that passes for sunset around here. The daytime drunks were being replaced by the nighttime junkies, prostitutes, and assorted creeps and misfits. It was the other side of the coin, but it was the same coin.

I still had a couple of hours to kill, and I was starting to get hungry. Since I had to go to the Strip anyway, I decided on Fernando's.

The restaurant was on one of those semi-crummy business streets off of Sunset Boulevard that go dead after 5 P.M. It was far enough away from the action to get none of the fashionable crowd, but the food was good and you only paid for the food, not some fancy address.

"Fernando" was a fat German who was just the right age to have been a Hitler Youth. He greeted me with enough oil in his voice to fry potatoes, showed me to a table, and took my order.

The lighting was low to hide the fact that the tablecloths were dirty, but I could see the place was doing good business.

The waitress brought me my drink. She was Fernando's daughter, and looked like someone out of a German opera. She was large, but her flesh was solid. Her hips were so wide that they made her thick waist look relatively small. The off-the-shoulder Mexican blouse she wore accented her truly enormous breasts, which bounced in front of my face like twin Germanic basketballs as she bent over the table. One of these days it might be fun to give it to her on top of one of the tables, especially with Herr Fernando watching. He'd probably give me a year's free dinners for the experience.

My dinner came quickly. As she leaned over my shoulder to serve it, she made sure that one of her tits pressed against the side of my face. I put my arm over the back of my chair and placed my hand on her ample rump. She started to wiggle it, but when I pinched her hard, she gave a small scream of surprise and hurried back into the kitchen.

My two-inch-thick porterhouse was good and cooked just the way I liked it—charred black on the outside and bloody raw in the center. They still remembered the time they served me a well-done steak and I threw it on the floor saying that was where shoe leather belonged. The service had been pretty good since then.

After I finished my second cup of coffee, I was feeling all right and beginning to look forward to what lay ahead that evening. I was going to have another meeting with my young witches or warlocks or whatever the hell they called themselves, and I had a feeling that this encounter was going to be far more satisfying—for me if not for them.

FIVE

I got into my car and drove up to Sunset. As usual the traffic was hardly moving. Carloads of hicks were there to disgust themselves with the creatures that inhabit the Strip at night. Carloads of freaks were there to see and be seen by their buddies on the street. Past the pulsating discos, the chic coffee houses, and the not-so-chic porno palaces, the sidewalks were a solid stream of the stuff that feeds off and is fed to the Hollywood dream machine. Pot heads, coke sniffers, hash eaters, speed freaks, skag shooters, bikers, draggers, racers, pimps, pushers, prostitutes, religious fanatics who have been saved, homicidal maniacs who never will be, yogis, Krishnas, Buddhists, Maoists, urban guerrillas, neo-Nazis, drag queens, butch dykes, leather boys, chain-mail girls, starlets hoping to be discovered, has-beens hoping to be rediscovered, and those who are there because there's no place else to go. All the scum of the city flowed down the street, and I was going to have to wade through it to get some answers.

I finally reached the place I was looking for, Scorpio Rising, and managed to find a parking place in front. A red neon scorpion sprawled across the black exterior of the building. The heavy double doors were black leather and decorated with astrological signs formed out of brass studs. Each of the innumerable places on the Strip had its own gimmick. Scorpio Rising's was the occult.

I went inside and my nostrils were immediately assaulted by the odor of unwashed bodies, booze, incense, and the sickly sweet smell of burning grass. The feeble lighting emanated from plastic skulls mounted on the black walls. A transvestite band filled the small room with the sound of a jet engine as they exploded smoke bombs.

A few people writhed on the dance floor in the center of the room, but most sat around tiny tables, unmoving, unseeing, unhearing, wrapped in some inner fantasy.

I moved through the room, roughly pushing bodies out of my way, but the bodies did not even notice.

At the back of the room was a door marked PRIVATE. I started to open it when someone grabbed my arm.

"Can't you read? It says 'private.' That means you can't go in."

It was the bartender. He was a head shorter than me, but must have weighed 250 pounds, with the build of a weight lifter gone to fat. His immense beer belly hung over the top of his pants.

"Thanks for the explanation," I said, "but I'm expected."

He moved in front of the door.

"I don't think so."

"I do."

I moved suddenly and caught him by surprise. A short quick punch into his protruding belly. My fist sank in up to the wrist. He just stood there. His face turned bright scarlet, then white, then green. I pushed him aside and he crumpled to the floor, a trickle of vomit starting to ooze from his mouth.

I looked around. No one had noticed. I opened the door and went in.

There were six of them sitting around a table in the center of a room that had strange signs and markings scrawled on the walls. Up against one wall was an altar of some kind, surmounted with an upside down cross. I don't know if they believed all that black magic bullshit, but they sure seemed to have all the props.

They were all about the same age—nineteen or twenty. There was one girl among them—at least I thought it was female. Anyway, they all looked the same with long, stringy, dirty hair; yellow, pimply complexions; and dull, sneering eyes sunk in dark sockets. Most of them I had seen before. Two of them were passing joints, and one of them was snorting up a spoon of cocaine. This was apparently my lucky day—the coke sniffer was George Lansing II.

One of the ones I had met before, who seemed to be their leader, had turned around when I entered.

"What the fuck do you want? Can't you read? This is private. Get the fuck out of here!"

It was the voice of a spoiled, rich brat who was used to getting his way instantly.

"After I get some answers to a few questions."

"Oh, it's the private pig. Hello, Mr. Private Pig. Oink. Oink. Georgie, this is the oink that was asking questions about you." Georgie raised his dull eyes, but showed no greater interest. The spokesman continued, "Now, Mr. Oink, you have no questions to ask, and we have no answers to give. You are trespassing, so get the fuck out of here!" His voice had risen to a shrill scream.

I stood, not moving, staring hard at him. My knuckles were starting to itch, and I had that metallic taste of expectation in my mouth. I was going to enjoy this. I kept my voice even.

"Who is Domingo?"

"You no longer amuse us, Mr. Oink. You amused us once, but you no longer do. So you had better leave while you still can."

"Who is Domingo?"

"Mr. Oink." It was the girl speaking. "Why don't you lick my cunt, motherfucker."

I stared at her until she turned away. I knew what was going to happen, and it would be a pleasure.

"If Mr. Oink insists on staying, we might as well have some fun with him." It was the spokesman again. "Jimmy, lock the door."

One of them got up and threw two bolts across the door. Better and better.

"Mr. Oink, you're a very lucky man. You're going to get to take part in our ceremony. You're going to be the star attraction." Someone giggled. "A little pig's blood is just what we need. Slit the pig!"

With that, Jimmy and another of them pulled switchblades and started advancing toward me.

I felt the total calm I always get in situations like this. My reflexes were tightened to the point where I could move with lightning speed. Even though my gun was under my arm, I wouldn't show it because that would scare them off, and I wanted them to come on. I wanted to feel their skins rip and their bones snap beneath my fingers.

I backed up against the door trying to make myself look scared so as to encourage them.

Jimmy came forward. His lips were parted and a drop of

spittle fell from the corner of his slack mouth. He made a short thrust with his knife, expecting me to jump back. Instead, I grabbed his arm and slammed his hand against the wall. The knife fell to the floor. Twisting his wrist, I straightened his arm and rammed the heel of my palm into his elbow. His arm snapped like a matchstick. Before he could scream I drove my elbow into his ribs and felt them crack. My fist came up and caught him square in the jaw, shattering it, the force of the blow causing teeth to fly out of his mouth as he fell to the floor.

The other one moved at me. His eyes had the crazy gleam of the meth shooter. They showed sadistic pleasure. He rushed, the arm holding the knife straight in front of him. I sidestepped, caught his wrist and slowly bent his arm back toward him. I covered his hand so that he could not let go of the knife, and as the blade moved closer to his head, the look in his eyes changed to terror. I let the knife blade rest on top of his ear for a second so that he would be sure to know what was going to happen. He started to scream as the blade cut into him, and as the ear was severed, warm blood gushed over my hand. He fell to his hands and knees, whimpering, and I brought my heel down hard on one of his hands, crushing it. I rotated my heel before lifting it.

The girl threw a heavy ashtray at my head. I ducked and it broke against the wall. As I was standing up, someone jumped on my back and tried to put his fingers around my throat. I backed into the wall as hard as I could. That knocked the wind out of him, and he let go of my neck. I turned around and hit him in the solar plexus. As he doubled up, I gave him a chop across the back of his neck and he collapsed on the floor.

I looked up and saw their fearless leader frantically trying to get the door open. I pulled him around so that he faced me. Terror showed in his face. His mouth worked but no sound came out. A stench hit my nostrils and told me he was literally scared shitless. I laughed. His face contorted and he tried to kick me in the groin. I caught his foot and flipped him on his back. Still holding his leg straight up, I said, "Is this what you tried to do?" as I buried the toe of my shoe in his crotch. Yellow foam frothed out of his mouth.

The girl came at me, screaming wildly, looking like the witch she pretended to be. She had picked up one of the fallen knives and was holding it over her head. She tried to plant it in my chest, but I grabbed her skinny arm with one hand. My other hand grabbed a tit and twisted it until she dropped the knife. She was glaring at me, spitting like a wild animal. She might have been the worst of the lot.

I put my hands at the top of her dress and ripped it off her. She wore no underwear. Naked she was even worse-looking than before. She was very thin except for full breasts that seemed out of place on that bony frame. She was dirty, and her skin was covered with welts and scratches and insect bites. She stared at me defiantly.

"Now what should I do with you?" I said.

"Eat me, motherfucker! Eat me!"

I was suddenly tired of all this. Before she had a chance to react, I hit her on the point of her chin. Her knees went rubbery and gave way as she slumped down, unconscious.

I looked around. There, in the corner, was George Lansing II.

"Well, Georgie, here we are. Just the two of us."

"Leave me alone. I don't know you. I don't know anything."

"But Georgie, you must. You're the reason all this happened."

"I told you, I don't know anything. Don't hurt me." He sounded like an eight year old.

Someone groaned and I looked around. When I turned back to Georgie he had a small gun in his hand. No matter what he sounded like, he had tried at least once to kill his father. He was unpredictable, and I figured I had to act fast.

"Georgie, that's just stupid," I said, and keeping my eyes on his face, I suddenly went low and threw a roll block at him, hoping I would be able to come in beneath his gun. He fired as my shoulder slammed into him. I felt the heat as the bullet passed just above my back. The second time I bounced into him he dropped the gun.

I kicked it across the room. Georgie was looking as though nothing had happened. I studied his face. His nose was running and he had the frozen upper lip of the chronic coke sniffer. His eyes were vacant and imbecilic. All that showed was viciousness, and the only way to get the truth out of him was the threat of pain.

"Who's Domingo, Georgie?"

"I don't know what you're talking about. Leave me alone."

"Who's Domingo?" I asked very quietly.

He turned his face away, bored.

"WHO'S DOMINGO?"

I shouted into his ear and at the same time reached up between his legs and grabbed his balls hard and squeezed.

He screamed and turned to look at me. I finally had his attention.

"Let me go! Let me go! You're killing me!"

I squeezed harder.

"Who's Domingo? Tell me quick or I'm going to crush your balls."

"I don't know. I never heard of him. Please let me go." He was starting to sweat and roll his head.

I squeezed harder still.

"The truth. Tell me the truth."

"Stop! Stop! That is the truth. I swear. I swear."

I let up the pressure. He relaxed a little.

"What about that big gorilla you sent to scare me off?"

"I didn't send anyone. Honest."

I jammed my hand hard up his crotch.

"Honest. I don't know anything about it. Let me go."

I relaxed my grip. I believed him. Very few men can lie under those circumstances. Georgie wasn't likely to be the exception to that rule.

"You know your father hired me, Georgie?"

"What for?"

I squeezed again.

"Because he doesn't want to be murdered by you. I think he should have killed you or put you away a long time ago. But that's his affair. My affair is to see that you won't send him any more presents or do anything stupid like try to kill him again." I squeezed very hard. "Understand?"

His face was white and covered with sweat. He was close to passing out.

"I understand. I understand. Please stop."

"Because if I hear that he's received any more funny packages, or any threats, or he has any kind of accident, you better believe that I'm going to come after you. I'm going to rip your balls off, and I'm going to smash both of your knees, and both your ankles, and both your elbows and both your hands. And every minute you live after that will be nothing

but pain—ask your friends about it. You better believe me,
Georgie. Do you believe me?"

I shoved my hand up hard one more time, nearly lifting him
off the floor.

"Yes! Yes! Yes!"

I let him go and he crashed to the ground, clutching himself
and crying in pain and fear.

I went to the door and drew the bolts. As I opened the door
I heard that the band was still playing. That was good. They
were so loud I could have set a bomb and no one would have
been the wiser.

I went into the main room, pulling the door shut behind
me. Directly in front of me stood Fat Belly, a wicked-looking
sawed-off shotgun cradled loosely in his hands.

"Okay, tough guy. Let's see how tough you are now."

I noticed that he didn't even have his finger on the trigger.
Obviously he was not used to guns and thought the sight of it
alone would be enough to put me out of business. He would
be easy to take, and I doubted if I would ever get a better
opportunity than I had.

He was still smirking, thinking about what he was going to
do to me, when I ripped the gun out of his hands. Surprise
showed on his face, and then fear, and then pain as I jammed
the stock a good six inches into his stomach. He doubled up,
and, holding the barrel like a baseball bat, I clubbed the side
of his head. I put my foot on his fat ass and pushed him
toward the wall. He hit it face first. Blood poured from his
broken nose as he fell backward to the floor. He was out cold,
spread-eagled. I shoved the business end of the gun down into
the front of his pants. If he wasn't careful when he came to,
he might do himself some more harm.

As I left the place, I looked at my watch. Hardly five
minutes had passed.

I went to my car and saw that some burly biker was sitting
on the front fender. He was an ugly son of a bitch with a
shaven head and an earring in one ear. His torso was bare
except for an open, sleeveless denim vest. He was heavily
tattooed with snakes and skulls, and he was busy impressing a
couple of teeny boppers with how tough he was.

"This is my car."

"So what?"

"So get off it."

"I don't think so, man. It's pretty comfortable." He slammed the fender with his hand.

Christ, I thought, doesn't it ever end?

"Suit yourself," I said. I got in and started the engine.

He was laughing it up and mugging for the benefit of the girls. Quite a comedian.

I waited until I saw a break in the traffic. I turned the wheels hard and floored it. He sat on the front of the car until centrifugal force took over. He went flying off, landing on a parked car.

I didn't bother to look back as I drove down the street. All I wanted was to get off the Strip, get home, and have a scalding hot shower and a big glass of gin.

Things were starting to sort themselves out.

And I had been right.

It had been a pretty good evening.

In my apartment, I turned on my answering machine to see if there were any messages.

There was one from a happy-sounding Clarissa Acker: "Hey, Hunter. I've been thinking about your ass."

Shit.

I had been thinking about hers.

SIX

I woke up early to the sounds of summer in Los Angeles. Through the cardboard walls of my apartment I heard some clown on the television screaming about how you should be shot for using the wrong laundry detergent. From the apartment on the other side, some woman was screaming at her husband that she would shoot him if he ever came home drunk again. A radio somewhere was screaming about a series of unsolved shootings in the San Fernando Valley. Down in the back alley kids were firing cap pistols at one another and yelling insanely.

It was only seven o'clock and already it felt like it was more than 80 degrees. It was going to be another bitch of a day.

I had a dull ache at the base of my skull and in my right shoulder from when Domingo's messenger threw me against the wall, but other than that I felt okay. A lot better than those punks from last night were feeling, I knew that. Just thinking about it made some of my soreness disappear.

I got up and stood under a cold shower until I was fully awake. I thought about getting dressed but decided to put it off as long as possible because of the heat. Wrapping a towel around my waist I made breakfast.

Four eggs scrambled with a handful of burning-hot jalapeño chiles, toast, and a couple of cups of double-strength black coffee, and I felt my system begin to function again.

I washed up the dishes and settled down to read the paper with another cup of coffee. I usually don't pay much attention to the news since it hardly ever seems new. I mean, anyone with any sense at all knows exactly what's going to be in the paper. The names change from time to time, but the stories stay the same. Anyone who is surprised at "surprising developments" is either a congenital idiot or has been living in a soap-opera fantasy world. The news that morning was the usual mix of violence in the streets, corruption in high places, and incompetence everywhere, along with what passes for human interest in L.A.—a woman raped by a love-starved Great Dane, a deranged millionaire who wanted to be buried at Disneyland, some joker who was crushed to death by the giant ball of aluminum foil he had collected for thirty years—the usual stuff. I was glad to put the paper aside when the knock on the door told me Charlie Watkins had arrived.

Charlie never looked that good, always kind of harassed and jumpy, like he expected to be hit from behind at any moment. He'd been like this ever since his wife ran off with some hippie in a camper. Even though it happened a few years back, Charlie still acted as though it was yesterday, and every time he saw me, he told me about it, like it was a new development.

It had been a while since I had seen him, and he was looking even a little worse than usual. He had dark, puffy circles under his eyes. His synthetic seersucker suit hung limply on his body, dried sweat stains showing on the back and under the arms. It might just have been the heat, but, looking at Charlie, I got a feeling of incipient disaster. I didn't know why, but I didn't think it would be healthy to be around him for any length of time. It was starting to affect me after he'd been in my apartment for only a minute, and I was glad I was not his partner. Knowing what to expect, I nonetheless asked him how things were going.

"Not so good, Sam. Not so good. You know my wife left me. Ran off with some goddamn hippie. And in a camper! Jesus, I just don't understand it. She didn't even like to go into the backyard. Jesus." He shook his head in a bewildered way and put a couple of large, chalky-looking tablets in his mouth and chewed them with a small, rapid motion like a rabbit nibbling a lettuce leaf. Whatever he was eating seemed to foam up a little at the corners of his mouth, and his lower lip was flecked with stray bits of tablet. He made a sour expression and gingerly rubbed his stomach, leaving dirty smudges where his fingers had touched his white wash-and-wear shirt. He saw the dirt smears and shrugged his shoulders in a resigned, helpless sort of way.

Poor Charlie. We'd been pretty good friends in Viet Nam,

and it bothered me to see that he was such a mess, but there was nothing I could do to help him. If he was going to pull himself together, he'd have to do it himself. To change the subject, I asked how things were with the Narco boys.

He made a face. "Jesus, Sam, we're just going crazy. There's all kinds of shit on the streets—real good quality stuff—and we just can't get a line on it. And it's been like this for some time. Usually, you hear some talk—something—but we've got zero. So, of course, the word comes down from on high, they want some action. They sit in their air-conditioned offices, and maybe go home early for some cool drinks, but the statistics aren't so good, and they want some action, so we bust our butts for twelve–fourteen hours a day in 120-degree weather, and come up empty. It's really getting us down."

Charlie did take his work seriously, I'll say that for him. He wasn't very good at it, but he sure tried. And he was a hundred percent straight, which is something for a Narco cop. Some people said he was too dumb to be otherwise, but Charlie was just a decent guy doing a job he wasn't cut out for.

"And as if all that wasn't enough," Charlie continued with a shake of his head, "they're really coming down on me, giving me a lot of gas. I'll admit it, I've screwed up a few times recently, and they're telling me to get my act together. I've got to come up with something good pretty soon or it's bye-bye. But thanks to you, old buddy, I may have found just the thing."

"What did I do?"

"Well, you know you asked me to look into the Black Knight Club?"

I nodded. Of course I knew. Get on with it, Charlie.

"Well, I saw a couple of interesting names there. Names connected with some people we've had our eye on for a while. Nothing very solid, but something to consider."

"What names?"

"Now, Sam, you're a good friend, but I can't tell you that right now. I want to check it out before I talk about it. I think I'll even take a few days off, you know, do some work on my own time. If this turns out to be anything, it could be just what I needed to get back in good graces with the higher-ups."

He looked more enthusiastic than I'd seen him for some

time, so I decided not to press him on that. Instead, I asked if he'd gotten anything for me.

"I got you a couple of things, but there was hardly anything in the file—just a few notes and that. I brought you something, but, Jesus, Sam, don't tell anybody because I'll really be in the shit for doing this. Anyway, they had two copies, so I hope they won't miss one."

He passed across a single sheet of expensive paper, folded in half like a card, with elegant printing on the inside face. It was a prospectus for the Black Knight Club:

"The Black Knight Club is an exclusive club providing facilities for sophisticated gentlemen with particular and discriminating tastes.

"In an atmosphere of the utmost discretion, the member will find attention to detail and exacting service that will cater to his every whim and fancy.

"There are nightly shows featuring international entertainers in performances that are exciting, stimulating, and that display talents and abilities of considerable virtuosity and uniqueness.

"For the tired executive wishing to relax after a hard day, there are private facilities carefully appointed in a variety of styles—classic, contemporary, and exotic—in which the member will be able to make his dreams become reality.

"Additionally there is a full range of recreational services and equipment, and even the most particular member will find the precise diversion for which he is searching.

"Granted the fees are considerable, but membership is carefully limited to ensure complete exclusivity. When it is considered that the club provides all the pleasure that money can buy, the fees cannot be thought to be excessive."

I had to laugh. It sounded like some health spa, but it wasn't hard to imagine what went on there. They might just as well flash WHOREHOUSE in red neon letters. Still, everything was vague enough to keep them out of trouble if the wrong person saw the notice. And it seemed to be working. Very few people knew about the place.

"That's a help, Charlie. It confirms some things that I've heard. What else do you have?"

"Just this." He handed me a scrap of paper. On it was written the name Nicky Faro, and an address in the Hollywood Hills.

"Who's this?"

"It was a name in the file. The series of numbers that followed it looked like payoffs. I'd say that was the snitch inside the club."

"Now this might be useful," I said, grinning in a way that seemed to make Charlie uncomfortable.

"Jesus, Sam, take it easy with that, will you? If it ever gets out I gave that to you, there's going to be a lot of trouble. If that Faro guy's cover is blown, we're all in for it."

"I'll be careful," I said, though we both knew I wouldn't necessarily be.

"Jesus, that is one hell of a big favor I just did for you, old buddy." He still couldn't fully believe that he'd done it, and he popped another tablet in his mouth.

"I know, Charlie. Thanks," I said, and I meant it.

"I'll do you another favor," he said when the tablet had stopped foaming. "I'll give you some good advice. Be careful with that club. It looks like a very heavy operation, and you might upset some mean people." I looked questioningly at him and he continued. "Almost as soon as I got done looking at the file, this Vice guy, Ratchitt, comes to see me. You know who he is?"

"I've heard of him. He's dirty."

Charlie looked nervously around. "Jesus, old buddy, you said it, not me, but you may be right. He's got a big house and a yacht and fancy clothes and nice cars, and he's always bragging about them. Burroughs, my partner, hates his guts. Won't even stay in the same room with the guy. . . . Well, anyway, he comes down to see me. Says he heard I was asking about the Black Knight—he seems to hear everything, that guy. He wants to know why. I gave him a song and dance about checking an alibi, and so on, and he seemed to buy it. But then he said to make sure I stayed far away from that place—that there was a long-standing investigation going on, and that he didn't want anybody poking around and fucking it up. Can you believe it? A long-standing investigation? With about three pieces of paper in the file?"

"The rest is probably in a safe deposit box somewhere, drawing big dividends."

"Jesus, Sam. I don't even want to think about it. I just thought you should know, though, that this is Ratchitt's territory, and that's one mean son of a bitch. I wouldn't want to get on his bad side."

"I'll keep it in mind, Charlie."

"Yeah," he laughed sadly. "Sure you will. I know you, Sam. . . . What's this all about?"

I said I really didn't know, and then I told him about what had happened the day before. I asked him if he knew about any Domingo. He thought for a minute.

"No, no help. . . . Say, wasn't there a private eye on television a long time ago—when we would have been kids—that was called Domingo or Dominic or something like that? You remember that? I thought he was really cool."

"If you say so." Big help, Charlie. Shit. No wonder the city was being buried in dope.

"Maybe it was somebody else. . . . Anyway, I think I know who the guy is who threw you around."

"Yeah?" *That* would be a big help.

"Yeah. It's got to be an ex-wrestler who was called something like Mountain Cyclone, I think it was. Don't know his real name. But that was a long time ago. I think he killed somebody in the ring. If I remember the story right, the guy was incredibly strong, but really dumb. He couldn't absorb the fact that it was all phony—that he had to follow a script. One day he was supposed to throw somebody out of the ring. Instead of putting the guy over the ropes and letting him drop on his feet, Mountain heaved him into the tenth row. The guy's spine was broken in about four places and he died. Needless to say, Mountain didn't wrestle any more, and I don't know what happened to him, but it sounds like your guy. Any help?"

"It's someplace to start."

"Glad to help, old buddy. But just take it easy. These are some nice acquaintances you've got, real nice. Jesus. . . Well, I've got to go now. I got some things of my own to check out."

"You sure you should do that on your own? Shouldn't you bring your partner into it?"

"I can look after myself, old buddy."

Sure, Charlie. Fuck it, I had my own problems, and I didn't know why I should be concerned about him. I had only saved his life, I didn't own it.

Anyway, I thanked him for his help, and he got up. He seemed a little bit more determined than when he came in. I watched as he purposefully crossed the room, opened the bathroom door, and went in. A second later he came out, an embarrassed look on his face, went to the right door, and exited. I shook my head. Some detective—he can't even find the front door. Watch out, you dope pushers, Popeye Watkins is in town.

I still had plenty of time before I went to see Maycroft, so I decided to take another shower. It wasn't just the steadily rising temperature. Watkins had left me feeling vaguely depressed, and I wanted to wash his visit away.

I got in the shower and adjusted the head to the hardest spray. I let it run as hot as it would go, and after a couple of minutes the bathroom was completely steamed up. I turned off the hot and ran the straight cold. After I alternated hot and cold several more times, the last remaining kinks in my back had just about disappeared.

I wasn't singing arias or anything like that, but I still didn't hear my apartment door open. I didn't know anyone had come in until the bathroom door opened. I must really have been slipping to let something like that happen. Either that, or some of the incipient disaster that Charlie Watkins carried around had rubbed off.

I stuck my head around the shower curtain and saw that it could have been a lot worse. It could have been The Mountain That Walks Like A Man, or a number of other unwanted visitors. Instead, it was only the daughter of the woman who manages the apartment building. Her name was Candi or Cindi or Bambi or one of those goddamn dumb names that were dropped on kids by parents who were terminally warped by the Mickey Mouse Club.

She was sixteen and pretty delectable if you like them that young. I had no particular prejudices either way, though I usually preferred them a bit older. I had boffed her mother a couple of times. Not bad, but she tried a little too hard to look like her daughter's sister. She came close, but not close enough. The girl knew that I had made it with her mother, and she in turn had been trying to make me for some time now. Nice healthy mother-daughter competition. For no particular reason I had successfully resisted the girl's advances, and, as is nearly always the case, this only made her try harder.

So there she was in my bathroom wearing a bikini that can only be described as minimal—three very small triangles of cloth, strategically placed, and held there by thin bits of string. It was the kind of bathing suit that, except for L.A., the Riveria, and Copacabana Beach, was only seen in magazines. She was tall and pleasantly thin with nice firm flesh. Her breasts were small, but well shaped and perfectly suited to her body. Her nipples were erect and visible through the thin fabric of the top. Her belly was beautifully rounded, and she arched her back to thrust it forward in the provocative stance that many adolescent girls display. She was blonde and pretty in a slutty sort of way that exactly suited her name, Suzi or Sherri or whatever it was. I figured she must have had boys howling around her like tomcats.

"Hi, Sam," she said, grinning, displaying teeth that were a tribute to an orthodontist's skill.

"Don't you know it's not polite to come into a man's bathroom without being invited."

She shook her long hair. "I didn't know that. See, I told you there's all kinds of things you can teach me." She let the tip of her tongue run over her lips like she had seen some starlet do in the movies.

"I don't suppose your mother knows you're up here?"

"She's away all day."

"Do you think she'd approve?"

"Who cares? I'm old enough to do what I want—whatever I want." She said the last phrase in a way that left no doubt about the meaning of "whatever." "Why? Do you think she'd be jealous?"

We both knew her mother would be, and while I didn't give a shit one way or the other, I wasn't going to give the little bitch the satisfaction of saying so.

"Well? What do you want?" I said, although I knew the answer well enough.

"I was lonely. I wanted company, so I—"

"So you hung around outside, and when you heard the shower running, you came in, thinking I'd be at a disadvantage and I couldn't throw you out."

At least she could still blush, which she did, and which

served to make her prettier. But then to cover her embarrassment, she started to pout, and that didn't help her any.

"I thought your generation was supposed to be open and honest?" I said.

"Naw. That was the last generation. Mine is sly and devious." She grinned and I laughed.

"All right, sly and devious, what do you want?"

She took a deep breath, which did nice things to her bikini, and lowered her eyes as she spoke in a small voice. "I want you to invite me in."

What the hell, she was starting to get to me. What could I say?

"Come on in, the water's fine," I said.

For a second her face lit up, making her look about twelve, which was a little disconcerting considering the circumstances.

She crossed the small bathroom in a couple of steps, during which time I adjusted the water to a comfortably tepid temperature. She pulled back the curtain and stepped in.

Her eyes roamed over me and her mouth fell open slightly as her breathing slowed and deepened. Her hand reached out and very lightly touched the long scar on my ribs just below my chest, one of a number of reminders of Nam, my work, and a variety of what are known as youthful escapades. She touched several other scars, and I could see that they both frightened her and turned her on at the same time. Her hands went up to my shoulders and lightly down my arms, feeling the tautness of the biceps.

I was fully erect now, and as she looked down her lips seemed to grow puffy and her eyes seemed to cloud over. Her tongue ran over her lips, and her hand came up to the bikini top, pulled at the small bow that held it together, and it dropped off, revealing firm breasts with large brown nipples, straining and taut. Her hand dropped to her hip, untied the knots there, and the bottom triangle fell to the floor of the shower.

I cupped a breast in each hand and squeezed hard, feeling the tight young flesh. I put my thigh between her legs and she rode up and down on it, pressing her mound into my leg. Her breath was coming in harsh gasps, a low moan coming up from deep in her throat. She tensed, squeezing my thigh between both of hers, digging her fingers into my shoulders, small cries of pleasure being forced out of her. She relaxed, started to move on my thigh again, and almost immediately tensed again. This was repeated several more times. Her breasts were swelling within my grasp and were covered with gooseflesh. I dipped my head and sucked hard on one of her nipples, causing her to squeal with delight.

She stepped back, looking at me with the expression of mindless animal hunger I have often seen before. She bent over and ran the tip of her tongue lightly up my penis from the base of the shaft to the head which she lightly kissed. She stood up, and with a sudden growl of urgency, she clung to me. She reached down, maneuvered my penis between her legs and settled down onto me. Her hands went around my neck, and she lifted her legs and wrapped them around my hips. Her teeth were biting into my shoulder, and she was sobbing convulsively. Putting my hand under her buttocks I stepped from the shower, turning off the water with my other hand.

I easily carried her into the bedroom and laid her on the bed. I got her legs over my shoulders and pressed my full weight down on her as I moved inside her. As I continued, she started to shiver and shake uncontrollably, her cries of surprise and mounting pleasure growing higher until her body sagged, totally spent. I finished off quickly, and left her lying half off the bed, tossing her head from side to side, moaning quietly under her breath.

I went back to the shower, rinsed the sweat off me and toweled down. The girl was still lying there when I went back to the bedroom to dress. I put on some clothes and looked at my gun lying on the dresser, considering whether or not I should wear it. I decided I wouldn't need it for a while at least, and it was too goddamn hot anyway, so I'd just keep it in the glove compartment of my car. There are few things more uncomfortable than carrying a heavy piece on a scorching hot day.

By the time I was ready to leave, Lili or Lindi or whoever had entered the world of the conscious. She looked at me confusedly.

"You're not going out, are you?"

"Things to do, kiddo," I said as I walked from the

bedroom, seeing her mouth fall open in dismay. I crossed to the front door and called back to her. "Make sure the door's locked when you leave."

As I shut the door I heard a wail of despair. "Ohhh, Sammm . . ."

I hoped she wasn't going to turn out to be a pain in the ass.

SEVEN

I felt okay when I left my apartment, but the feeling soon deteriorated when I felt the full force of the heat. It was only a little after ten, but already things were starting to shimmer. Even the neighborhood's stray dogs found it too hot to scavenge around the garbage cans, and lay exhausted, panting, in small patches of dusty shade.

I got in my car, put my gun in the glove compartment, started up, and backed out into the street. The part of the Valley I lived in looked particularly dismal in the heat. The lawns were all brown and dry. The trees withered and drooped. Even the plastic bushes some people used for landscaping looked limp. Maybe they'd melted. A layer of dust had settled on everything, changing all colors to a uniform gray. And this was with water. Christ! What would it be like when the tap was turned off for good? All the natives would pack up their unsinkable Volkswagens and head across the Pacific for new lands on which to bestow the blessings of their civilization. The buildings would collapse, the pavement would crumble, the plastic palm trees would disintegrate, and it would return to the desert it originally was, where pitiful, mangy Indians dug and rooted in the hard ground for the grubs and beetles on which they survived. Looking at the endless rows of dumpy drive-in food joints broken only by the occasional used car lot, drive-in theatre, drive-in bank, drive-in supermarket, and drive-in mortuary—"Eternal Rest While-U-Wait"—I figured it couldn't happen soon enough.

I made pretty good time going across to the freeway, but as often happens, traffic slowed to a bumper to bumper crawl once I got on it. None of this made any sense to me. Here was the one city in the world designed as the exclusive domain of the automobile, with an extensive and elaborate highway system, and most of the time all you could do was about twenty miles an hour going into town. Rush hour was a bit slower. Another triumph for the planners and all the other assholes who think they know the answers because some machine told them which end of the pencil to sharpen.

We were moving about as fast as shit in a clogged sewer, but there was nothing I could do about it except relax and wait. I can do that when I have to, but some red-necked turkey in the car next to me had on a quadraphonic speaker system that was playing country-and-western garbage loud enough to be heard in Oklahoma. He was wearing a Hawaiian-patterned rayon shirt and puffing on a fat cigar which he didn't bother to remove from his mouth when he drank from a can of Lucky Lager. I scowled across at him and he laughed like he thought he was some king of the road. Since the traffic wasn't moving and it looked like I might be next to him for some time, I asked him to turn it down. He laughed again and told me to fuck off. It was too hot to put up with something like that. I reached across, opened the glove compartment, and pulled my piece from the holster.

"Hey, asshole," I shouted at him.

He turned and started to say something when I stretched my arm out and pointed the gun at his head. His mouth fell open and the cigar dropped out. His eyes grew wide and his lips moved, but no sound came out.

"Would you please turn it down," I repeated.

This time I had his attention. Without taking his terrified eyes off the gun, he leaned across the car, turned something, and the sound died away with an abrupt whimper.

"Thank you." I retracted the gun.

I turned back to the front, but I could tell that the turkey continued to stare at me, unable to believe what had just happened. What I did was, of course, grossly illegal, but who was to know. It worked, that was the main thing.

The guy suddenly gave a squawk of surprise and pain, and started bouncing around crazily. I guessed his cigar had started to burn him. Just then the traffic opened up, and I was able to pull away as the guy was frantically burrowing between his legs for the cigar.

About the time I got over the hill, the jam-up had thinned and I was able to make better time the rest of the way into town. I got off at Wilshire and headed for the fancy Beverly

Hills building where Maycroft had his office. It was one of those prestige addresses where all goods and services cost about fifty percent more than they would have a few blocks away. They weren't any better, they just cost more.

As soon as you walked in the entrance, you knew you were in a fancy place. You could tell because the air conditioning made it about ten degrees colder than was really comfortable. On an ordinary day it would have been unpleasantly cool, but in this weather, coming in from the stifling heat, you immediately felt chilled and clammy. But I guess money, like lettuce, wilts if it's not refrigerated.

I took the express elevator up to the twenty-fifth floor. Music played softly above the quiet hum of the elevator. For some reason the ceiling of the car was mirrored. Before I could come up with a plausible explanation for this odd feature I had arrived at my floor.

There were only two offices on the floor. One was the Eye of God Religious Foundation, Inc. I didn't know what they did, but they must have had access to the Purse of God to occupy this address. On the other side of the corridor, tiny raised letters on the wall spelled out SPODE, MAYCROFT AND BURBARY. If you were more than a couple of feet away, the letters would just look like specks on the wallpaper. There seems to be some sort of theory in effect that says the bigger the operation, the smaller and more discreet the sign announcing it should be. If I followed that rule, I'd have to use the whole side of my building. Of course it's all bullshit, but jerks who are impressed by the swell address will be doubly impressed by the tiny letters.

I opened a door that seemed as heavy as the doors to some bank vaults. The reception area looked big enough to hold a small African republic, and proceeds from the sale of the furnishings would have balanced the budget for that same republic. Everything was in shades of brown, from the palest beige to a rich sienna. There were a dozen Barcelona chairs against the wall, at about $1500 per. On one wall there were four canvasses hung, each about three feet square, and each covered with a slightly different shade of brown acrylic paint that had been applied with a roller. There was a small card that identified the paintings as a work called "Progression in Brown" by a currently popular artist. Through some work I had done for a dealer, I knew that the set had cost about fifty grand. At least the paint was put on nice and evenly.

The whole appearance of the office was designed to give the impression of solidity, sobriety, and success, and anyone encouraged by the little letters outside would be completely won over by the interior decor, and would fight to leave their money here by the bucketful. I knew better, though, and I would sooner keep my money in a sock under my bed than let these frauds get their hands on it. But there's no accounting for taste, as they say, and there are lots of people who are happy to go down the tubes while telling their friends about the swell Barcelona chairs in the reception room.

I waded through the ankle-deep, cream-colored shag carpet to the desk where the receptionist sat. She looked like she had been chosen by the decorator to harmonize with the interior. She wore an expensive beige two-piece silk outfit that too precisely coordinated with her light brown hair and brown eyes. Her skin was lightly but perfectly tanned. She had the cool, severe, thin appearance favored by high-fashion models which appeals to women, but rarely to men. She was obviously intended to contribute to the total effect of quiet elegance and superior class. The impression was spoiled slightly by the fact that she was energetically chewing gum. She was applying nail polish with the intentness and concentration of a diamond cutter working on a million-dollar gem.

"Just a minute," she said without looking up, as she finished off one long and perfect nail.

She carefully replaced the top of the bottle and turned to face me. Her expression of polite interest quickly faded when she saw me. Evidently she determined I was not a client, and therefore unworthy of any expenditure of charm. Just to make sure I knew my place, she very slightly wrinkled her nose, as if smelling some mildly unpleasant aroma. I sniffed loudly several times.

"Hope, it's not me," I said.

This caused her to sneer. She tilted back her head and looked at me from under drooping eyelids, as though my appearance was too shocking to be confronted fully.

"What do you want?" she said, barely moving her lips.

Before I could answer, the telephone rang. She announced the establishment and listened.

"I'll see if he's free," she said. She depressed the hold button and stared at the ceiling for about thirty seconds. She reconnected the line. "I'm sorry, Mrs. Spode. He's in an important conference and cannot be disturbed." An angry rattle came over the receiver. "I'm sure I don't know, Mrs. Spode. I'll tell him you called." Another angry rattle. The girl hung up the phone and looked at it as if it, too, smelled bad.

"What's Spode doing—laying a secretary on his leather couch? Or is it a wealthy widow client?"

"Really!" She started to sputter with the shocked indignation people display when you take a stab and come close to the truth.

"And who are you having it off with?" I said. "Maycroft or Burbary?"

"Now, look you—"

"I guess it's got to be Maycroft. Burbary has a decided preference for young boys."

Just then the door to the inner office opened and a blond, fair-skinned, slightly pudgy young man came out carrying a stack of envelopes. He hurried across the room, walking as though he had a dime between his cheeks and he didn't want it to drop, and went out into the corridor.

"Now that must be Burbary's playmate," I said.

A harsh laugh exploded from her, acknowledging the accuracy of my remark, but she quickly recovered herself and glared at me with considerable dislike.

"If you do not immediately state your business, I will call the security guards and have you thrown out."

"Does that mean you don't like me?"

She tried to look cool and detached—an ice princess from the pages of *Vogue*—but I wasn't fooled. She had the hollow cheeks and wide mouth of the inveterate cocksucker, and she had been speculatively eying the bulge of my crotch throughout our snappy repartee. I walked around the end of her desk and stood close to her, my crotch at her eye level. It was with difficulty that she raised her eyes to my face, and with even more difficulty that she tried to maintain her composure.

"Who do you think you—"

"I'm here to see Maycroft."

"I'm sorry, Mr. Maycroft is busy and cannot be disturbed. Perhaps you would care to—"

"Maycroft is expecting me."

"What's your name? I'll call—"

"Don't bother," I said, reaching across and stopping her before she could buzz his office. "I'll announce myself."

I walked to the door. She looked after me with a mixture of anger and confusion.

"You want to have lunch?" I said.

She sniffed haughtily.

I shrugged. "Too bad. I would have given you a nice lunch."

I went through the door to the office proper, where it seemed that some work was being done. At least there was the click and hum that is usually associated with a working office, and people were walking back and forth not completely aimlessly. The suckers that had their money there would no doubt be encouraged by this display of energy and purpose on their behalf.

I went down the hall to Ellis Maycroft's office and went in without knocking. He was leaning back in his chair, his Gucci loafers up on the desk. All his attention was concentrated on the smoke rings he was blowing to the ceiling.

"Sorry to disturb you, Maycroft, in the middle of your busy day."

He glanced at me without much pleasure. "Oh, Hunter." He also wrinkled his nose before he returned his gaze to the smoke rings. This could give me some kind of complex. Three showers this morning, and people were still acting as if I smelled bad.

His office was sparsely but expensively furnished. The big windows provided a panoramic view of L.A. that was slightly spoiled by the layer of yellow-green slime that hung over the city. Maycroft's desk was completely bare except for a telephone and a piece of pre-Columbian sculpture that he no doubt paid a genuine price for, but that I was sure was a fake.

The phone rang. Maycroft reluctantly lifted his feet from the desk, picked up the receiver, and listened for a moment.

"Yes, he's here. . . . No, that's all right. . . . That won't be necessary. Thank you, Carla."

He hung up and looked glumly at me. "That was the receptionist. You didn't make much of an impression."

"I must be losing my boyish charm."

"She wanted to call security and have you removed."

"The devotion of your staff is really something. Is she any good in bed? I bet she really loves to gobble you up, huh?"

He blushed—bull's-eye!—and then looked pained. "Hunter, is it really necessary for you to be so crude . . . And for the record, Miss Cavelli is an employee—nothing more."

"Fine. It's your record. I wouldn't want to scratch it. . . . Look, Maycroft, I already went through a dance with the delightful Miss Carla, and I don't want to do the same with you. I don't like being here any more than you like having me, so just give me the info I wanted, and I'll be on my way, farting and spitting and wrapped in my cloak of crudity."

He leaned back in his chair, folded his arms, and looked every inch the successful businessman. "Look, Hunter, I'm a senior partner in a large brokerage firm, and I don't appreciate your ordering me about when you need something."

"Did I do that? I called you as a friend for some assistance. I thought you'd like to help."

"Well, I'm sorry, but I wouldn't. Now if you'll excuse me, I have a lot of work to do."

Why do these assholes always make it so difficult? I tried to look beaten and unhappy, and Maycroft's dignity inflated a little bit more.

"I guess I'll just have to push off then."

"I guess so, Hunter."

"Could I use your phone for a minute?"

"What for?"

"Oh, I thought I'd call your wife. She might be interested in what's going on with Carla. She still controls all the money, doesn't she?"

"Now, Hunter—" he started to whine, perspiration beading up on his forehead.

"I'll call the SEC later. We both know there's stuff going on here that they'll be curious about."

That did it. He slumped in his chair, all the color drained from his face. He laughed in what was supposed to be a hearty, jovial way but sounded instead like a death rattle.

"Come on, Hunter, I was only joking. You know that."

"So was I, Maycroft." I laughed in a way that caused him to cringe.

"You won't be making any phone calls, will you?"

"Come on. Let's cut the shit, huh? Get on with it."

He could have been helpful, like I asked in the first place, and everything would have been simple. But he got to thinking about his $200 pair of shoes, and how big a man he is, and how his dignity is somehow on the line, and so he digs his heels in. I mean, who's he impressing? Himself, I guess. Maycroft's a jerk, but I didn't get much satisfaction from humiliating him. All I wanted was some information, which he was now about to give me.

He had taken a slim file folder from a drawer and placed it in front of him. As he flipped through the material to refresh his memory, the immersion in the familiar world of corporate dealings served to restore his confidence and composure. Our battle of wills was temporarily forgotten, and he spoke easily, the professional playing on his home field.

"You wanted to know about Medco Pharmaceutical Supplies, right?"

"Right."

"Ordinarily, I would not have been able to help you. Medco is a privately owned company, which means that their records are private, and I would not have access to them. It is also a small company, and we do not usually concern ourselves with small, private firms. However, I can give you a little information for two reasons. One, I am acquainted with Dr. Edmund Mustard, the former owner—we have played golf together on occasion. Two, because of the proposed take-over by Megaplex that you were asking about."

"Why that?"

"Because Megaplex is so large, so important a corporate entity, that anything they do—or think of doing—is of considerable interest."

"I see."

"I doubt it, but I will continue. As you probably know, Medco is a small firm that produces component chemicals for use by the bigger drug companies. At one time, this was, within its modest limits, a profitable enterprise, and Dr. Mustard was able to do very well for himself—he would not have been able to join our country club had it been otherwise. However, with time, many of Medco's biggest buyers began to produce the materials themselves, and Medco's business declined, as did that of several other similar firms. Dr. Mustard, who was sole owner of the company, was interested in getting into other fields, and when Megaplex made a fair offer for Medco, he was happy to accept."

"Why would Megaplex want a company that was going nowhere fast?"

"At the time that the take-over was considered, Megaplex was moving into the pharmaceutical field in a big way, and the acquisition of Medco would have served a purpose in conjunction with several other companies they were getting."

"Then why did the deal not go through?"

"I'm afraid I can't tell you. I remember meeting Mustard the day after he learned that Megaplex was calling off negotiations. He was most upset. Everything had looked definite, and then Megaplex simply backed out."

"Why?"

"They gave no reason. Or at least Dr. Mustard said they gave no reason."

"Who was negotiating for Megaplex?"

Maycroft looked in the file. "Adrian Sweet. He's a senior vice-president. A very sound man, if a little conservative. Perhaps he saw something in the books he didn't like."

"And then what happened?"

"As far as we were concerned, nothing. Once Megaplex lost interest, so did we. However, shortly after the deal fell through, I again saw Dr. Mustard at the club, and he was in excellent spirits. He had just sold his company to one of his employees."

"Simon Acker."

"That's right. And Mustard seemed to be overjoyed to be getting out, and also to be getting out with very close to his asking price."

"Which was?"

"I really couldn't say. Somewhere between half a million and a million, I would imagine. Not very much. The building was not owned, only rented on a long lease, and, as I said, business had been declining. If Mustard got anything around that, he had good reason to be happy."

"You may not think that's a lot of money, but Acker was only the managing director, and he didn't have that kind of dough. How did he do it?"

"Hunter," he said with some exasperation, "I'm not his bank manager."

"Okay, okay. Just asking. Got anything at all on Acker?"

"No, and there's no reason why I should."

"Why do you think Acker would want to buy the company? Wasn't it a losing proposition?"

"It seemed to be, but in business, people do strange things everyday. You wouldn't believe some of the colossal mistakes I've seen."

"But it wasn't a mistake," I said.

"What do you mean?"

"Medco's doing great. Acker has a great big house in Bel Air, and the company's soaring. At least, so I understand."

"Really! How surprising. I must make a note to look into that. Mr. Acker may be a man worth watching."

"Just what I thought," I said.

That seemed to be about all there was. As soon as Maycroft stopped trying to prove something, he turned out to be all right. As far as I was concerned, he was still a fraud, but even frauds have to know their stuff if they want to pull it off. I thanked him and said we'd be in touch, which soured him a bit. I made for the door and he leaped up, nervously saying he'd accompany me downstairs.

"What's the matter, Maycroft? Are you afraid I'll unzip my fly and expose myself to dear Carla. Shit! She'd probably follow me home with her tongue hanging out if I did that."

Maycroft cringed slightly and looked a little green. It was an unnecessary comment on my part, but, fuck, I get so tired of his type. Twits like Maycroft think they're so civilized they can handle anything, but their guts turn to cat puke when they encounter a barbarian like me. Like my father said, I believe in playing my game, not theirs.

Maycroft nervously ushered me across the reception area. I noticed that he and Carla exchanged meaningful glances. When I reached the outer door, I turned and grinned at her.

"Don't worry, honey. I fixed it so the bruises wouldn't show, though he may not be much good for a few days."

Her eyes grew wide with alarm, and I laughed as Maycroft pushed me through the door. We didn't exchange any conversation while waiting for the elevator to arrive. The doors opened and he followed me in. Too much!

"I may not be a hot-shit stockbroker," I said, "but I can find the ground floor in an elevator."

Maycroft didn't answer. His eyes were turned upwards and he was delicately fingering his scalp, making certain his hair piece was in place. I laughed. At least I had found out the reason for the mirror on the ceiling of the car.

EIGHT

I drove through town to my office. The temperature felt like it was rising by the minute. All movement was slowed down to about half normal speed, and the heat haze made everything look as though it were seen through a distorting mirror. It wouldn't have been too bad, but the exceptional heat combined with the exhaust fumes of a million malfunctioning automobiles, and the result was that pleasant effect of greasy heat. You find the same thing in traffic-clogged Bangkok during hot season, and a few other fortunate locations around the world.

After a lot of stop-and-start driving I finally made it to my neighborhood. As usual there was no place to park, so I left the car at the back of the local used-car lot. I wasn't much worried about anyone being tempted to buy the thing—rust-rimmed bullet holes haven't yet caught on as a popular decoration.

On the way to the office I went into a submarine-sandwich joint. I had a fresh Italian roll filled with lots of extra-spicy chorizo sausage and covered with a burning-hot chile verde sauce. It was so hot that even my forehead started to sweat a little, and I felt the fiery tingle from my teeth all the way down to my belly. The proprietor, an oily little Turk, watched with amazement as I munched on some pickled serrano chiles as I ate the sandwich. I washed it down with a couple of icy San Miguel beers from the Philippines.

I lit up a cigarette as I finished the second beer. I was convinced there was something going on with Simon Acker and Medco. I didn't know what, but there were too many abrupt reversals for it to be completely legit. There was going to be a take-over, and then there wasn't. The company is going under, and then it seems to be quite successful. The Ackers have no money, but then he comes up with some very heavy dough and buys the company. He shares his problems with his wife, and then he becomes secretive. There was something there, but what? And what any of this had to do with the man-monster and Domingo was still a mystery. I'd had problems like this before, though, and I knew I just had to keep stirring things up, making noise, and getting people nervous, until all of a sudden—zap!—things fell into place.

I stood up, dropped my cigarette on the floor where it joined the numerous generations of butts already there—the Turk wasn't very strong on cleanliness, which probably accounted for the potency of the chile verde—and went out into the afternoon.

By the time I had covered the two short blocks to my office building, my already limp shirt was even more so. I stepped over the wino who was prone in the doorway, either dead or laid low by the heat. The elevator again had a crudely printed sign, Owt of Oder, on it, so I went up the stairs. On the second-floor landing another drunk had passed out in a pool of oddly colored vomit.

I went into my office to be met with a nice friendly greeting from Maria. At least she didn't wrinkle her nose at me. In spite of the heat, she was looking pretty cool, or as much so as that hot tamale ever got. She was wearing a skimpy cotton halter that left her middle bare and showed her heavy breasts off to great advantage. Her skirt was just about long enough to cover her ass. Not your standard office attire, but who was complaining? The outline of her nipples showed clearly through the fabric in a way that started my jaws aching, but I decided to pass for the moment. When I got this situation sorted out, we'd have a couple of nice weeks in Mexico. If this was what she wore to the office, I wondered what she'd wear on the beach. A smile, probably.

I asked if there were any messages, and she said Mr. Argyll had called. At first I didn't know who that was, and then I realized she meant Stubby. It was probably the first time since World War I that anyone had referred to him as Mister. Stubby Argyll had been a P.I. for about a hundred years. He smelled bad and most of his teeth were gone, but he was smart enough to never cross me, so we got along. He said he'd be in Jack's around 3:30, and I should stop by if I could.

I looked at my watch. That left me a couple of hours which I could put to good use. I went through the connecting door

to my office. I was surprised to see that everything had been
turned right side up and reassembled. The desk was a little
the worse for wear but otherwise was about the same as it had
been before Godzilla had tried his hand at redecorating.

Maria had followed me in and stood grinning at my
surprise.

"Are you pleased, Sam?"

"Yeah, Maria. That's swell, How'd you manage?"

"I got the janitor to help. He was very upset at the
damage."

It figured. Janitors, who are paid in pigeon shit and a small
spoon, always act as though it's their property, and not a tax
write-off for some asshole relaxing in the Bahamas. I got five
dollars out of my wallet and handed it to her.

"Get him a bottle of something strong and cheap, and tell
him thanks."

"That's not necessary. He was happy to do it—for me."

No doubt, the horny old bastard.

"I bet he made you pick up all the little stuff, though."

"That's right. How did you know?" she said, surprised.

"Hey, baby, I'm a detective. Remember?"

It wasn't hard to figure. Maria was more stimulating than
any cheap whiskey, and the sight of her bending over in that
tiny skirt would be enough to inspire the dead, or at least the
comatose. The janitor was probably still groaning and salivat-
ing at the recollection of it.

"Never mind. Give him the bottle, anyway. I've a feeling
he could use it about now."

Maria shrugged and turned to go. Halfway to the door she
bent to pick up a small scrap of paper. The transparent
panties she wore left little to the imagination. Yep, the janitor
had been well paid for his assistance.

"Say, Maria," I said, and she turned around. "You want to
go down to Mexico with me for a couple of weeks? We'll find
a quiet beach someplace where I can do some fishing."

Her face lit up and she ran across to me, her breasts
bobbing gently in the halter. She kissed me quickly on the
mouth, let her hand lightly run up my thigh, and then ran
from the office, grinning over her shoulder. I guess she
wanted to go.

I checked the addresses of some gyms where pro wrestlers
worked out, and I saw I could visit a few of them before it was

time to meet Stubby. I told Maria to stay around for another couple of hours and then lock up. She seemed genuinely disappointed that I wouldn't be back. A nice trait in a secretary.

I went to the used-car lot and found that some bozo had put a card on my windshield saying "Must Sacrifice—$750." I kicked my front tire and decided I wouldn't pay it. I put the card over the official one on a two-year-old Cadillac and drove off.

I got nothing at the first two gyms I visited. Hardly surprising since the grunters that were hanging around needed cue cards to get their own names right. One of the guys was trying to read a comic book. He took a liking to me when I helped him with several of the tougher words and told me I should try the Regal over on Fifth.

I still had time, so I drove over there. The sign over the door was so chipped and faded as to be nearly illegible. With effort you could read that it said "Regal Gym—Training Ground of Champions." At one time that might have been wishful thinking, but now it was only the grossest irony. The closest the Regal had ever come to training a champion was in '35 or so when some sixth-ranked contender worked out there before he was kicked out of boxing for throwing too many fights. The guy took so many dives that he should have practiced in a swimming pool. Since then it had all been downhill for the Regal. Now a few has-been wrestlers hung out there, hoping to get on a card in Turlock or some other armpit town, and low level goons worked out there, honing their reflexes so they could intimidate seventy-five-year-old shopkeepers. It was a class operation.

I went through the door and up the narrow flight of stairs that led to the gym. Halfway up I was met by an almost visible locker-room smell of stale sweat, unwashed underwear, and cheap cigars that had been accumulating for five or six decades. The rivers of raw sewage in a Saigon slum gave off a no less appealing aroma. Lighting up a cigarette and being careful to breathe through my mouth, I pushed ahead.

The gym itself was small and dominated by an ancient, sagging ring in which a couple of overweight candidates for a retirement village were sweating heavily as they threw one another around with a maximum of noise and grimacing and a minimum of skill and realism. Off to one side a pair of greasy young punks with sloping foreheads and vacant, moronic expressions were trying to flip cards into a hat on the floor about six feet away from them. I thought that was only done in '40s gangster movies. That feeling was heightened because they were both dressed in shiny black shirts and skinny white silk ties. No one had told them that this was the age of denim.

I walked over to them and asked if they knew a monster named Mountain Cyclone, but they didn't look at me and just continued to toss their cards. I stood in front of the hat and repeated the question.

"Hey, man, you're in the way," the one with no chin said.

"I asked a question."

"Fuck off. We ain't no information service."

They thought that was pretty funny, and started braying and snorting like a pair of mules.

"I'm looking for this Mountain Cyclone, and I heard he hangs around here," I said, suppressing the impulse to kick in their stupid faces.

A look passed between them that told me they knew him. They whispered together a minute, and the one with a squint yelled to the back of the gym.

"Hey, Cueball, ya better come out here."

A door at the back opened and this thing appeared. I could see why he was called Cueball. He was short and damn near as wide as he was tall. He had a huge barrel chest and a belly to match. His waist measurement must have been equal to his height, and his arms were as thick as most people's legs. There was a lot of fat there, but there was also a lot of muscle. He was an albino, and his skin was that pasty white-pink that you sometimes see—so white that it seemed to blend into his T-shirt and white canvas trousers. He was a giant white ball, and as he rolled over toward me I saw that he was also completely hairless. No hair on his scalp or face, no eyebrows, not even any fuzz on his arms. It wasn't shaved off; he just didn't have any hair. He rolled to a stop close to us. His small red eyes flicked at me and then turned to the two punks.

"What is it?" His voice was high and squeaky and totally out of keeping with his appearance. It sounded like he might be a eunuch.

"This jerk is asking about Mountain," one of the punks said.

"So?" Cueball squeaked.

"So we thought you should know."

Cueball gave the punks a scornful look which made them squirm, and turned to me.

"Class material," he said. "They need a diagram to know which end to shit out of."

I shrugged. "They say good help is hard to find these days."

"You want to discuss the employment situation, or what?"

"I want to find Mountain. You can tell me where he is."

"Who are you?"

I told him my name, and he laughed with a sound like fingernails being scratched across a blackboard.

"Yeah, I heard about you. Mountain did a little number on you." He laughed again. "Mountain's really something, isn't he?"

"He's something, all right, but you see, he did some damage to my office, and I figure somebody's got to pay for it."

"That somebody's you." He laughed again, and I shook my head. "Pal, you're really stupid, you go looking for Mountain. People who are smart stay out of his way."

"Where is he?"

He looked at me with his little red eyes. "Interview's over, pal. Clear off."

"Where's Mountain?"

Cueball turned to the two punks. "Boys, this guy's really stupid. He can't even find the way out. Why don't you show him where it is?"

I shook my head sadly, and the two punks yucked it up a little. The chinless one reached under his chair and came up with a baseball bat. He swung it a couple of times as he walked toward me.

"It's nice to see youth taking an interest in sports," I said, standing still, completely relaxed and alert.

The punk looked pleased that I wasn't running. He stood a few feet away from me with the bat cocked over his shoulder, excitement shining in his rodent eyes. He took a hard swing for my head, but he completely telegraphed his move and I easily stepped aside.

"You'll never hit big league pitching with a swing like that," I said.

He came running at me with the bat held over his head. As he swung down at me, I ducked under the blow and flipped him over my back. He hit the floor hard and the bat fell from his hands. I picked it up just in time to see the other one running at me with a length of lead pipe. He swung down at my head with enough force to crush my skull, but I pulled out of the way and then quickly turned back in as I swung the bat with all my force. It struck him dead center on his knee and I heard the kneecap shatter. He crumpled to the ground, screaming in agony and writhing in pain.

The first one was on his feet. He looked at me shaking the bat, willing him to come on, and then he looked at his friend crying and groveling on the ground. He ran for the stairs and out of the building.

I looked around for Cueball, but he had vanished. The two old groaners in the ring clung to one another in a sweaty embrace of mutual exhaustion, unaware of what was going on. I heard heavy footsteps going downstairs in the back. I got to the door in time to see Cueball turning the corner at the bottom of the stairs.

I gained ground going down the stairs, and when I got to the back parking lot, he was only about ten feet ahead of me. I ran after him, and when I got close enough I threw a tackle that would have been respectable from a Ram linebacker. He went down, but his momentum carried him out of my grasp and he rolled upright just like one of those kids' inflatable punching bags with a weighted bottom. I jumped up ready to continue the chase, but he wasn't running. He stood facing me in a karate stance that looked like he knew what he was doing. I shook my head. It figured.

He started advancing slowly toward me, his red rabbit eyes shining. I backed up, but I soon ran into the side of a parked car. I wasn't worried, but I tried to look like I was, hoping to make him overconfident. He smiled a little and then suddenly kicked his foot high and slashed back at me, trying to plant his heel in my stomach. I moved to the side just out of reach, but he immediately followed with an overhand chop aimed at my head. I ducked just in time and the side of his hand came down on the front fender of the car. The fender crumpled nearly in half as it was torn away from the body. It was an old car, but still . . .

He instantly turned and his other hand slashed out with a horizontal chop going for my throat. I moved enough for the blow to miss its target, but it still caught me on the chest just below my shoulder, knocking me back about six feet. He sensed a kill and came charging at me full speed, his thick arm straight out at his side, planning to cut me in half. At the last second I turned sideways, caught his wrist in both of my hands, and swung him away from me. His speed and the suddenness of my move propelled him into the wall of the building, and he hit it face forward, arms spread out, unable to break the impact. He hit with a tremendous splat and seemed to stick there.

I was upon him before he had a chance to recover and got one of his arms in a brutal hammerlock, bringing his hand up nearly to his head. When I pulled him away from the wall, there seemed to be an outline where his body had struck the stucco. He twisted and squirmed his massive body, and he tried to reach behind with his free arm, but my hold was too good, and the only way he would get out was by dislocating his shoulder.

I applied still more pressure and there was a high-pitched grunt of pain.

"Now, what about Mountain?"

"Fuck you," he squeaked.

Maintaining my hold, I slammed him into the wall. He grunted again. I repeated my question. He repeated his answer. It looked like we could keep up this routine almost indefinitely, but I was starting to grow numb from where he hit me, and I knew I couldn't hold him much longer. I looked around and got an idea.

Being careful to keep my grip, I got my fingers in the neck of his T-shirt and pulled hard, ripping it completely down his back.

"Hey!" he squeaked in surprise.

I took advantage of his brief disconcertion to pull the shirt off him without losing my position of control. His upper body was as round, smooth, hard, white, and hairless as that which gave him his name.

"What are you—"

I cut him off by roughly turning him around. I marched him into the parking lot, away from the building. As we approached the edge of the shadow cast by the building, he understood what I had in mind, and he started to struggle and plead in panic.

He tried to dig his heels in, but I pushed the albino out of the shadow and into the powerful, brilliant sunlight. I turned him around to face the sun.

"Stop! You'll kill me! You'll kill me!" Almost immediately his skin started to turn pink.

"Talk. Tell me about Mountain."

"I don't know anything." His already high voice rose in panic as he tried unsuccessfully to struggle free.

"Talk, or I'll keep you here until you fry and turn black and shrivel up like a sausage."

"Okay, okay! I'll talk. Only let me get into the shade. You'll kill me." His skin was turning bright red in spots.

"Talk."

"Yeah. I know Mountain, but I don't know anything about him. He comes in once in a while. He was in yesterday, that's how I heard about you. That's all. Please."

"Who does he work for?"

"I don't know."

"Who does he work for?" I applied more pressure to his arm.

"I don't know. For the love of Christ, I'm telling you the truth! I don't know."

I pushed his arm some more.

"I swear to you, I don't know. Look. He used to work at a place called the Black Knight—some kind of private club—but there was trouble there, and he don't work there anymore. Please! Let me into the shade."

"Keep talking."

"Jesus Fucking Christ, there's nothing to say. Only that he didn't seem bothered at losing his job. Got a better one. For somebody real big, he said."

"Who?"

"I don't know. Look, you got to believe me. If I knew, I'd tell you."

"He ever say anything about Domingo?"

"Nothing. Mountain don't talk much, except about guys he's torn apart. He likes to talk about that."

"What else is there?"

"There's nothing. I swear. I'm dead if you don't let me into the shade. Please." His voice was going weak. He was red all over now and his skin was blistering in places.

"If that's all there was, why did you put up such a fight?"

"I don't know. I'm sorry I did it. Only Mountain, he don't

like people talking about him. And I don't want to get in bad with Mountain. You got to believe me!"

I did. Cueball was telling me the truth because he knew if he didn't I'd keep him out there until he burned up.

I gave him a hard shove as I released him, and he scrambled into the shade where he collapsed. He was starting to swell up and go all puffy. They'd have to call him "Tomato," at least for a while.

He looked up at me from eyes that were nearly swollen shut.

"You're fucking crazy, man," he said weakly in that high voice that sounded like a recording played at too fast a speed.

I looked down at him. I shook my head. I didn't know why everybody felt they had to take the hard route today. Maybe it was the heat.

NINE

I was feeling a little grubby after my exertions. Since my office was on the way to my meeting with Stubby, I decided to stop off there, wash up, and put on a clean shirt. On the way I thought about the fact that Mountain had once worked at the Black Knight Club. I didn't think a lot about it because it wasn't very much to consider. It was suggestive, but of what I didn't know. If I kept pushing, I was sure it would reveal itself.

The cops were in the process of hauling away a car from the tow-away zone in front of my building, so I hung back and pulled in as they were leaving. They gave me a dirty look through their rear window. Fuck 'em.

There was still a body sprawled across the entranceway, but it was a different one. Somebody had stolen the son of a bitch's shoes. It he wasn't careful, something was going to come along and eat his feet.

The elevator seemed to be "in oder" again, so I rode it, clanking and grinding, up to my floor. The door was locked, so Maria must have gone home. There was a note that Charlie Watkins had called. Also someone selling life insurance. Something about that struck me as being funny in a not very pleasant way.

I've got an old stained sink in a closet in my office that occasionally spits rust-colored water. After a noise like the starting line at Indianapolis, some stuff came trickling out. I took off my shirt, noting I was going to have a nice bruise where Cueball had hit me, and sponged down. The water was never hot or cold, always unpleasantly tepid no matter the weather, but it served to wash off the sweat and dirt even if it didn't refresh.

I stayed stripped to let the air dry me as I poured a tumbler of gin. I took half of it in a swallow, lit a cigarette and sat down, letting the gin relax me and ease the throbbing of the bruise. I sipped at the rest of the drink, thinking of nothing in particular, or maybe about life insurance. I tried to call Watkins at the station but nobody knew where he was. I gathered that people were looking for him at that end as well. I found a clean shirt in the file cabinet, put it on, and went downstairs. Almost as soon as I went outside, the shirt started to cling to me, and my thoughts skipped to a breezy Mexican beach.

My car was still there, but a mongrel dog was eying it speculatively. My approach made him reconsider. I eased into the sluggish stream of traffic just as the police tow truck pulled up behind me. I waved at them and headed the short distance across town.

My neighborhood was not so swell, but there was a steady block by block deterioration as I proceeded. The area where Stubby hung out was undecided whether it was Chicano, black, or down-and-out white. The only thing it was sure of was that it was dirt poor and getting poorer. Everything and everyone there had a tentative quality, always looking nervously over their shoulder for the cops or the immigration or the flood of urban renewal that would one day sweep over them and wash them all away.

I parked the car and gave a kid who was standing around two bits to make sure no one took anything other than what was easily removable. He pledged eternal loyalty, or something to that effect.

Stubby Argyll's "office" was a table at the rear of Jack's Pool Palace. He had used these facilities for longer than anyone could remember, and his tenancy had seen an endless series of Jack's come and go. He gave the proprietor a few bucks a month, and for that he got his table, a small closet in which to keep his stuff, and his own telephone line. Jack answered the phone when Stubby was out and took messages. The arrangement seemed to work pretty well, and none of the parties concerned had ever seen any reason to change it.

The current Jack was a large Polynesian woman who looked up from her copy of *Ms.* and gave me a sour nod as I walked to the back. Stubby was at his table, looking over yesterday's racing form, trying to figure out what had gone wrong.

Stubby was a little scrawny guy who looked about 150-

years-old, and not an especially well-preserved 150. His face was all nose and chin that nearly met somewhere in front of his toothless mouth, and his brown, wrinkled skin made his head look like it was a dried up apple. He was wearing a three-piece plaid suit, but each of the pieces was a different color and pattern, and they were all so large and hung so loosely on his shrunken frame that it was difficult to believe there was a body within. His polka dot shirt and striped tie complemented the rest of his outfit, giving him the look of a demented race track tout. But appearances were deceiving, and Stubby was still tough and fast and had a great nose for things that weren't as they should be.

Stubby's nose, however, was not very sensitive to his own distinctive scent. He believed baths sapped your body's vitality, and consequently he took only about one a year, whether he needed it or not.

Stubby looked up from his paper and an expression of amazement crossed his face, as though my presence was totally unexpected. This was just Stubby's way, and if you had gone to the john and come back a minute later, he would have greeted you with the same look of surprise.

I sat down opposite him, tilted my chair back in an effort to stay as far downwind from him as I could manage, and waited.

Stubby thought for a while before speaking.

"Hot enough for you?" he said.

I waited.

"You know, it's not the heat but the humidity," he said, as though that was an original idea.

I waited.

"It's this damn smog. It keeps all the moisture in," he said.

I waited. It was almost over.

"This place used to have a nice climate, but not any more." He shook his head disgustedly and spat with a loud ping into the brass spittoon next to his chair.

This was Stubby's standard conversational opening, with slight variations depending on the season. Someone once told me this was because Stubby originally came from Canada, where you couldn't talk about anything else until you had taken care of the weather, but I didn't know one way or the other.

Somebody dropped a beer down next to me, and I drank it

and had a smoke as I looked around the pool hall, waiting for Stubby to get around to whatever it was he wanted.

Like everywhere else in this heat, business at Jack's was slow and there were only a few customers. A pair of hookers who were long past their prime—if they ever had a prime—were draped over another table, looking as though they were hoping they wouldn't have any clients until about autumn. Considering their appearance, I thought they might get their wish.

At one of the front pool tables a couple of guys were finalizing arrangements for a game. I could see that a little one-armed black man was pretending to let himself be hustled by some dude. The black man was called One Arm Shifty, and the dude was obviously a stranger because no one around here would ever shoot pool for money with Shifty. But the mark must have thought a game with a one-armed man was a pretty good bet. The mark broke and then Shifty went to work. It took him about nine shots to clear the table. The balls were racked up, another nine shots by Shifty, and the balls were racked and cleared for the third time. The dude watched with growing disbelief and anger as Shifty hopped around the table, contorting himself into strange positions, using his nose for a bridge, and never missing a shot.

After the third rack, Shifty held out his one hand to be paid. The dude refused and Shifty complained to Jack. The big woman reached under the counter, pulled out a Maori war club that looked like an intricately carved cricket bat, and lumbered toward the dude shaking her weapon. The dude took one look at her, quickly paid up, and ran out the door.

A loud hawking noise followed by another ping in the spittoon told me that Stubby was about ready to start talking.

"Say, Sam, I got something that might interest you."

I nodded, and Stubby chewed his gums a bit, like he was trying to find the right words in the corner of his mouth.

"You know somebody named Acker?"

"Male or female?"

"Male. Runs some kind of drug company."

"I'm working for his wife." Only when Stubby mentioned the name did I realize that Clarissa Acker had been nestling at the back of my brain all day. I wasn't sure I liked the feeling. "She's interested in his activities," I said.

Stubby shook his head. "Yeah, so I heard."

"Where?"

"From the party in question—Acker, male."

I must have showed my surprise, because Stubby's apple-head bobbed vigorously.

"Yeah, I know," he said. "Sort of strange. Yesterday, this Acker calls me up, and when I see him, he tells me that you're investigating him and he wants me to keep my eye on you."

"What for?"

"That's what I asked him. He said he wanted to know what you were getting on him so that he'd be able to counteract it in time. He says his wife is after his money, and he doesn't want her to get a dime more than is absolutely necessary. You might say the love has gone out of their relationship."

"Yeah. You might say that. How did the setup seem to you?"

He shrugged. "I don't know. I've heard of things like this before—and it's not a bad idea—cautious, careful, maybe save a lot of money. But somehow it just didn't seem right, though I can't say why. I know one thing, though. That Acker is a tough customer, so cool he's a little scary."

"You took the job, I assume."

"Of course." He looked shocked that I thought he might have done otherwise.

"Did you say you knew me?"

"He asked. I said I knew who you were, that's all."

I thought for a minute. The situation might be legitimate; Acker's explanation might be real. But I didn't think his wife was after money. One thing seemed certain, though; if Acker hired Stubby, he didn't send Mountain after me. There'd be no point.

Out of curiosity I asked Stubby what he was getting for the job. He looked only slightly embarrassed when he told me a figure that was nearly four times his usual fee. Stubby laughed when he saw my reaction, and said that Acker accepted without any hesitation.

"This is a man who's so careful and cautious, so tough and cool, and he agrees to pay an outrageous fee like that?" I said.

Stubby thought for a second. "Yeah, you're right. It is curious. I didn't think about it at the time. I guess I was too happy at landing a big fish. What's up?"

"That's what I'm trying to find out." I told him about the warning I had received.

"You think Acker sent the monster?"

"It doesn't look like it, but I don't know. Do you think Acker might have hired you, not because he was worried about his wife, but because he was worried that I might find out about something else?"

"That could be." He thought for a bit. "You know, I think there's something strange going on at that factory or whatever it is."

"Like what?"

"I can't say. It just doesn't feel right. That's supposed to be a pretty successful operation, isn't it? Well, it didn't feel that way. It seemed a little like a place where a fire's going to start, you know, sort of accidentally on purpose."

"You think that's what it is?"

He shook his head from side to side. "No, it's not that. I been in enough places like that to know—I even helped torch a few in my younger days. But the place just feels wrong in some way, like those other places felt wrong, and my instincts are pretty good."

I knew they were, and that helped along the feeling I had that Acker was into something more than long-legged girls who didn't mind being beaten a little. Stubby and I agreed to help each other out on this, since it looked like it might be mutually advantageous. Stubby clearly didn't feel much loyalty to his Acker, especially if there was a chance to get more out of it than his fee.

I took out a smoke and saw that I was out of matches. Stubby dug around in a pocket, pulled out a book, and pushed them across to me. I lit my cigarette and started to pass the matches back when I noticed the cover. It was shiny black with an embossed chessman on the front. Tiny gold letters on the spine said "Black Knight."

That seemed to be coming up a lot lately, just like when you see a new word for the first time, you keep running across it for a while. I asked Stubby where he got the matches and he shrugged.

"Come on, think," I said. "Where'd you get them?"

"Why?"

"Just tell me."

He screwed up his dried-apple face until it was nothing but creases and wrinkles, his jaws chewing away like mad. He cleared his throat and spat loudly.

"Acker," he said.

"You sure?"

"Must have been. Why? What's it mean?"

I shook my head. I didn't know, but somehow I wasn't too surprised at the connection.

"Okay, Sam, I know you. You never give anything away."

"Not if I can find a buyer. And I don't know if this is worth anything."

Stubby knew better than to push it, and we discussed how we should proceed.

"Acker won't be expecting anything from you for a while," I said, "so we'll get together in a couple of days and work out something to give him. We'll make it good so he'll think you're earning that ridiculous fee."

Stubby tried to look offended. "It's not so ridiculous. The client wanted results, and he's going to get them."

"If not in the way the client intended."

Stubby made a face and spat. "Screw the client."

Not a bad philosophy in this business, particularly since most of our clients would try to do it to us if we gave them the chance. Most of the time, being honorable meant getting fucked . . . or not getting paid. But for some reason I was going to try to be straight with my Acker.

"In the meantime," Stubby said, "I'm going to nose around a bit and try to find out what Simon Acker's up to. I'll see if I can see what makes his business seem so funny. What are you going to do?"

"I'm not sure yet."

I was sure, but there was no percentage in telling Stubby. I'd let him follow his own line and I'd follow mine. Maybe they'd meet somewhere, and if not, I didn't want Stubby getting in my way.

We agreed to keep in touch and pass on anything of interest.

I left Stubby sitting at his table. The two hookers had fallen asleep across theirs. One Arm Shifty was practicing a difficult three cushion shot and making it look easy. Jack didn't bother to look up from her magazine as I went out.

TEN

Since the Black Knight Club popped up every time I turned around, I figured I'd better keep on with it to see where it took me. You don't have to be in my business very long before you begin to appreciate the importance of accidents and coincidence. You can plan fully, prepare carefully, and work hard, but an awful lot of the time, coincidence will make you or break you. You look really hard for the key piece of information, and when you stop looking because you decide it doesn't exist, you trip over it and everything falls into place. A lot of veteran cops know this, and it turns them into gamblers or mystics.

I wasn't either, but I follow signs when I see which way they're pointing, and that was why I was up in the hills looking for Nicky Faro's house.

I went by it twice before I found the number. It was easy to miss since all you could see was a small mailbox next to a narrow driveway that was mostly hidden by thick shrubs. The house was one of those little bungalows found throughout the Hollywood Hills, stuck down below the road and completely screened from everything by trees and bushes. These houses used to be some of the few cheap places in L.A. where you could have nearly total privacy, but they've become pretty popular now and are no longer so cheap.

I parked up a ways on the road and walked back down to the driveway. There was a car parked at the bottom of it, so it looked like somebody was home. I didn't bother to call first because I figured this Faro guy was another one of those that it's better to visit unannounced.

I walked on the thin strip of grass next to the gravel drive so I wouldn't make any noise and quietly started moving around the house, looking in the windows. The third window I went to looked into the living room, and I saw that someone was indeed there.

Rock music was playing very loudly and a couple were dancing around pretty actively. They were both naked. The woman was short and had a heavy, pale, fleshy body that was starting to lose its firmness, and a pair of the largest breasts I had seen in a long time. "Cantaloupes" was an understatement, but her breasts seemed to bounce in an unnatural way, and I figured they were shot full of silicone. Her hairdo and her heavily made up face told me she was a pro.

The guy—who I took to be Faro—was dark complexioned with wiry black hair. Tall and bony, his body was seemingly without either fat or muscle. He also had a huge, erect cock that must have measured fifteen inches, and was the kind of attribute that was only seen in stag films—usually on bulls or donkeys.

They danced around a bit with the forced enthusiasm common to paid relationships. Her enormous breasts looked like they were balloons about to lift her off the ground. He looked like he could win a three-legged race by himself.

He motioned her to get on her knees. He came up and jammed his cock between her breasts, which she pressed around it with her hands, and he started pushing and thrusting. It looked like it was a good time to make my entrance.

I went around to the back, where I had seen the door was open. The screen door was unlocked and I silently went in. I crossed to the living room.

His back was to me as he worked away, and the woman saw me first. She screamed. He whirled around.

"Sorry to interrupt," I said. "Census Bureau."

"What the fuck do you want?" he spat at me.

Before I could answer he was moving across the room to a desk in the corner. I had seen movements like that often enough to know what was coming next, and I started moving as well. I was at the desk as he got the drawer open, and by the time he pulled out the gun—a good old .45 automatic— I was throwing a hard right that caught him flush on the jaw. He crumpled joint by joint like a marionette until he lay in a pile on the floor. Oddly enough, his cock remained stiff and straight.

The woman was no longer screaming, but was glaring angrily at me. She seemed used to this sort of occurrence.

"What do you think you're doing, buster?"

"It's not your concern," I said, "but your friend will be all right."

"Man, I don't care if you off the schmuck. It's just that—" She cut herself off, came over next to me, and tried, but failed, to look seductive. "I like you. I like strong men. He'll be out for a long time. Why don't you and me have some fun. I'm really special, baby. I'm worth it."

She took my hands and put them on her breasts. They felt like overly inflated beach balls. She started to rub her belly up against me. I gently pushed her away.

"Maybe later," I said. "Now you'd better go."

"Shit! You goddamn son of a bitch. How's a working girl supposed to get along?"

She was right. I asked how much she was going to get.

"A bill."

I saw Faro's wallet on the desk. I took out four fifties. "Here's two bills. Forget you were here."

"I been at the beauty parlor all afternoon. You're okay, honey. Sure you don't want me to take care of you quick? On the house. I really am good."

I told her good-bye. She shrugged, threw on her clothes, and was out the door in about a minute. I heard her go up the drive, and soon a car started on the road.

Faro was still out, and looked to be for some time. I lifted him onto a straight-backed chair and tied him securely with a couple of neckties I found. I wanted to look around without worrying about him coming to and sneaking up behind me. I pocketed his gun. You never know when a loose weapon might come in handy.

There was nothing to be seen in the kitchen, bedroom, living room, or bath, except that Faro was a piss-poor housekeeper. There was also a door that was locked. I could probably have found the key in about two minutes, but what the fuck, who can be bothered? Two good kicks and the door splintered open.

Behind it was an elaborate darkroom setup, with lots of good quality equipment and some expensive cameras on a shelf. Faro hardly seemed the type to have this kind of hobby, but then I saw the prints on the drying rack and everything came a little clearer.

The pictures might be called action shots, but the kind of

action that goes on behind closed doors. Each picture involved a couple—not always of different sexes—engaged in
some not-too-conventional sexual practice, often employing
exotic costumes or implements. The pictures were not posed,
and, from the lighting and the angle, I gathered that they
were candid shots taken with a hidden camera. I only
recognized one face in the bunch, that of a well-known
Hollywood actor who was entangled in a complicated posture
with an extremely young girl. I began to get a clearer notion
of the Black Knight Club.

There was a metal file cabinet with a heavy padlock on it.
In view of what I had already seen, its contents were
tantalizing, but I couldn't open this without a key, and I
decided it was time to have a chat with Faro.

He was just coming around and was not especially pleased
with his condition. He yelled and cursed and threatened me,
but he was hardly in a position to do anything about it. I
asked him about the club. We danced around that a bit and all
I got out of him was that I was in big trouble, and that if I
didn't let him go, there wouldn't be enough of me left to feed
to a small dog. Hardly the kind of cooperation you expect
from someone who is tied bare-assed to a chair with his hose
hanging over the seat.

"If anyone's going to be dog meat, pal," I said, "it won't be
me."

"Oh yeah, fuck face?" Clever, very clever comeback.

"I wonder what your boss would do if he found out one of
his trusted employees was a police snitch."

"He'd laugh," he said somewhat uncertainly.

"Would he? Not if he knew that that trusted employee was
playing it cute with Detective Thomas Ratchitt of Vice." Faro
paled and his bony face took on the appearance of a skull.
"Tell me what I want to know, or I'm going to throw you to
the sharks."

He protested some more, but finally realized that he had no
choice.

Faro had been at the club just under two years—it had been
operating for about three or four—and he said he was a kind
of general assistant. He then confirmed some things that I
already knew or had suspected. Basically, the Black Knight
was a very expensive whorehouse that specialized in fairly

kinky stuff. They put on fancy sex shows for the members, and there were a number of back rooms for more personal endeavors. There was a lot of S-M, a good deal of elaborate costume fantasies, and a fair use of children. In all categories there were hookers of both sexes, depending on the clients' persuasions or momentary interests, and the club's specialties could be combined in any variety of ways to meet all possible scenarios. Naturally all this came high. Faro didn't know for sure how much, but it was a lot, and you had to be pretty wealthy or want it very badly to indulge yourself. Faro recognized a few celebrities who made use of the facilities, but other than that, he had no idea who the members were. One of the features of the club was the guarantee of complete security. I let that pass for the time being.

A guy named Freddy Lascar ran the club. Faro stayed with that story for a while, but after I put on some more heat, he said that Lascar was just fronting for someone. Lascar ran the day-to-day operation, but if there was a big decision to be made, it was referred somewhere else. Faro didn't know who was behind Lascar. He said he had never heard of anything or anyone called Domingo, and I believed him.

He had heard of Mountain, though. When I mentioned the name he went pale again and started to sweat. Mountain had served as the club's muscle for a while, but there were a couple of incidents where he used a little too much of it. He had broken up one of the club's girls pretty badly while he was taking his pleasure with her. I had trouble imagining what that monster liked to do, but I knew it would have to be rough on his partner. It was, and the girl was in an institution for life. But Faro said that was more of an annoyance than anything else. The real trouble came when Mountain messed up one of the members—the host of a TV game show. Faro didn't know the reason behind it, but the guy had to spend a lot of time with a plastic surgeon before he could face the cameras again. It was hushed up pretty well, but some of the other members heard about it and got nervous. Mountain was yanked soon after that. Faro didn't know where he went, but Mountain still came to the club every so often. He would spend a few minutes with Lascar and then leave. I showed Faro the picture of Linda Perdue, the missing girl, but he said he'd never seen her.

Naturally there was a big fix in, and Ratchitt was getting to be a wealthy man as a result. Faro was on the payroll because the Vice cop wanted to know about anything unusual going on at the club. Faro figured Ratchitt wanted to be able to up the ante if something happened, but Faro said he'd only given the cop garbage.

Throughout all this, Faro had grown increasingly nervous.

"Hey, man, that's all. I don't know any more. It's a very tight operation there. If they hear I talked to you, I'm finished."

"Then you better make sure they don't. And if I find out you haven't been straight with me, you're just as finished."

"I've been straight," he said. "Now will you let me go? My arms are killing me."

"A couple more questions."

"Hey, man, I don't know anything more."

"Tell me about the blackmail."

"What blackmail?" His voice rose an octave and he started to sweat again.

"Don't play cute. I saw your darkroom."

"Photography's my hobby."

"Smarten up, or your only hobby will be growing flowers from the bottom up."

He sighed. "Okay. Some of the rooms have hidden cameras, both video and still, but I don't ever see the videotape. Every once in a while they give me some film to develop and print. Like I said, photography's really my hobby. I just give them what they want. Swear to God, I don't know what they do with the stuff."

"But you make extra prints, right?"

"Hey, I wouldn't do that."

I laughed in a way that made him cringe and repeated my question.

"Hey, okay. I make some extra prints. But I haven't done anything with them . . ."

". . . yet." I finished his sentence.

"Okay . . . yet. . . . I sort of figured I'd get some security for my old age, kind of a pension. Put a little black on those guys. They can afford it."

"Faro, the way you're going, I think your old age is the least of your worries."

"I can handle myself, but your future won't be much if you mess up the deal at the club. It's a very serious operation."

"Your concern touches me." I paused long enough to get him off guard. "Now give me the membership list."

"What!" He jumped enough to nearly tip over the chair to which he was tied.

"I . . . I . . . told you. I don't know who the members are. . . . I don't have any list."

"Then it'll be tough for you to blackmail them if you don't know who they are."

He looked puzzled for a second. "Hey, I never thought of that. You're right. Pretty stupid of me, I guess. Ha ha."

"Never mind the list, give me the key for the padlock."

"The key?" He was jumping again.

"The key."

"I don't know where the key is. I guess I lost it. I've been meaning to get a hacksaw and cut it. But there's nothing in there anyway. Just some chemicals and paper, stuff like that. . . . Hey, where are you going?"

I had walked into the kitchen. I opened a couple of drawers until I found a large, heavy knife, and went back into the living room.

"What are you doing?" Faro squirmed in the chair.

"Unless you tell me where the key is, sucker, I'm going to start cutting pieces off that long prick of yours and make you eat them. We'll keep it up until you tell me, or until you have nothing left."

"Hey, man, that's not a very funny joke." His voice cracked and broke, and he was sweating profusely.

"Depends which side of the knife you're on."

His eyes were wide as I brought the knife toward his cock. When the blade just touched him he screamed.

"No! No! Stop! The key's in the desk. Taped on the bottom of the middle drawer."

I smiled at him and found the key. He was shaking and crying. Suppose he had really lost the key?

I opened the cabinet. There were folders containing photos similar to the ones I had already seen. The folders had no names on them, only numbers. The numbers went up to about 150, but there wasn't a folder for each number. I looked at some of the pictures. There was one of a super-tough cowboy star dressed as a ballerina. He was being whipped by a small woman clad only in knee socks and a black mask. He seemed to be enjoying himself.

I flipped through the folders. At the back of the cabinet, under some papers, was a plain envelope. In it were two sheets of paper, each with three typed columns of names. The names were numbered up to just over 150. Some of the names had check marks that coincided with the presence of folders. Very orderly.

I looked over the list. I found Simon Acker's name. That certainly didn't surprise me. There was no check next to his name.

It almost didn't register when I saw the name Adrian Sweet, but then I realized that was the guy who had been in charge of the proposed merger of Acker's company. Now that was interesting. There was a check next to his name, and a folder to match. There were only a couple of pictures in it. In each there was a thin man in his late thirties with a young boy of about twelve. They were both naked. In one the man was spanking the boy with a large wooden paddle. In the other, the positions were reversed. The man looked keen and intent. The boy seemed mildy bored.

I took the folder, along with the membership list, and went back to the living room.

Faro was composed again, but looked very pale and drawn.

"Interesting stuff you've got there," I said.

"What are you going to do with it?" he said weakly. "I'm a dead man."

"Not if you act smart. I took one file. You can keep the rest for now. I also took the list, but since you didn't have it, you won't miss it. Now there's one more thing you've got to do, and if you play it easy, nobody'll find out about you—at least not from me."

"What do you want?"

"I want to get into the club tonight. I want to see Lascar."

"Are you crazy? I can't do that. That'll blow everything."

"Not if you do it right. You'll tell Lascar that you met me somewhere, and that I've got a business deal for him."

"What kind of deal? It'll have to be good."

I thought for a minute and suggested something to him. He wasn't happy, but he thought it would work. We worked out our story, and I told him when I'd be coming by the club.

I cut the neckties with the knife. He stood up, but immediately fell to the ground. He had cramped up from being tied so long.

I turned as I got to the front door. "Remember, Faro, you cooperate and you'll come through this. If you try to fuck with me, I'll pull the plug on you."

He looked at me with a scared, mournful expression as he tried to work some life back into his knotted limbs.

Lying on the floor in a twisted heap he didn't look like much.

He wasn't.

ELEVEN

It was early evening by the time I got back to my apartment. A lot of the sun's power had diminished, but the heat that had been soaking into the ground all day was now radiating back up in an effort to compensate. There was no wind at all to provide any cross ventilation through my apartment, and it was about as comfortable as a sauna bath.

I took a tall glass, put a few ice cubes in it, and filled it up with gin. I swirled the ice around a couple of times and drank off half of it. I don't know if it cooled me off or just made me less sensitive to the heat, but I started to feel better. I put in another ice cube, refilled the glass, and took it into the bathroom. I stripped and got under the shower, letting it run hot and then gradually turning off the hot until it was running straight cold. Periodically I stuck my head out and took a pull on my drink. After about ten minutes of this I was feeling okay. The soreness where Cueball had hit me had completely gone, but it looked like the bruise would stay around for a few days.

I lay around for a while until it got dark, letting the events of the day flow around, waiting to see if any clear patterns emerged. I was starting to see some outlines, but there was nothing very firm. I had a feeling, though, that it wouldn't be too much longer.

I got up to dress. I looked in my closet. I didn't have anything sleazy enough for the part I was going to play, so I decided to dress for comfort: a pair of hopsacking trousers, a loose-fitting shirt and a lightweight sportcoat to cover the gun I would wear on my belt at the back. I looked in the mirror. I didn't exactly look like a porn merchant, but it'd have to do.

I went out into the night, which had turned very muggy without getting any cooler, and headed back to town. On the

way I decided I felt like barbecue, and when you feel like
that, there's only one place to go.

Mama's Bar-B-Que is not located in a black neighborhood,
but it's good enough for a steady stream of blacks to cross
town to eat there regularly. For a couple of blocks around the
place, the streets were lined with pimpmobiles—those cus-
tomized chrome and pastel hybrids with Cadillac fins in the
rear and Rolls-Royce grills in the front that cost their owners
over 50 K.

Inside, Mama's was crowded as usual. The owners of the
cars were there, each with an elaborate display of gold and
diamond jewelry, each surrounded by his stable of ladies.
The tables that weren't occupied by pimps were full of the
biggest numbers men or dope movers, each trying his hardest
to look like the pimps. Most succeeded. I couldn't have stood
out more if I had come in wearing a white sheet and carrying
a burning cross, but I had once helped Mama out of a jam,
and she liked me, so my presence was usually tolerated.

The place wasn't much to look at—a few rooms crowded
with tables covered with red-checked tablecloths. Sawdust on
the floor. Old ceiling fans that didn't do much good. Beer
advertisements that alternated with old travel posters for the
Rhine Valley provided the only decorations. Not much of a
place except for Mama.

Even with all the fancy ladies and their fancier men, Mama
dominated the place like a cat in a cage of canaries. A shiny
black woman, enormous, ageless, who dressed like a southern mammy, she was everywhere at once, her gravel voice
shouting orders to the cooks, telling the busboys to move
faster, trading jokes with the customers. She helped out at the
huge stove, ran the cash register, and moved with the grace of
an Olympic gymnast.

Mama had run the restaurant for more than forty years,
and she was an institution that was known in every ghetto in
the country. Like all institutions, she inspired a lot of wild
stories. Most concerned her immense wealth: everybody said
she had a ton of money buried under her house, but she said
she was just a poor cook. She laughed when she said it, and
no one believed her.

The best story, though, went back a long way. One day
Mama had found that her current old man was cheating on

her. She didn't like that since she'd given him all kinds of presents. There was only one thing to do. She hatcheted him, and for the next couple of days he was served for dinner. They said he was pretty good. Nearly every day since then, some fancy man would come in and ask Mama if she had any of that special long pig. Mama would just laugh and say, "Not unless you're offerin' your services, honey."

I sat down at one of the few vacant tables. Mama knew what I wanted, and soon a large platter was put down in front of me. There were enough ribs on it to make up half a pig, along with homefries, greens, rice and beans, and a lot of cornbread. The sauce on the ribs was a combination of sweet and hot, and no one had ever figured out what was in it. The hot burned your throat, but right away the sweet soothed it like honey. Mama had turned down a lot of money for the recipe, and there was nothing else like it.

I washed the whole thing down with some cans of Tecate beer and felt pretty good. I lit up a cigarette and watched Emile, the black dwarf newsie, walk by with his odd rolling gait. Up front he had a newspaper stand, but he ran the biggest book in the city. His clothes were always torn and dirty, but he owned a lot of Beverly Hills real estate, and he came to Mama's in a chauffeur-driven limo.

After one of Mama's dinners, about all you want to do is curl up with a nice soft woman. I had one in mind, but I had other things to do. I paid and drove to the Black Knight Club.

The club was in a big house on one of those old quiet streets south of Hollywood Boulevard. There were no signs on the place. The windows were boarded up, and it looked dark and deserted.

I went up the walk and rang the bell. Nothing happened for a while, and then the peephole opened up and an eye looked at me for a long time. I wondered what would happen if I suddenly jammed my finger into the eye. Maybe next time.

The door opened about a foot and a beefy guy with a bulldog face blocked the way.

"Yeah?" he said.

"I'm here to see Lascar."

"Mr. Lascar don't see nobody."

I was saved further stimulating dialogue when Faro came over, moving nervously like a gimpy stork. Bulldog reluctantly let me in, and I saw that he had a twin standing next to him. They were both wearing badly fitting dinner jackets that were too small for their large shoulders, causing them to hunch over awkwardly, a pair of penguin weight lifters.

Faro led me down a long hallway, not saying anything or even looking at me. On the way we passed a large room that was set up like a lounge with lots of couches and chairs facing an elevated stage. Even though the room was extremely dark, I could see most of the seats were occupied by men looking expectantly at the empty stage. A number of the men were being fondled by women who wore little or nothing.

At the end of the corridor we came to a door. Faro knocked and we went in. He introduced me to Lascar and quickly left.

Lascar was lean with unhealthy pale skin. He had a black patch over one eye and an ugly-looking scar ran up his cheek and disappeared under the patch. He was dressed in a black suit over a black turtleneck. He was smoking a long, thin Brazilian cigar. He was the perfect image of a tough, sophisticated sex club manager, but somehow he didn't quite make it. It was a role he didn't look comfortable with, and he knew it, which made him seem even more awkward. He tried to appear relaxed, but he made a nervous movement with his head, continually twisting it to the side and looking over his shoulder with his good eye.

We looked at each other for a while until he felt compelled to break the silence.

"I understand you're selling something we may be interested in." He had a surprisingly soft voice that almost had a stutter in it.

I told him I represented a group of South American gentlemen who sold some very special goods and services to selected clients around the world. From what I knew of the Black Knight, I said, I was certain they would be interested in purchasing the full range of products. Up to this point, Lascar was looking bored. I then said I was selling a series of snuff films. At those two words his attitude changed, and while he tried to look uninterested, I knew I had him.

In the sexual underground, snuff films have an almost mythical quality attached to them. Stories about them abound, but few people have actually seen them. Each new rumor of the existence of one sets off a frenzy of activity to locate it. Very simply, snuff films are like most stag films except they end with the torture, mutilation, and murder of the woman. The thing that gives them their high market value is the fact that they are real—the leading lady does not come back to make a sequel.

Lascar questioned me closely about the films I was selling, not believing at first that they were the real thing, but I described them in detail and soon convinced him.

"The broads are really offed?" he said, and I nodded. "How much you want for them?" He had difficulty remaining cool.

"Ten thousand apiece, and you have to take all five."

He started coughing and choking.

"That's way out of line," he said after he recovered himself. "I can get stuff like that for a lot less anywhere."

I stood up. "Bullshit. If you can get the genuine article anywhere else, be my guest. I thought this was the right kind of operation, but I guess I wasted my time."

I moved to the door. His head was jerking and twisting around like a weather vane. He called me back.

"Wait a second. I might be interested, but I'll have to think about it."

"You mean you'll have to ask the boss?" I said with a lot of contempt.

"I am the boss." He failed to sound very convincing.

"Bullshit. If you were the boss the deal would be made already. With the kind of place you run here, you could get your bread back two or three times over, easy. These are quality goods."

"Take it easy. That's a lot of dough. I'm interested, but I've got to talk to a few people first."

"Why don't you just tell me who the man is, and I'll deal with him direct. Otherwise no deal. I don't like talking to jerks who have no authority."

He was getting pretty upset. "I can't tell you. The man likes to stay behind the scenes. If he wants to talk to you, he'll talk to you."

"You're blowing it. I wonder what the man'll say when he hears you fucked up?"

"Take it easy. We'll work this out. It'll take a couple of days is all. Besides, there ain't no place else in town you can move films like you've got."

"Maybe not," I said. I looked at Lascar and decided it would be a good time to send out a feeler. "Meanwhile, maybe you can help me out. One of my clients is looking for a girl, a particular girl. She ripped him off or something, and he wants to see her again. If you could get a line on her, I'd be willing to sell the films cheaper. Your boss wouldn't have to know, and you could have the difference."

Lascar started to look more comfortable. This was more in his line, and he could always use a little extra. His kind never had enough. "You came to the right place. I can locate any broad. If she's in the trade, I can get her. Who is it?"

I took the picture of Linda Perdue out of my wallet and handed it to him. "That's her. She looks like somebody's virgin daughter, but take it from me, she's a lot of trouble. A whole lot of trouble."

As soon as Lascar saw the picture, all the color drained from his face, he started coughing again, and his head twisted around almost completely. I was obviously onto something, but I decided to let it rest for the time being. Lascar looked at me, and I could see that he was really frightened. I just stared back at him without any expression until he started to relax.

"Never seen her," he said when he'd calmed down enough, "but I'll ask around. Maybe I can come up with something."

"Okay, do that. I'd appreciate it, and, like I said, it would be worth your while."

Lascar couldn't figure out what was going on, but, since I was moving to the door, he was breathing easier. I decided to rock him one more time.

"Say, I almost forgot," I said. "My clients wanted a little technical assistance."

"What about?"

"The kind of cameras you use in your private rooms."

"Cameras?" The word barely came out, and he was twitching again.

"Yeah. The hidden cameras that you use for the blackmail pictures. My people haven't been getting very good results with the setup they use, and they wondered what you had. They also wondered how you monitor the rooms. Do you use closed circuit video, or do you have something else?"

"Who the hell are you?" He was pretty scared.

"What's the matter?" I said as ingenuously as I could. "Wasn't I supposed to know about that? Oh, sorry. I just figured every place like this had a similar arrangement—good for maximizing profits, as the schoolboys from business admin. say. If you don't want to share trade secrets, that's okay."

I was opening the door by this time.

"Wait a second," he said. "How do I get in touch?"

"Don't worry about that. Tell the man my name. I've got a feeling he'll be contacting me. If not, I'll get back to you."

I shut the door behind me. Lascar had a funny expression on his face as I left. I was still operating in the dark, but I thought my performance might turn some lights on for me.

I looked into the lounge on my way out. The show was just beginning. An oily little bastard was announcing it was something called "The Spanish Inquisition." From the murmured reaction of the audience, it was obviously a big favorite around here.

A spotlight came on to reveal a pretty blond girl who was completely naked. Her skin was very white and her nipples very pink. She was lifted above the stage by ropes attached to her wrists. She was surrounded by three men in dark red cloaks with hoods over their heads. She screamed as they began to poke and scrape at her fair skin with various metal implements. From where I was, I couldn't tell if it was real or fake, but I wasn't much interested. I left before the performance was over. I had a fair idea how it came out.

I made good time getting home.

I turned on my telephone answering machine. There was a message from that asshole who was trying to sell me life insurance. If I ever ran into him, he'd damn well better have hospitalization.

There was a message from Clarissa Acker. She said hello.

Hello, yourself.

Shit.

There was also a message from Stubby. Even on the tape he sounded excited. "Hey, Sam, I'm onto something big. Boy, is it ever. We're going to be golden. I can't talk now. Somebody might be tailing me, but I can get free. We got to get together soon. This is big, big . . ." The tape clicked off.

I didn't bother even to wonder about what Stubby had found. I'd get in touch the next day.

Just then I heard a noise in my bedroom. I pulled out my gun. I turned on the tap in the kitchen sink to cover my movements, took off my shoes, and silently went across to the bedroom. In one motion I threw on the overhead light, jumped clear of the door, and pointed the gun in the direction of the sound.

It was Bobbi or Debbi or whatever her name was. She was lying on top of the bed, naked. Her knees were bent, and her thighs were open wide. She was pinching her erect nipples between the thumb and forefinger of each hand. When she saw me with the gun, she raised her hands over her head.

"I give up," she said quietly.

Shit. She *was* going to be a pain in the ass.

I shrugged. I'd deal with it later.

TWELVE

It was pretty late by the time the girl snuck downstairs to her own apartment. She was even more eager than her mother. Ah, the vitality of youth.

In spite of the heat I managed to sleep in later than usual. When I got up, the apartment was already an oven and I was covered in a film of sweat. A shower, and I was ready to ease into the day.

While I was brewing some double strength coffee—three parts Colombian, one part Kenyan for an acid bite—I called up Stubby. Jack answered and said he hadn't been around since the previous afternoon. I asked her if she knew where he lived and received a snort of laughter for a reply. It was a stupid question. For more than thirty years no one has known where Stubby lived. There were a few theories on the subject, but no evidence to support them.

I fried up some flour tortillas with cheese and a lot of chiles inside and ate these along with a papaya sprinkled with lime juice. While I was sipping my coffee, I looked up the number of Megaplex. After a couple of transfers I reached Adrian Sweet's secretary. He was in conference, his line was busy, he was on holiday, he was not to be disturbed. Very protective, these secretaries, but I kept insisting. Finally she agreed to take my name.

"Just tell him I heard he was interested in photography," I said, "and that I'm a dealer with some curious specimens he'd want to see."

She wasn't very happy about that, but agreed to pass on the message. Almost immediately a nervous-sounding voice came on the line.

"Who is this and what do you want?"

I told him I had some pictures that I found amusing, but

that others might not appreciate. He denied any knowledge of what I was talking about, and I had to threaten him a bit.

He groaned. "Oh God! Another one. What do *you* want?"

"Look, Mr. Sweet, I've got some idea about the problems you're having, and I may be able to help you, but I've got to see you, and soon. If you're not interested, I'll just send the pictures to some parties who may be."

He didn't sound thrilled by the prospect, but he agreed to meet me for lunch at the Pheasant d'Or.

Soon after I hung up, I heard the knob of the front door turn, but the door was locked. There was a soft knock. I figured it was Vicki or Ricki or whatever, back for more. Christ, what a nuisance.

I crossed the room and opened the door about a foot. I saw two hefty men standing there. The one in the front put his arm through the door and stuck a gun in my face. Shit! I hadn't even had my second cup of coffee.

I just stood there, trying to look surprised and frightened, and suddenly I slammed the door with all my force. I caught his wrist between the door and the jamb. I heard a loud crack that wasn't the door breaking. The gun dropped out of the hand and there was a scream of pain. I yanked open the door, grabbed the guy's arm, pulled him in, and flipped him over my back. He hit the floor hard enough to rattle the windows.

I turned around and the second one was racing in, reaching under his jacket for a gun. I didn't hesitate but threw a punch at his jaw with the full weight of my body behind it. From the way it went all soft at impact, I knew I had shattered his jaw. He flew through the air a few feet. As he hit the floor, a spray of blood came out of his mouth, followed by three or four teeth.

The first one was starting to groan and sit up. I jumped on top of him, knocking him back down. I put my hand at his throat and was just about to crush his windpipe when I heard a voice behind me.

"All right, Hunter, that won't be necessary."

I turned around and saw a large man with a dark tan. He was dressed in an expensive beige summer suit and wore a high-quality Panama. He was smoking a ten-inch cigar. He looked like an ad for a Caribbean resort.

"I'm Ratchitt of Vice," he said.

"And what's this garbage?" I motioned to the two bodies.

"Just a couple of my boys."

"They make a nice entrance. Didn't anyone ever teach them to identify themselves? If they had, I could have saved them some doctor bills. On the other hand, I just might have killed them if I'd known they were vice cops."

He laughed, briefly and coldly. "I guess it's my fault. I told them you were a tough guy and that you might not be too keen to talk to us. I guess they were a little too enthusiastic."

"It happens. No harm done."

He laughed again and looked disgustedly at the two cops. The one with the broken wrist was sitting up and staring stupidly around.

"Benson, get yourself out of here, and take Phillips with you."

The one with the broken wrist struggled to his feet. With his good arm he took the arm of the other one and dragged him through the door. I heard a few thumps that must have been Phillips's head hitting the steps as they went downstairs. Ratchitt shut the front door.

"Hunter, we've got a few things to talk about."

"Fine. What'll it be? The weather? Or the declining quality of those who are making law enforcement their profession?"

"Don't try to be smart, Hunter. You don't make it."

I hoped I looked suitably abashed.

"I'll tell you just this time," he said. "Stay away from the Black Knight Club. You are impeding an important police investigation."

"Is that what I'm impeding?" I shrugged. "It's okay with me if that's what you want to call it, but I would've thought there were more precise terms—bribery, take, graft, protection, probably a few others."

"Hunter, don't be stupider than necessary, huh? Stay away from the Black Knight."

I was obviously stepping on some toes, and my visit to the club had brought a quicker response than I had expected. I said as much to Ratchitt, but he ignored my comment. He looked around my apartment, an expression of distaste curling his upper lip.

"What a dump," he said.

He wasn't far wrong. My apartment's decor could be described as "early motel," but, fuck it, I didn't care.

Ratchitt held up his cigar. "Look at this. Made special, by hand, from Cuban tobacco brought in through Mexico. Can't buy them anyplace. I spend more on my cigars in a week than you spend on rent in a month." To make the point, he dropped his cigar on the floor and crushed it with his foot.

I didn't react. I knew I could have broken Ratchitt in half, but it wouldn't have accomplished anything at this time. I was sure there would be another opportunity. "Your success story is an inspiration to us all," I said mildly.

He sighed heavily. "Hunter, I'll try to explain it so that even you can understand. You're a two-bit shit kicker of a P.I. who thinks he knows some stuff, and who's trying to make waves in the pot so he can get some of the drippings. Well, you don't know sweet-fuck-all, and you never will. But I know you. You're a bum and a punk. Let me tell you—I've got a great big house in the hills with a pool. I've got a forty-foot cruiser at the marina. I spend more on suits in a year than you earn."

"And they say that crime doesn't pay," I said with a shake of my head, but Ratchitt just continued.

"No cheap P.I. or anybody else is going to fuck that up. Get it? You might be able to deal with jerks like Benson and Phillips who are even cheaper and stupider than you are, but you've never come up against anyone like me. You fuck with me, and I'll bury you. You can count on it."

I just smiled at him.

"Like I said at the beginning, Hunter, stay out of police business."

"As in, 'Crime is the business of the police'?"

He shook his head. "So long, sucker. Just remember—if I have to see you again, it's your ass." He stopped at the door. "Oh yeah. You might pass the message on to your buddy, Watkins. He's poking his nose into things that are none of his concern, and if he keeps it up, he's going to be in deep shit."

He left.

I don't think much of cops, but to be fair, there aren't many like that asshole. Of course, it doesn't take many like him to stink up the whole force.

Ratchitt was right about my not knowing what was going on, but people were starting to be bothered, and that was what I wanted. In spite of the way he sounded, even he was getting upset, and I liked that. With his house and his boat and his Cuban cigars, it would be a positive pleasure to take him down, that slimy creep. And I would. Yes, I would.

I picked up his broken cigar. It did look like a good one.

THIRTEEN

The Pheasant d'Or was one of those supposedly classy restaurants around La Cienega. As far as I could tell, the main thing it had going for it was the reputation of being one of the three most expensive restaurants in the city. Apparently lots of jerks impressed themselves by eating there. I would have preferred to meet Sweet for a hot dog somewhere.

I pulled my car into the entranceway, and a kid dressed like the palace guard from the court of Kublai Khan came over to park it. He looked at the car and then at me.

"Are you sure you're at the right place?" he said.

I snarled at him and he jumped. He looked as though he thought it would be beneath his dignity to have anything to do with my heap, and he hesitated before getting in it.

"Don't worry," I called to him, "I got most of the dog shit off the seat."

He leaped out and wiped the seat down with a rag he carried.

I went in, and a guy who looked a little like Bela Lugosi on a bad day ran over to block my path. He, too, looked like he thought I was in the wrong place.

"I'm here to see Sweet," I said.

"Gentlemen usually prefer to wear neckties in here," he said without moving his lips, as though to do so would somehow compromise his stature.

"That's all right. If I was a gentleman, I'd probably prefer it as well. But I'm not, so there's no problem."

"Sir, we have extra neckties. I will bring you one," he hissed at me.

"Sir," I hissed back, "if you do I will shove it up your tight little asshole."

"Well, really—"

"Now, move aside, you greasy toad, or I will pick you up and throw you into the middle of the buffet table."

I had spotted Sweet over at one side, walked across to him, and introduced myself. He looked the same as he did in his pictures except a little more drawn around the eyes, and he didn't seem to be enjoying himself nearly as much.

Bela came hurrying over to the table.

"Is everything all right, Mr. Sweet?"

"Yes, André," he said, not too sure if it was.

André asked if we wished drinks. Sweet ordered a Scotch. I asked for a lot of gin in a tall glass with a little ice. André shook his head as if to say he should have known. He handed us leather-covered menus that were nearly as large as the table and as thick as the telephone book for a medium-sized town. André asked if we wished to order now or later. Sweet said the abalone was excellent and we both said we'd have that. André looked pleased to leave.

I said, "If that guy's an André, my name's Chou En-lai." After that, we both sat in silence. Sweet tapped his fork on the table.

The drinks arrived. Sweet looked relieved, drank his in one gulp, and signaled he wanted another. I tasted my gin. It was cheap and might have been watered. More silence.

The food came. Sweet seemed happy for the diversion and attacked with enthusiasm. The abalone was frozen, tough, and badly prepared. I'd had much better at the shack next to the Santa Monica pier. We ate in silence. Halfway through the meal, André came over and asked Sweet how everything was.

"Fine as ever, André."

André smiled and bowed slightly forward.

"The gin is cheap and the food's lousy," I said.

André's smile froze. He pulled himself erect.

"The gin is the finest imported English gin," he said.

"You may use imported English bottles," I said, "but the stuff inside is the finest domestic cat piss."

André sputtered for a minute and then hurried away.

Sweet looked pained. "That wasn't necessary, you know. I frequently eat here."

"That's one of your lesser problems." Sweet cringed as I said that. I looked at him steadily. "Look, Sweet, you may not believe it, but I'm not here to fuck you over. I came on hard because I wanted to get your attention, and that seemed to be the easiest way to do it. I'm a private investigator, and the Black Knight seems to figure in a case I'm working on, but I can't get much information about it. That's where I want your help. In return, I may be able to do something for you. I don't know yet, but we'll see how things turn out."

He hesitated. "How do I know I can trust you?"

"You don't, but what do you have to lose?"

He thought about that for a minute and shrugged helplessly.

"You're being blackmailed?"

"Yes. I thought you knew that."

"I assumed it. I didn't know for sure. How can they blackmail you? I know what they've got on you, but that seems to be pretty mild stuff these days when nearly anything is tolerated."

"I wish that was the case, but I'm pretty vulnerable. You see, the people who run Megaplex are Mormon and very conservative. They'd prefer that their top executives didn't even smoke or drink, but they know that's unrealistic, and so those 'vices' are tolerated. They'd have no such tolerance for my . . . uh . . . habits." He paused and I nodded. "I also have a wife and family whom I love very much. They have no idea that I like . . . certain kinds of things . . . and I know it would destroy them and our relationship. I don't want that to happen."

"So how much are you paying out?"

"That's the funny thing. I'm not. Well, I am, kind of, but basically I'm not."

This started to get confusing, so I had Sweet explain it from the beginning. After a lot of questioning from me, and a lot of digressions for self-pity and self-justification from him, I finally got most of the story.

Sweet's obsession for discipline dated from the years he spent at an English boarding school in the early '50s when his father was working in London. Homosexuality among the students was traditional at the school, and mildly sadistic forms of punishment and abuse were among the main diversions. For years after Sweet returned to the States, those experiences were forgotten, but under the pressures of work and family life, cravings to experience those pleasures again began to assert themselves. He tried to suppress his feelings, but the harder he tried, the stronger the urges became, until they were nearly tearing him apart.

One day an acquaintance managed to get the truth out of him. Instead of being shocked, the acquaintance understood completely, and he told Sweet there was a place where he could do anything he wanted—a private club that made fantasies real, and not only that, but did so with complete security and discretion. For Sweet it was a dream come true, and he soon became a member of the Black Knight Club. It was expensive—ten thousand dollars to join and a thousand dollars a month membership fees, plus extra charges for the use of the private rooms—but Sweet had the money, and for the first time in years he felt completely satisfied. His work improved as well as his relations with his family, and no one had any idea about his secret life.

Suddenly all that changed. Sweet received a phone call telling him that photos existed and would be made available if Sweet didn't cooperate. The caller didn't want money, but only wanted Sweet to queer the take-over of Medco that he was currently negotiating. Sweet didn't believe about the pictures and refused. Shortly afterward, he was visited by the biggest, ugliest man he had ever seen—friend Mountain, of course—who showed him a couple of photos and exercised some none-too-subtle persuasion. Sweet was terrified that his whole life was about to fall apart, and saw no choice but to cooperate. The take-over was a comparatively small matter for Megaplex, and Sweet had little trouble in canceling the deal. He never understood why anyone would want to stop the merger, and he never knew who was blackmailing him. Other than the voice over the phone, he never had contact with anyone except Mountain.

The whole episode scared Sweet shitless, and he stopped going to the club. He still paid a thousand dollars a month, though, and he lived in terror of another telephoned demand.

The one thing Sweet did was talk to the man who had introduced him to the club. It turned out that the man was similarly coerced into enlisting Sweet—not Sweet specifically, but anyone in a position of power and influence. That man had since committed suicide, and Sweet confessed that the uncertainty of his situation, plus all the guilt he felt, had led him also to consider that escape.

Sweet said that of course he knew Simon Acker who had taken part in the negotiations. He was surprised when Acker bought out the owner of Medco after the take-over fell through, but Sweet was deeply involved in his own dilemma and did not think much about it. He didn't know Acker belonged to the Black Knight and was startled to hear it. No, he repeated, he didn't have a clue about what was going on.

"Does this help you at all?" he said after he had finished the story.

I thought. Had it? I knew more than I had before, but it seemed that the more I got, the more complicated it became. I didn't know if I was getting closer to or further from the answers. The Black Knight was sure some operation, though —taking it in from all sides and directions. Money from one end, power and influence from another. Whoever was behind the club must have enough people in his pocket to do just about anything he wanted. Quite a setup. I could see why Ratchitt would fight pretty hard to protect his piece of it.

And what was the situation with Acker? He seemed to be right in the middle, or close to it. Was he being blackmailed? Faro had no pictures, but there might be something else. And if Acker was being blackmailed, what did he have to do? And where did he get the money to buy the company? And why? Too many questions. Maybe Stubby would have some answers when I got in touch with him in the afternoon.

Sweet was watching me closely as I thought about all this, despair, hope, and expectation crossing his face.

"Do you think you can do something?" he said. "It'd be worth a lot to me." I bet it would.

"I don't know yet, but I'll make you a deal. Let's see, you're paying twelve grand a year now in membership fees. I don't want anything up front, but if I can get you free, give me half of that—six K. One time payment, and that's it. Fair enough?"

He nodded. "But you'll have to be careful. I mean, I don't know what would happen if they found out I was talking with you. I'm sure they wouldn't like it, and I could be in an even worse position than I already am."

"Don't worry. Your secret is safe with me, as they say." And I meant it—if it was possible. I'd sacrifice Sweet if necessary, but I'd try to avoid it. He seemed okay, but, fuck it, I didn't owe him anything—only a shitty lunch.

I grinned at him in what was supposed to be a reassuring way. He didn't look reassured. I'd have to work on that.

I told Sweet I'd be in touch and got up.

On the way out I saw that André was holding a gin bottle, deep in discussion with the bartender. They both looked daggers at me as I passed. I smiled.

The car jockey didn't look happy to see me coming.

"I know which one is yours," he said, trying to make it an insult.

I heard the engine roar, and I saw my car race through the lines of parked cars like a pinball off a bumper. He pulled up with a squeal of the brakes.

The jockey looked real pleased with himself as he got out and held out a hand for a tip. I put a puzzled expression on my face and kind of leaned around to look behind him.

"It looks like you got something on the seat of your pants after all. A big grease stain or something."

"Oh, no," he said, and got to looking real worried. He twisted around trying to see what was on his fat butt. Of course there was nothing there, but he kept twisting even harder until he was slowly turning around, like he was trying to corkscrew himself up his ass.

I got in my car and started moving slowly forward. The jockey was so intent on his problem that he didn't notice he was right in front of the car. I gave a short, loud blast on the horn. He gave a surprised yelp and leaped out of the way, landing in a small mud puddle and soiling his fancy gold trousers. He looked disbelievingly down at his pant legs and then stared after me with his mouth hanging open. Meatball!

FOURTEEN

I made fairly good time back to my office. For a change there wasn't anyone passed out in the doorway. There was just an old pair of broken-down shoes. That was odd. It was usually the other way around—bodies without shoes. I didn't bother to figure out if there was any symbolic significance to the change.

Maria was happy to see me. In spite of the heat and the stuffiness, she looked as cool as ever. Charlie Watkins had called again, but there were no other messages. The insurance salesman had stopped by. Maria said he had chatted her up and tried to get a date.

"Did you accept?"

She wrinkled her nose. "He was a turkey. And besides, I said we were going to Mexico." She tossed her shiny black hair in a haughty gesture. ". . . I was thinking, Sam. I know this small village near San Blas. It's got the best beaches and the best fishing in all of Mexico, and no *turistas* ever go there. We can rent a house right on the beach. Would you like that?"

"Sounds great." Perfect, in fact.

"Look. I got this dress yesterday, especially for the trip. Do you like it?"

She stood up. She was wearing a yellow cotton sundress that beautifully set off her smooth olive skin. The top of the dress was cut in such a deep vee that it was hardly more than a pair of straps that only partially covered her large breasts. She bent forward slightly to make sure I appreciated the design of the dress . . . and the design of the wearer. I did. She did a quick pirouette, causing the skirt to flare up. It was extremely short and didn't have far to go. I was treated to a shot of transparent lemon-yellow panties that made my throat go dry. The temptation was very strong to say fuck it and leave that minute for Mexico. As things turned out, it would have been better for a number of people if I had, but I don't operate that way. I patted Maria's plump bottom, then dragged myself away and went through to my office.

I poured out a glass of gin and drank it down in an effort to wipe out the taste of the swill I had been served at the restaurant.

I sat down at my desk and was just about to call Stubby at the pool hall when the phone rang. I identified myself.

"There's something on page seventeen of the afternoon paper that might interest you. If you are wise, you will follow the advice that is obvious, even if it is not stated."

Before I could say anything the line disconnected. I didn't recognize the voice, but it somehow sounded familiar. Not from recently, but from a long time back. It's no good struggling with these things, so I let it drop, and sent Maria out for a paper.

When she brought it in, I immediately turned to 17. It was the traffic accidents page. The lead story was about a big rig that overturned carrying a load of watermelons. The watermelons fell on a sports car, crushing it and killing the two occupants. An interesting photo accompanied the story. At first I didn't see anything, but in one corner, sandwiched between stories about several multiple fatality crashes, there was a small article.

Private Detective
Hit-and-Run Victim

In the early hours of the morning, the body of Francis Eugene Argyll was found in an alley between Cedar St. and Wilson Ave., the year's 57th hit-and-run victim.

Police say that Argyll was a licenced private investigator who was something of a local character. His age and current address are not known.

A spokesman for the police said they are questioning residents who might have witnessed the crime, but they are not optimistic about the outcome.

Argyll was the 57th hit-and-run fatality since January 1, making the total to date ten ahead of the record set last year.

I sat for a minute and then got up and poured a drink. I raised the glass in a silent toast and tossed it back. That was it for Stubby. No use mourning him further.

Apparently Stubby had been right about some things and wrong about others. He must have been right about finding out something. And he was right about being followed. He was wrong about being able to get away.

He was obviously murdered—in just about the best way to avoid causing suspicion. There was no point in my going to the cops. I had nothing hard to give them, and even if I had, I probably wouldn't. Partly on principle, mostly because I was afraid of everything getting back to Ratchitt. No, I'd have to take it on my own.

It wasn't a question of avenging Stubby's death. I'd known him for years, and we got along okay, but I didn't owe him anything. We were both in it for ourselves, and if something happened, tough shit. That's not being hard, that's just the way the game is played, and Stubby would have been the first to agree. However, I was getting tired of people threatening me and warning me off. I wanted to find out what was going on. If, in doing so, I could settle the score for Stubby, so much the better. If not? Rest in peace, Stubby.

The situation was definitely heating up. The only way to deal with pressure is to meet it with more pressure. I still didn't know what it was all about, but people were starting to get nervous—Ratchitt's visit and Stubby's death made that clear. And when people are nervous, it's easy to make them more so. The more noise you make, the higher they jump.

I thought for a minute and got a nice idea. I looked up a number, dialed one of the newspapers, and soon got an old acquaintance, Harold Ace. He didn't have much of a calling for journalism, but with a name like Ace, he figured he had no choice. He answered the phone in the way that always amused him, putting the pause in the wrong place.

"Harold, Ace reporter."

"Hunter here. Would you be interested in a story about an exclusive private club in Hollywood that sells kinky sex? Some of the members are big-name stars. There are also a few politicos and the heads of some big companies. Not to mention big-scale police bribes to keep the wheels moving. Your paper interested?"

"Are we ever!" It sounded like he was bouncing in his seat.

"I kind of thought you might be."

"Well, you know nothing sells papers as well as the combination of sex and celebrities, and the kinkier the better. But we really look for those stories where we can adopt a tone of moral outrage."

"I know. You're a family newspaper."

"That's right," he laughed. "Some comment on the American family, isn't it. . . . But tell me more about this place."

I told him about the Black Knight. He kept interrupting to shout "Wow!" or "Too much!" or other cogent journalistic remarks. When I finished there was a silence on the other end of the line.

"That's dynamite," he finally said. "But can you provide some evidence to back up this story?"

"I didn't think your paper bothered about things like that."

"Sam! This is not some sleazy tabloid."

"I hadn't noticed much difference."

"Well there is. We're responsible journalists, for one thing."

"You mean you sell fewer papers."

"That's right," he said sadly. "But I do need solid information."

"How about somebody who works at the club?"

"Great! Can he provide anything to support the story?"

"Photos of the famous enjoying the club's facilities."

"No shit?"

"No shit. But you'll have to come up with some money. A fair amount considering what this will do to your circulation."

I had a couple of reasons for doing this. Newspapers, like everyone else, place a greater value on what they have to pay a lot for than on what they get for nothing. Also, though I knew I could get Faro to cooperate, I wanted him to be at least willing. His game at the Black Knight was almost played out, and if I could give him a stake so he could get out of town, he might be more helpful.

Ace thought the request was reasonable but said he'd have to get authorization from the higher-ups. I told him to get on with it and to keep the next afternoon free. I'd make the necessary arrangements, and we would get together with the source at that time.

I hung up. I could feel that my lips were twisted into a grin. There were some people that might not find it a comforting expression.

I called the cop shop and asked for Watkins. Instead, I got Burroughs, his partner. Burroughs didn't know where Watkins was. Charlie was taking a couple of days off—said he was onto something that might be big, but he wanted to check it out on his own, that he needed to come up with something to compensate for his screw-ups. Burroughs said he tried to get more information, but Watkins just acted mysterious. Did I know what it was about? Why should I? I said. Burroughs said that Watkins had mentioned my name. Fucking Charlie, that was all I needed!

I told Burroughs I'd call later. He didn't sound enthusiastic. He didn't much care for me. It happens.

There was no answer at Watkins's home. Damn.

I looked at my watch. There was still some shit I wanted to stir up before the afternoon ended.

I told Maria to buy some more things, only this time to get some clothes that weren't so prudish. We were going to Mexico, not fucking Buckingham Palace. I said it looked like we might be leaving pretty soon. Her eyes gleamed.

FIFTEEN

My first shit-kicking stop was a crummy, windowless warehouse off of Santa Monica. The sign on the door said Mound
of Venus Films, Starr Monroe, Producer. I had been there
once before looking for Linda Perdue. I hadn't gotten
anything from Monroe then, but that time I hadn't realized
there was a connection between Venus Films and the Black
Knight. Maybe this time would be better.

You stepped through the front door into a ten-by-ten
cubicle that had been partitioned off from the rest of the
warehouse with two-by-fours and plasterboard. They hadn't
even bothered to paint the plasterboard, and the manufactur-
er's name, repeated at intervals, was the only decoration in
the room. Impressive.

There were a pair of flimsy metal folding chairs that didn't
look very trustworthy and a cheap, phony wood desk. Behind
the desk sat a plump, gray-haired woman reading a copy of
Variety. She wore a balloony, floral print dress from the '40s
that was partially covered by a faded gingham apron. She
looked like everybody's grandmother until you noticed the
hard glint in her eye. The thin cigarillo that dangled from her
lips didn't help much either.

"I want to see Monroe," I said, standing in front of the
desk.

She looked up appraisingly. "Are you the new beef?"

"No."

"Too bad. You look like you might have potential. Are you
well hung?"

"I'm not here for a job. I want to see Monroe."

"Can't. Starr's busy. Shove off, toots." She turned back to
the copy of *Variety*.

I leaned over the desk. "What's a nice girl like you doing in
a place like this?"

116

"What's that supposed to mean?"

"I just wondered."

"I like to help out. I'm Starr's mother." It figured. "Starr and me are going places. Right to the top." Christ!

"I'll give you some advice. If you don't want to spend your golden years in the slammer, dump the son of a bitch."

"Who the fuck do you think you are, asshole?" She glared at me.

"I'm the guy that's going to put him there unless he cooperates. Now, I'll go and see him."

I was past the desk and through the rear door before she could say more than "Hey!"

The warehouse was large and wrapped in darkness except for a circle of bright lights off to one side. I crossed to this, being careful not to trip over any of the cables that were lying around.

When I got close, I saw that it was a set for a bedroom. The props seemed to consist of a giant round waterbed and not much more. There was a cameraman and a few technicians. Close to the camera Starr Monroe was calling instructions to the performers on the bed.

The center of attention was a big guy on his back in the middle of the bed. He had the overly developed muscles of a weight lifter and the blank expression of a plastic doll. Two very small girls who looked about thirteen were climbing around on top of him, exploring his body. Like the guy, they were naked, and their breasts had only begun to develop. One of the girls worked her way down his belly and looked surprised to discover his stiff cock.

"Now look at it like you don't know what it is," Monroe shouted.

The girl tried to do that, but looked more like a hungry dog eying a bone.

"Now start to lick it," Monroe said. "No! More slowly. Start at the bottom. Get your tongue farther out. Good. Get the camera in there close. Got it? Okay. Now, Cathy, you come in and start to suck on it. Jennie, you keep licking the length of it. That's right. Just like you're sharing a Popsicle. Harry, are you getting all that? Good. Keep it up. That's right."

The girls worked enthusiastically, occasionally kissing one another when they met at the top of his cock. The recipient of

all the attentions stared at the ceiling, looking like he was
trying to do long division in his head.

I moved forward another few steps and shouted as loudly
and roughly as I could. "All right. This is a raid."

The girls jumped up, startled. All the crew whirled around
to face me. Only Muscles didn't react.

"What the fuck is this?" Monroe said. "Who's there?" He
stepped in my direction. "Who're you? Oh, it's you. What the
fuck do you think you're doing?"

"I want to talk to you." My voice was hard and my eyes
held his.

He was about to protest but then saw something in my
expression that made him think better of it. He turned back
to the set.

"Okay people, take ten."

The crew shuffled off to the side. The girls looked at one
another and giggled. They put on robes and started to flip
through movie mags. Only Muscles did not move. I began to
wonder if he might be stuffed.

Monroe led me to his office, which was in one corner of
the warehouse. He was wearing a sky-blue velour jumpsuit
that was open to the navel. His chest was thin and hairless
and he was starting to get a belly. He had about half a
dozen gold—or gold-colored—chains around his neck with
heavy medallions on the ends. He jingled slightly when he
walked.

"I don't know why you interrupted like that. You ruined a
good take." His voice was nasal and whiny.

"What're you calling the epic?"

"*What the Gardener Taught the Girls.*" He said it with a
straight face.

"I'll look for it when it comes out."

"You won't see it. Private clubs only, and mail order."

"Clubs like the Black Knight?"

"Never heard of it." He spoke without turning around, but
I thought I saw his shoulders twitch briefly.

We reached his office and he flicked on the light. The walls
were covered with posters: *Teenage Lust, Incest Bride,* and
Hostage of Love were a few of them. These were the movies
that played in theatres. There were also stills from other
productions—the ones that were even raunchier and were

sold and shown privately. Mound of Venus Films didn't look like much, but somebody was making a lot of money from it, and I had the feeling that it wasn't Monroe, Mother and Son.

Monroe rattled his chains nervously as I glanced at the stills on the wall. I recognized my good friend Nicky Faro in one of them. The lighting wasn't very good, but his equipment was unmistakable. Interesting. I also recognized someone else in one of the pictures.

I stared at Monroe. He held my gaze for a minute and then looked away. He continued to play with his chains.

"So what do you want?" he said. "You were looking for some runaway girl, weren't you? I already told you, I never saw her."

"I know you said that, but I found out different. She worked here."

"You're mistaken."

I walked over to the wall and pulled a still down. It was Linda and another girl, naked, playing with each other. The fucking, stupid jerk, Monroe, leaving the picture on the wall. Incredible! But if people weren't so dumb, my job would be a lot harder.

I shoved the picture in his face. "You still don't remember?"

"Oh, her." He was nervous, but he was disguising it pretty well. "Is that the one? I didn't recognize her from the picture you showed me. She had clothes on. Anyway, I can't remember every cheap hooker who comes through here. What difference does it make?"

"It might make a difference to some people if you use minors in sex films."

"Would it?" He laughed. "Besides, she told me she was eighteen."

"And you believed her?"

"Why not? Who's got time to check? I got movies to make. There's a big demand for my pictures. What am I supposed to do, ask to see a birth certificate? All I want to see is a pair of tits and a cunt."

"That's an attitude that's going to get you in trouble. Haven't you heard? They're coming down on kiddy porn."

"Yeah? I'm not worried," he said. "It's all taken care of. It's all fixed, and you won't be able to unfix it."

"Maybe not, but I bet I could provide a few embarrassing moments for you and your friends—and your friends wouldn't like it."

He thought for a minute. "Okay. The girl was here. She made a couple of pictures. She left. That's a wrap."

"Where'd she go?"

"How do I know? You think I keep track of all the meat that comes through here? Does the butcher know where every steak he handles goes?"

"You passed her on to the Black Knight."

He jingled his chains. "I told you, I never heard of it. You got that place on the brain."

"What do you do, pimp for the club? You see good talent coming through here, you send it along? I know you're connected to the club."

"I don't know what you're talking about." Rattle, rattle, rattle.

"Who do you work for at the club? Who runs this operation?"

"I run it." Jingle, jingle.

"You couldn't run an electric train. No, you're tied to the club, but the club doesn't run it. Of course! There's the same guy behind both operations."

"You're crazy, man." Rattle, jingle, rattle.

I took a shot: "You tell Domingo I'm going to send all of you down the tubes."

At the mention of Domingo, the hand stopped playing with the chains, and Monroe's eyes opened wide. I've got to hand it to him, he recovered pretty quickly, but the instant of recognition was there. "Who's Domingo?"

"No one."

I could have pushed further, but it was liable to be counter-productive. I made a couple of good guesses, and Monroe thought I knew more than I did. If I carried on, I probably wouldn't get anything more out of him, but he might find out I was bluffing. No, I'd leave it. He was jumpy, and the word would go up the line pretty quickly.

I walked out of the office and through the warehouse. Muscles still hadn't moved.

Mother Monroe glared at me from her desk. I saw the light flash on that showed one of the telephone lines was in use. Monroe didn't waste any time. I considered picking up the phone and saying something cute, but somehow I didn't want to wrestle the old woman for it. It looked like she'd fight dirty.

SIXTEEN

As I drove across town I tried to think things through.

The puzzle was starting to come together. The picture wasn't clear, but I was beginning to get some idea of the pieces that were there.

Domingo was the man behind Mound of Venus Films and the Black Knight Club, and there were other links between the two that I knew about—Linda Perdue and Faro to start with. Mountain had worked at the Black Knight. Did he now work for Domingo? Seemed likely. Domingo used the club to set up marks for blackmail. Acker was a member of the club. Was he being blackmailed? What did Domingo have on him? What was the price? Was he in fact even involved? And where did Linda fit in—if she fit in—and what happened to her?

I began to see how I had gotten into all this. I was looking for the girl and touched on Venus Films in the process. At about the same time, Acker finds out I'm looking at him. They both lead back to Domingo, and Domingo starts to get nervous. Coincidence, sure, but lots of things are set off by meaningless coincidence. It made sense . . . and it didn't. Considering what I had done, the warning I received seemed to be a real overreaction, and Domingo, whoever he was, didn't seem like the kind to overreact. There obviously were still things I didn't know about—that I'd overlooked or hadn't yet seen—and they must be big. Stubby said he was onto something big. And Stubby was killed. And Stubby was looking into Acker. Acker. Acker and the Black Knight. Acker and Domingo. Acker. Acker? I had a couple of answers, but I had more questions. Well, I'd soon see.

I pulled into a no-parking zone opposite the four-story building that housed the offices and production facilities of Medco Pharmaceutical Supplies.

As soon as I was inside the building I saw what Stubby had meant. The place felt funny. There was none of the activity and energy that is associated with a successful concern. I knew Medco was not a big company, but Acker seemed to be making a bundle out of it. However, there was no feeling of movement, only treading water. It was dull and lethargic, and the heat wave was not the explanation because the temperature was comfortably cool in the building.

I rode up to the top floor, where the executive offices were located, and found that Acker occupied one corner. His secretary was staring out the window when I came in. She looked bored and welcomed the opportunity to do something, if only to send my name in. The reply was prompt and I went through the connecting door.

Acker stood up as I entered. Of course I had seen him before, but never this close, and I was struck by the cool hardness of the man. He was about five-ten or -eleven and slim, but his taut muscular development was evident under his well-cut fitted shirt. His skin was lightly bronzed and contrasted with his pale blond hair, which was short and cut close to his head. His eyes were a washed-out milky blue—the eyes of a Siamese cat—and it looked as though they would never give away secrets or betray emotions. He reminded me of pictures I'd seen of the Aryan robots of the SS. Stubby was right about Acker being a tough customer, and I began to get an idea about what the excitable personality of his wife found so hard to take.

"Won't you sit down, Mr.—uh—Hunter, isn't it?"

I sat and stared hard at him. "There's no point in pretending you don't know who I am." He raised his blond eyebrows in a question. Very cool. "I'm the one you hired Stubby Argyll to investigate."

"Stubby Argyll? Is that a person?" He was very good.

"That was a person. He's dead."

Acker blinked. That was the only reaction he had, and I couldn't tell if he already knew or if the news came as a surprise to him.

"I should say 'I'm sorry to hear that,' but, since I don't know the man, there seems to be no point to it."

"No, you shouldn't be sorry," I said. "Stubby was killed because he found out something about you—something big. I came here to tell you that I'm going to find out the same thing. . . . And I won't be nearly so easy to deal with."

An unpleasant smile played around the corners of Acker's mouth. Damn. He seemed to be enjoying this.

"I'm sorry, Mr.—uh—Hunter, I do not quite understand why you should be interested in me."

"No? Okay. At first I was only interested because your wife hired me to be interested. She doesn't much like you, Mr. Acker."

At the mention of his wife his icy composure broke for the first time. His jaws clenched together and his lips grew thin and bloodless. His hands gripped the edge of his desk with enough force to make his arms tremble.

"That stupid, whoring bitch," he hissed through tight lips, not really talking to me, just talking. "She thinks she hates me. She doesn't know what hate is. She thinks she's being clever. She's in for a big surprise. She'll get nothing. Nothing. Tell her she's liable to end up peddling her ass for cigarettes if she doesn't smarten up."

Anger flared inside me. I felt like leaping over his desk and throwing him out the window. Or slapping his face and telling him, "Pistols at dawn." I couldn't believe it. One tumble on a fur rug, and I was ready to defend her honor or something. Shit! I didn't need this. I'd kept myself clean and clear and empty for a long time, and now that woman had me acting like some moon-mad, infatuated adolescent, and I didn't much like the feeling. Mexico was what I needed. A couple of weeks on the beach with Maria would clear away all that stuff.

At least I wasn't so far gone that I let my anger show, and, as quickly as he lost it, Acker also regained his coolness.

"You said 'at first.' There is now a difference?"

"Yep. When I started to smell that something funny was going on, I became very interested—for myself. It was the smell of big money. I like that smell."

"You think that something funny is going on? What? If you tell me, perhaps I can disabuse you of the idea, and you will stop wasting your time."

"Okay. Maybe you can." I didn't mind telling him what I knew. My only problem was making it seem like I knew more than I did. "I think it was funny that the take-over by Megaplex suddenly fell through."

"You obviously do not know much about business, Mr.

Hunter. There is nothing unusual there. Mergers are considered and then rejected all the time." He was smiling.

"But it is unusual that the person responsible for the arrangements is blackmailed into queering the deal." I grinned back at him.

Acker's smile froze, but he responded smoothly. "If what you say is true—and I doubt it—I know nothing about that." He sure was good.

"Then it must just be coincidence that right after the deal fell through, you came up with the money to buy out the company. You didn't have money like that."

"But I did have a silent partner. That, too, is very common."

"Why would he want to own Medco? The company was going under."

"On the contrary. The former owner had lost interest in the company, and as a consequence it was poorly run, but it had significant growth potential. As managing director I saw the potential, and I was able to secure the backing to take over and implement my ideas. In a very short time Medco's situation has been considerably improved."

"Has it? It doesn't look to me like anything's happening here. Everyone's asleep."

"Things are slow at this particular moment, but I can assure you that our balance sheet is very healthy."

"So your backer's confidence in you has been justified?"

"Completely. It may be immodest of me to say so, but that is the case."

"Who's your partner?"

"If I told you, he would no longer be silent." Acker smiled in mock apology.

I was getting nowhere. I could continue to fence with Acker all day and it wouldn't change. I had to take a shot.

"Domingo is not so silent, and he's getting louder all the time."

No reaction. Acker had complete control, but somehow the atmosphere in the room changed. The tension increased, or something, and I thought my remark had hit home, but Acker was tough.

"Domingo? Domingo? That's another name about which I know nothing, I'm afraid."

"No? He's the one behind the Black Knight Club. He

specializes in kinky sex and blackmail. He's probably got something on you. I'm sure your wife would like to know what."

"Really, Mr. Hunter, you are most entertaining, but I'm afraid your imagination is too good. I've never heard of this Black Knight Club, and certainly no one is blackmailing me. My charming wife would like to, I'm sure, and that's why she hired you—" He quickly caught himself and smiled. "—if, as you say, she did. But you will find nothing. I am merely a businessman."

"There are all kinds of businesses, Acker, and I'm going to find out just what yours is."

Acker raised his shoulders and let them fall. "If you wish to persist with this foolishness, I doubt that I will be able to stop you. Of course, you will find nothing, but I am a man who values his privacy. Therefore, I'll make you a proposition. If you will desist in this pointless investigation, I will pay you whatever you were going to get from my wife, plus, shall we say, a bonus of two thousand dollars. I think that is fair. What do you say?" He pulled a checkbook from his desk and opened it up.

"Thanks, Acker."

"Then you agree?"

"No. I was thanking you for making a stupid move. You're smooth, but you just made a mistake and confirmed my suspicions."

"What do you mean?" A shadow passed behind his pale blue eyes.

"Men with nothing to hide don't pay two grand to buy off an investigation."

"But I said I value my privacy, and—"

"Nor do they hire other P.I.'s to look after the first."

"I thought it would be interesting to thwart my wife's plans." A note of urgency was creeping into his voice.

"So you admit you hired Argyll. Did you also have him killed? Or was that Domingo? Or his big gorilla, Mountain Cyclone?"

"I do not know what you're talking about." He had to work hard to keep his voice level, and I noticed his knuckles were white from gripping the edge of his desk.

"You people are getting very sloppy. Everything is starting to unravel. One good pull and it's going to fall apart."

"Then you will not accept my offer?" He maintained his control. He was tough.

"Two's not enough. Make it five."

"Very well." He smiled coldly and put his pen on the check.

"Forget it. If you're willing to go to five now, you'll go much higher later. That's when we'll talk."

His eyes got very cold and hard. "You're making a mistake, Hunter, and it's going to cost you."

"Not me. You're in big trouble. You don't realize it yet, and that means you're in bigger trouble."

"You don't know what trouble is." He suddenly sounded tired.

"Tell me."

For a second I thought he wanted to open up, but the hard surface was quickly restored. "I think we've exhausted this conversation."

"We'll be in touch," I said. "You're going to need me soon, and you better believe that it's really going to cost you when you do. You can pass that on to Domingo. I'm bringing him down."

I got up and went out of the office. As I passed his secretary's desk I noticed one of the buttons on her phone light up. I smiled.

Ah, Hunter, you really make the phone lines hum.

SEVENTEEN

My car was still there, but something was stuck on the windshield. I figured I'd gotten a ticket, but it must have been my day. It only turned out to be a flyer advertising three rooms of furniture for $250—terms could be arranged. I was sure they could. I treated the flyer with the same reverence I would have given the parking ticket. I threw it away.

The freeway back to the Valley was tied up with the normal perpetual traffic jam. The sun was a brilliant red ball cutting through the brown haze that hung over the city, the bloodshot eye of a town that's had a few too many. The traffic wasn't moving, and I had lots of time to look at the sun. It didn't tell me anything.

My shirt stuck to the back of the seat. My skin was covered with the invisible grit that passes for air here. What a fucking lousy place to live. Was there even such a place as an empty beach in Mexico? The bus in front of me gunned its engine with the sound of a dying dinosaur and said, "No way, buddy, this is all there is." A gust of diesel exhaust blew into my open window. Swell.

In front of my apartment building a bunch of kids were playing a game they called Muggers in the Park. In a few years they'd be playing it for real—on one side or the other. Whatever happened to cowboys and Indians? Maybe that was what I was playing.

I parked my car. Somewhere close by a woman with a voice like a banshee was screaming, "If you go out that door now, don't you fucking bother coming back." I heard a door slam. I guess he wasn't coming back. I could see why he wouldn't.

Fifty-five minutes on a crowded freeway is just about what it takes to make my apartment look good. I was hardly through the door before I had stripped, poured myself a big glass of gin, and jumped into the shower.

128

I finished the gin and the shower at the same time. I tried to phone Watkins, but he wasn't at the cop shop or at home. I lay down on my bed to relax. I must have been tired because I went out pretty quickly.

I dreamed I was chasing shadows. They looked familiar but I couldn't quite place them. Suddenly they turned and started chasing me. I tried to turn around to see who it was, but they kept moving out of my vision. I was tripping over bloody corpses—a lot of them. Stubby Argyll popped up, saying, "It's not the heat, but the humidity." I listened as though it meant something. One Arm Shifty kept asking, "Do you want to play a game, sport?"

I woke up and it was dark. I was covered in a thin film of sweat and I felt chilled. Either I was getting spooked or it was a mild flare-up of malaria, another memento of Nam. After I was awake for a couple of minutes, I knew I wasn't spooked, so I took a couple of the pills I keep around. By the time I washed off the sweat, the pills were starting to work and I was feeling hungry.

I would have liked to stay in, but I still had one more call to pay in my shit-stirring program. I dressed and went out.

I let my stomach lead me to the Golden Dragon, a greasy little Chinese restaurant between a topless bar and an auto-parts shop. There were a few clowns at the Formica tables who thought they were being daring and exotic by eating chop suey and some deep-fried crap in bright-pink sweet-and-sour sauce, the usual North American Cantonese garbage. I'd rather starve than eat that stuff. Somewhere along the line, though, I discovered that the cook really knew his Szechuan food and would fix me things that weren't on the menu.

I sat down at a table and sent the cockroaches scurrying for cover. They were large and obviously well fed. I shrugged. If the food was good enough, I didn't mind competing with a few dozen insects for it. I figured I was more than their match.

The waiter came over, giving me a big smile that showed a lot of gold. I told him to have the cook make me three dishes, whatever he felt like, just so it was good. If it wasn't, I said, I'd see to it that he'd never wok again. The waiter looked at me blankly. Inscrutable.

In a very short time the cook himself brought out the dishes. He was just over four feet tall and humpbacked. On his chin there was a mole with several three-inch-long hairs

growing out of it which he lovingly pulled at from time to
time. He looked like a refugee from an opium den, and was
said to be the best Mah-Jongg player on the West Coast. He
put the plates down, squawked "Hot! Hot! Hot!" like a
malignant parrot, and went back to the kitchen chuckling to
himself at some unknown joke.

The food was good as ever. There was a dish with thinly
sliced chicken, dried orange peels from Shanghai that cost $25
a kilo, and a big handful of dried hot chiles. You took a piece
of chicken, a piece of orange peel, and a chile into your
mouth at the same time and let the flavors explode. There was
a dish of matchstick beef and shredded carrots stir-fried with
lots of crushed chiles. The sweetness of the carrots enhanced
the hotness of the chiles, and the pieces of beef absorbed it
all. The third dish was bean curd covered with a soupy ground
meat sauce filled with *fagara,* the aromatic Szechuan pepper-
corn. Not bad, and a nice contrast in texture to the other
dishes. I had three large bowls of rice and a couple of beers. It
was all right.

On my way into town the various flavors and the hotness of
the chiles lingered in my mouth. My belly felt full and warm. I
was ready for the third installment. After this I would wait for
them to make their move.

The door to the Black Knight Club was opened and I was
admitted without comment. Bulldog I glared sullenly at me.
Bulldog II stood at his shoulder and did the same.

I looked them up and down. I fingered the lapel of Bulldog
I's jacket. Polyester.

"Hmmm. Nice. Who's your tailor?" I said. "I need a
tuxedo for my performing chimpanzee, and this is just what
I'm looking for."

I heard a growl in his throat. I shrugged and moved off.

I stood in the entrance to the lounge. The night's performance was getting under way. It was announced as "The Revolt
of the Slaves."

Three immense black men clad only in loincloths, their
bodies oiled to show off their incredible musculature, advanced toward a small blond girl wearing a frilly white
hooped skirt. She looked like the same girl from the previous
evening. She seemed to have survived the Spanish Inquisition
okay. The black men grabbed her and began to prod and

poke her with quizzical expressions on their faces, as though she were some species of strange animal.

I felt a touch on my arm. It was Nicky Faro. He was looking terrible. His long body was stooped over, and there was a terrified expression at the back of his eyes. He drew me off to one side.

"Jesus Christ, Hunter! What have you been doing?"

"What's going on?"

"All hell is breaking loose. Everybody's nervous. Lascar is jumping around like a spastic. He's on the phone all the time. I try and find out what's going on, and nobody says anything. They just look at me kind of funny."

I nodded. Things seemed to be progressing nicely.

"Come on, Hunter." Faro seemed near to cracking. "You said you would keep me out of it. I don't like what's happening, I'm getting pretty scared."

"That's too bad, Faro."

"Hunter!" My name was almost a wail. "You can't do this to me."

"Faro, you're a stupid, slimy schmuck, trying to play a big boy's game. I owe you nothing. I love to see punks like you go down the toilet."

"Hunter!" Panic.

"But you're lucky. I'm going to help you."

Relief.

"Not because I think you're worth saving—because you're definitely not—but because it happens to be worth my while to do so."

Gratitude.

"Now listen close. Everything's going to come down in a crash. I don't know if there'll be any survivors, but if there are, you can be damn sure you won't be one of them."

Panic.

"You are in deep shit. I can get you out, but you have to cooperate. If you do, you'll get a stake so you can clear out. What you do after you leave is your business."

"What do you want me to do?" His throat sounded dry and his voice was a barely audible croak.

"You'll talk to someone, tell him what you told me."

"Cop?"

"Reporter."

"Jesus Christ, Hunter!"

"And you'll turn over all your pictures."

"They'll kill me!"

"You're already dead. This is your only chance."

He swallowed hard a couple of times. "Okay."

"Be available tomorrow afternoon."

He nodded miserably. His face looked like a death's-head.

"And lighten up or you'll blow everything. In twenty-four
.ours you'll be clear."

He shook his head. "What are you going to do now?"

"I'm going to goose Lascar and see how high he jumps."

Faro groaned and shuffled off, a bent beanpole.

I went down the corridor and opened the door to Lascar's
office without knocking. He was sitting behind his desk,
motionless, staring into space. He seemed somewhat the
worse for wear from the previous evening. He was still
dressed all in black, and, while he was still immaculate, the
impression was that he was covered with a fine layer of dust
and dandruff. He jumped when I came in.

"Who!— Oh!— What do you want?"

"I wanted to find out how our deal was coming."

"I don't know who you are or what you're trying to do, but
you're not wanted here."

"Does that mean the deal is off?"

"You're funny."

"Why didn't you tell me the girl I wanted had been in the
club?"

"She wasn't. Who says?" His head started twisting and
jerking on his neck.

"I hear things around. She was seen."

"You been talking to your friend Faro? If he doesn't watch
it, he's going to end up a grease spot in somebody's garage."

"It wasn't Faro. Other people saw her. What happened to
her?"

"Nothing happened to her 'cause she wasn't here. Understand? Never here. That's where I want you to be—never
here. Now get out or you'll leave carrying your ass in a sling."

"That's no way to talk to someone who's here to do you a
favor."

"The only favor you can do me is to leave. Now."

"You've got trouble."

"You're my only trouble, but you won't be in about thirty seconds."

"You poor sucker," I said, shaking my head.

"What do you mean?" he said between twists of his head.

"They're setting you up."

"What are you talking about?"

"Jesus, you really don't know, do you?"

"You got something to say, say it."

"The whole thing's coming down. The club—everything. It's going belly up, and you're going to be left holding your cock and pissing into the wind."

"You're full if it." He didn't sound too confident.

"No. You're going to be closed up."

"Can't happen. We're safe."

"You were safe. Ratchitt's cutting you loose. Things are getting too hot."

"You're lying."

"And Domingo's clearing out as well."

"Now I know you're crazy." His head was twisting so hard it was pulling his body around.

"You keep saying that up until the time they throw you in the joint. Domingo's not stupid. He knows what's coming, and he's getting out, clean and healthy. You're being left to take the fall. And it's a good one. Shit! Is it ever! Prostitution, running a bawdy house, use of minors for immoral purposes, corruption of minors, white slavery, probably Mann Act violations, blackmail, bribery of law enforcement officers, possession and distribution of pornography. And there are a dozen or two more charges they can throw at you if they want. And you're going to be the only one left around to pin it on."

"Where do you hear all this?"

"It's all around. Man, you must be the only one who doesn't know. It'll probably be in the papers tomorrow."

"Yeah? Now listen to me. That was a good number you just ran by me, but I been told about you. I been told you're full of shit, and that I should deal with you like any other piece of garbage I find." His finger pressed a button on his desk.

"Who told you that? Domingo? Well, of course. He knows I'm after him. He's just making sure that you're going to stand in the way. You think he cares what happens to you?"

The door opened and the Bulldogs appeared.

"Show this jerk out," Lascar said. "Hard."

"Okay, Lascar," I said, "but you'd better look into it."

I went through the door between the two heavies, shutting it behind me. I took a couple of steps and stopped.

"Hold on a second, I forgot something," I said, and quickly turned and opened the foor. Number three. Lascar was on the phone and froze when he saw me. "Give him my regards," I said and shut the door.

A Bulldog took me by each arm and muscled me toward the door. On the way I looked in to see how the revolt of the slaves was going. Progressing nicely. All parties were naked and the southern belle had each of her openings filled with thick black cock. The girl looked busy. The men looked bored. The audience was shouting requests.

The front door was opened. I was clubbed between the shoulders by a heavy fist and given a hard punch to the kidneys. It hurt. I was then pushed out onto the walkway where I fell to my hands and knees. My trousers ripped at the knee. Son of a bitch.

I got in my car, started it, and drove around the corner. I parked, waited about ten minutes, and then lit a cigarette and walked back to the club. I knocked and pressed myself against the door so I couldn't be seen. The spy hole opened. I stood up and blew a big mouthful of smoke into it. There was a puzzled exclamation followed by some loud coughing. In a second the door flew open and Bulldog II came charging out, but I was ready. I buried my toe in his crotch. As he doubled over I put my hands on the back of his head and pushed downward, hard. His face met the concrete walk with a satisfying sound and he was still. That took about four seconds.

I jumped into the shadows next to the door. Bulldog I came out. One hand was furiously rubbing his eyes, which were watering badly. His other hand held a gun. I sadly shook my head: that was a definite escalation of the conflict. He looked around angrily, trying to see me through his blurred vision. I grabbed the barrel of the gun, catching his finger in the trigger guard, and twisted it until I heard the bone snap. I yanked the gun from his hand and, with the butt, hit him solidly on the bridge of his nose. He fell straight forward onto his face. I found his wallet and took out thirty-five dollars.

That would cover a new pair of pants.

No one had heard anything. Too engrossed in the performance, I guess.

I went back to my car and drove home.

I checked the bedroom and was glad to find that no one was there.

The only message on my answering machine was from Charlie Watkins. He wanted to talk to me. He said it was important.

I tried but couldn't reach him. I was starting to get bothered about not being able to reach people. Tinny voices on my machine and then nothing.

There was no message from Clarissa Acker. Shit.

I threw my trousers in the garbage and went to bed.

EIGHTEEN

I was draining my second cup of coffee when the phone rang.

A voice I didn't recognize said that if I wanted the goods on Domingo, I should be at a parking lot near Venice Beach at eleven o'clock. I tried to get the caller to identify himself and tell me what this was all about, but he hung up.

I thought about it. It sounded phony, like I was being set up. On the other hand, my agitating might be bringing in dividends. I weighed both sides, figured I could take care of myself if it was a setup, and decided to keep the appointment. I had nothing else planned for the day anyway except to wait and see what developed.

I heard a key turn in my front door lock. I started moving to the bedroom for my gun, but the door opened before I got halfway. I was lucky again—or maybe not, depending on how you looked at it. It was the woman who ran the apartment building, the mother of Miki or Kiki or whoever. I couldn't remember her name either, but I began to see where her daughter got the habit of coming into my apartment uninvited. Damn these women.

"Whatever happened to knocking?" I said. It wasn't a very good line, but I was standing in the middle of the room with only a towel wrapped around me, and it was the best I could manage.

"Then what would be the point of having a passkey?" She grinned and stood with a hand on an out-thrust hip. The resemblance to her daughter was striking, except the mother had a few extra pounds. They had accumulated mostly around the breasts and hips, and did her no harm. She worked hard to create the illusion that they were sisters. It even looked like she wore her daughter's clothes. She had on a long T-shirt, and from the way it clung to her, there was nothing under it.

136

The front of the shirt said, "If love is the answer, what's the question?" I could think of several.

"Well?" I said. I was really sharp this morning.

"I guess you're wondering why I'm here."

"Not really." I had a good idea. Two, in fact.

"I gather you've been screwing my daughter." Right on one count. It figured the girl would brag, being locked in competition with her mother.

"Guilty," I said. "But could you accept that she seduced me?"

She laughed. "I could . . . that bitch. But you're not going to tell me you were an unwilling participant."

"Well, my heart wasn't in it—"

"Something else was though," she cut in with a harsh laugh.

"—and it was unpremeditated."

"Hey, Sam, I'm not complaining. If she's going to fuck around, she's going to fuck around, and she might as well learn from the best, which is what you are, baby." Another entry for my book of testimonials. "All I want is my fair share of the goodies. I haven't seen you for a while." I was right on both counts.

She grabbed the bottom of her shirt and pulled it over her head. She was naked, and she stood there with her legs apart and her hands on her hips, looking like she meant business. She was fleshy but still firm. Her breasts were slightly cone-shaped, capped by hard, pointed nipples, and they swelled slightly with each breath she took.

"I'm not so bad, am I?" she said hoarsely.

She wasn't. I said so, though the movement of the towel I had on made my answer unnecessary. She hungrily eyed the mounting bulge.

"And I still know a few tricks that the girl hasn't had time to learn yet," she said as she crossed over to me. She pulled away the towel. "Oh, Sam!" She fell on me like she was dying of hunger and I was the Christmas turkey.

What the hell. I had a couple of hours before my appointment.

She wasn't as good as she thought she was. They never are.

Somewhere in the middle of the performance I decided I'd have to find a new apartment. The mother-daughter routine was getting to be a drag. The goddamn bitches.

Not without a struggle, I managed to get the woman off me in time to shower, dress, and leave for my meeting.

It was hard to believe, but it seemed hotter than the previous days. Life in the city had been reduced to a crawl. The freeways were littered with cars that had overheated. The emergency wards of hospitals were filled with people who had collapsed from the heat. The water shortage was severe and growing worse. The massive use of air conditioners had created power shortages and there were blackouts in parts of the city. The sun was an ochre smudge behind the veil of smog and dust. The forecast said no letup in sight. For once, the weathermen were probably right.

It wasn't even any cooler at the beach which usually provided some relief from the heat, but that didn't seem to make any difference, and the place was packed. Every foot of sand that wasn't covered with the results of the latest oil spill was occupied by some overweight bozo eating chopped egg sandwiches and turning bright red.

The beach smelled like a garbage dump from the corpses of thousands of oil-clogged fish and sea birds that had washed ashore and were cooking in the sun. Welcome to L.A., the playground of the stars.

I got to the place I was supposed to be and waited. Nothing happened. I stayed around for about half an hour and still no one showed. I started to get an uneasy feeling in my gut. I was cursing myself as I went to a phone booth. I dialed my office, and there was no answer. There should have been. It might be nothing, but the feeling in my gut was getting stronger.

I got the car going and headed into town. For a change I was able to make pretty good time. Most of the traffic was heading west, toward the beach, and I didn't run into much congestion until I got close to my office.

I found a place to park, ran to the building and up the stairs. The door was unlocked and I went into the outer office. No one there. I crossed to my office. I found Maria.

I'd had this feeling, so it wasn't a total surprise. I've also seen a lot of death in my time, but this hit me like a rifle butt in the stomach.

Maria was naked on top of the desk, her legs spread wide, hanging over either side of it. The inside of her thighs and her genitals were ripped and bloody, insanely mutilated. Her body was crushed and flattened, seemingly every bone bro-

ken by a great weight. She was like a rag doll with half the
stuffing removed. A note was on her breast, held in place by a
large safety pin driven into the soft flesh. It said, "Back off or
you're next."

I saw white then yellow then red. A howl of rage filled my
head and expanded into my body, growing, intensifying,
swelling until I felt I would burst. I opened my mouth and it
exploded, a scream of anger and agony, a wild, ferocious,
insane animal noise. My belly felt like it was in the grip of a
giant claw, squeezing and tearing at my insides. I just made it
to the sink in the closet in time to heave my guts up. I heaved
and heaved and heaved until I was empty, empty of everything. I washed my face and the water helped to revive me.
The madness was gone, but it had been replaced by a cold,
intense, determined hatred, the like of which I hadn't known
since Viet Nam.

I went back into the room. In a corner I saw the shreds of
what must have been another new dress that Maria had
bought for our trip to Mexico.

It had to have been Mountain. No one else could have
broken her body like that. And he didn't act on his own. He
was sent by Domingo. Domingo, who I chased like the
faceless shadow in my dream, who had turned and was now
striking out at me.

But he'd made a mistake. Before, it had been more like an
exercise, a puzzle. Now it was personal—deeply, intensely
personal—and I would make him suffer and pay for this. I'd
make them all pay.

Stupid. Stupid and pointless. Why Maria? They were afraid
to take me on directly, but they wanted to scare me off. So
they got me out of the way and let Mountain go to work.

I looked again at what was once the lovely body of Maria.
She had been okay—as a woman and as a secretary—and
there weren't too many of that kind around. I spat curses,
both at myself for letting it happen and at them for doing it.

But they would not succeed. I would exact vengeance. Not
for Maria—it made no difference any more to her—but for
myself. I would shatter their plans. I would shake their
power. I would destroy their riches. I would shoot fire into
their bellies and make them puke and squirm on the floor. I
would splatter the walls with their brains. Vengeance! I could
taste it in my mouth. A red haze dropped before my eyes, and

I saw vengeance, red vengeance. It would be mine. It would be good.

"Hello there. Anybody here?"

A voice came from the outer office. Who the fuck was it? Footsteps crossed the room to my door. Shit. I kept my back turned.

"Ah, Mr. Hunter. There you are. I've been trying to get you for several days. I'm Al Allen of Acme Life and Casualty—'You can trust the people who trust in you.' Have you considered the benefits to be obtained from a three-way life insurance policy—"

I whirled around in a crouch. It felt like my eyes were blazing fire. My lips were curled back and a growl escaped my throat. I must have looked pretty frightening because he stopped his patter, his eyes grew wide, and his Adam's apple bobbed up and down in his scrawny throat. His eyes left my face and took in the body on my desk. He started to back up.

"I see I've come at a bad time. Well, I'll just be going now. I'll leave my card, and you can get in touch when it's more convenient." He was almost to the door.

"If I ever see your face again, you won't have it anymore," I said with complete sincerity.

He turned and fled. I heard his footsteps retreating down the hallway.

I felt I should have crushed the worm and was sorry I hadn't. I took a couple of deep breaths and realized that was stupid. I got hold of myself. If I was going to do what I had to do, I would have to stay cool.

I tried to force myself to think about my next move. I hadn't gotten very far before I heard police sirens tearing down the street. They stopped in front of my building, and I knew they were coming to my office.

Of course the cops would have been alerted. It made sense. Domingo and his crew weren't worried about anything coming back to them. They felt secure about everything except me. But they knew that if I got into a dance with the cops, I'd be so tied up I'd never get back on the trail. Or when I did, there wouldn't be any trail.

I made up my mind in an instant. I had no choice. I had to get away. I wasn't worried about the cops pinning the murder on me, but I wasn't a great favorite of theirs, and they might keep me locked up for a while until they decided I was clean, just to remind me of my place. Certainly, they'd hassle me all they could, and I had enough to do without dealing with that. I realized it wouldn't do me any good to tell them what I knew. There was hardly anything tangible. What there was was centered on the Black Knight, and Ratchitt had that sewed up.

No, if I was going to do anything, I'd have to stay loose. The cops would sure want to talk to me after they found the mess in my office, but I figured I was better off with them looking for me than with their knowing I was nice and available in a cell downtown, to be hauled out at leisure.

I heard the elevator grinding away and footsteps coming up the stairwell as I went down the back way. I was glad that no one had thought to cover that exit, or they'd have been after me for assaulting an officer along with everything else. I was in no mood to take any shit from anybody, in uniform or out.

NINETEEN

After I got onto the street, into my car, and away, I realized it was probably a good thing the cops came when they did. Otherwise, I might have kept sitting there, getting nowhere, having no ideas, growing crazy-mad again, seeing red, and running in circles until I paralyzed myself. At least I was moving now. I didn't know where or to what end, but it was better than foaming at the mouth and howling at the walls. At least movement kept me in the game.

I knew I was going to get pretty hot pretty quick, and I'd have to get some of that heat taken off. Charlie Watkins could help with that, and I needed to find him anyway to see what he'd been trying to talk to me about. I had a feeling it was tied in with all this, but the thing was, first I had to find him.

I got to a phone booth and made a couple of calls with the same result I'd been getting. Shit. What to do? It was starting to get to me, and I was even beginning to feel exposed standing in the phone booth.

Then I realized what I ought to do. I'd go to Watkins's house and wait there. It would keep me off the street, and Charlie would have to show up eventually.

Driving back into the Valley, I was feeling very conspicuous. If I'd had a new car like every other jerk in the world, I'd have blended right in, but the age and condition of mine made it stand out. Or at least that's the way I felt. Christ, I *was* getting spooked. I tried to comfort myself by saying that you're not paranoid if someone really is after you. What a comfort.

Watkins lived in one of those crappy tract houses that look the same wherever they're built. Six- or seven-room flimsies with all the character of a parking lot. The tract that Watkins lived in was especially bad. About a year after it was fully occupied, the houses started to disintegrate. Plaster cracked and fell off the walls. Electrical wiring burned out. Plumbing backed up and stopped working. Roofing material fell off and the roofs leaked. All the appliances and equipment were factory seconds with a life-span measured in months. And if all that was not enough, it turned out that the soil had some odd chemical composition that killed anything that was planted. A few varieties of weeds seemed to thrive, but that was all.

Naturally, when all this came out there was a big scandal followed by an investigation. It revealed that at every possible opportunity the developer used substandard material and workmanship. If a nickel was to be saved, he saved it, and almost nothing in the houses met even the minimum standards of the building code. To get away with all this, there were big payoffs to inspectors up and down the line. The investigation resulted in enough indictments to wallpaper most of the houses in the tract. But by the time this happened, the developer and the others who had made all this possible were comfortably residing in Costa Rica. Meanwhile, nobody would buy any of the houses at any price, and payments still had to be met every month. Those that were smart abandoned their houses to the banks and finance companies, took their losses, and got out. Those that weren't smart stayed. Obviously most people were still there. If they'd been smart, they wouldn't have bought in the first place.

Driving through the streets with the barren, weed-choked lots surrounding the faded, dilapidated houses, I felt I was on a deserted army base or one of those temporary villages that spring up around some big public-works project and are then left to rot when the project is completed. This village was still inhabited, but by people who wished that they were elsewhere. If for no other reason, I could see why Watkins's wife left him. A sleeping bag in a swamp would be preferable.

I passed the remains of a gopher that had unsuccessfully tried to cross the road, and slowed down to look for Watkins's house. I could never remember if his was the phony Cape Cod or the phony Tudor. It was the phony Tudor, and it looked like I was in luck. His car was in the sagging garage.

I parked, and as I walked up the pitted drive, I noticed that he was sitting in the car, like he was getting ready to go out. I waved and went over to him.

He wasn't going anywhere. He was sitting upright, held in place by his seat belt and shoulder harness. His head was drooping forward and his chin rested on his chest, as though he were looking at something on the seat next to him. At first I thought he was, and then I saw the two-inch hole in the top of his skull. I put my head through the window and looked up. A circle of dried blood and brains was stuck to the roof of the car, radiating around a bullet hole in the roof liner. His hand was beside him. It held his revolver.

I went around to the passenger side. Being careful not to leave any prints, I opened the door. I saw that his jaw was hanging open, a slimy trickle of blood still oozing from the hole in the roof of his mouth. Not much doubt about what had happened, but there were some questions about why. And why had he been trying to contact me? To tell me what he was going to do? Possibly. Even though I could see Charlie offing himself, in view of everything else that was happening, it didn't seem right.

I carefully picked through the litter of rubbish that covered the car seat. Maps, old newspapers, candy wrappers, empty bags from fast food joints, all the kinds of stuff that remain from long hours on stakeouts. I finally found the note. He was sitting on half of it and his arm was covering the rest of it. I maneuvered it out from under him.

Holy shit! It looked like it was Charlie's writing, but very labored and awkward. The note was short: "Hunter got me involved in something. It was too dirty and I couldn't take it anymore. This is the only way out. Tell Rosie I'm sorry."

Charlie didn't commit suicide any more than Stubby was a hit-and-run victim or Maria died of natural causes. The first part of the note was total crap. I knew it, but the cops probably wouldn't. Whoever killed Watkins not only rigged it to look like suicide, but fixed it to implicate me. If Maria's death wasn't enough, here was something else to tie me up.

I also knew that Charlie fought it, but he was forced to do it. That's what the last line meant, but I was the only one who would understand it. Rosie was a Saigon whore who Charlie had spent a lot of time with. One time he'd had it fixed up to meet her, but he'd gotten a last minute assignment. He'd tried hard to get out of it, but he had no choice. He asked me to tell Rosie he was sorry he couldn't make it.

It looked like Charlie might have been drugged and forced

to write the note. He'd had no choice, but a part of him had held out, and he put in that last line just for me. Charlie had more spunk than I thought—not any more brains, but more spunk. So long, Charlie.

I looked over the setup. Somebody was sure working hard, and it would have gone down fine, except I got lucky and got there before the body was found. Otherwise, I was supposed to have been picked up at my office. I would have been in custody when Watkins's body and the incriminating note were found. And then I would really have been in for it.

Without any hesitation I pocketed the note. That was against the law, but there was no point in being lucky if I left the damn thing lying around. That improved the situation, but not much. There might still be other stuff concerning me that I didn't know about. I was being more and more isolated, made more and more vulnerable. I was dancing to somebody else's tune, and I didn't like the feeling, but I was not at all sure how to change the music.

Although I would have liked to do a thorough search to see if I could get a line on what Watkins had been doing, I was getting nervous. There was some kind of timetable in operation, and there was probably only a short time before a "neighbor" reported the suicide. My being found at Watkins's house would be even worse than having the note found.

I thought I heard sirens. It might have been my imagination, but I couldn't afford to wait and see.

I quickly started going through Watkins's pockets. There was nothing of interest in his wallet or his notebook. Odds and ends of garbage in his other pockets. The sirens were getting closer. In his outer left jacket pocket there was a crumpled ball of paper. Three rooms of furniture for $250—terms can be arranged. The same flyer that was stuck on my windshield when I went to Medco.

Did it mean anything? Fuck if I knew. An army of rummies had probably plastered half the city with the things. Still, it was something.

No time to look further. The sirens were definitely getting closer. I ran to my car. I drove away at a nice legal speed.

TWENTY

When I got close to my apartment, I had a hunch. I parked a few blocks away, and casually walked the rest of the distance. I turned the corner onto my block and quickly ducked behind some bushes. I saw that I was right. A patrol car with two cops in it was parked in front of my building.

Shit. They didn't waste any time. I knew I'd have to stay out of sight for a while, and I wanted to pick up some things first, but they could see both entrances from where they were sitting. I thought that if they were distracted for even a moment, I could get up the driveway without being seen. I only had to cover about twenty feet, and then the side of the building would hide me. But the cops looked young and alert, and I couldn't see how I would manage. I decided to wait a few minutes to see if anything developed.

It did. Sandi or Mandi or whoever came walking by my bush. She was wearing cutoffs that were cut to reveal half her ass and a tiny halter top that halted nothing.

I hissed at her. She looked around, puzzled, and when she saw me she squealed with delight and ran around to join me.

Before I could say anything, she said, "Do you want to do it right here?" and started to pull down her shorts.

Her shorts were around her knees and she was attacking my waistband by the time I restrained her. She looked disappointed, but when I told her I needed her help, she was quite willing. I explained that I wanted her to distract the two cops so I could get into my apartment without being seen. She said it sounded exciting, but she didn't think she could do it. I looked at her. She still hadn't pulled up her shorts. Fuck!

"You won't have any trouble," I said, and told her what she should do.

She went into the building and I saw the cops' heads turn to

146

follow her. I smiled. In a couple of minutes she came out carrying a beach towel and wearing the bathing suit she had had on when she invaded my bathroom the other day. Even from this distance she was pretty spectacular. Poor cops, they didn't stand a chance.

She walked by the cruiser nice and slow to catch their attention. She did. I started moving up, being careful to stay in the shadows as much as I could. With a great deal of movement and wiggling, she spread the towel on the skimpy front lawn and settled down on it on her belly. She untied the thin string that fastened the bikini top and let it drop. She then started twisting and turning around, trying to get into a comfortable position, seemingly unaware of the cops' presence and of the fact that she kept revealing tantalizing glimpses of her bare breasts.

I made it up the driveway and around the side of the building with no difficulty. Hell, I could've driven a tank up and the cops wouldn't have noticed.

My apartment seemed the same as when I had left it. The way things had been going, that was not so small a blessing.

I flipped on my answering machine. Harold Ace, reporter, wanted me to call him. He didn't sound too happy. Who did?

I gathered up some clothes, some weapons, some ammo, and whatever else I thought I might need for a few days and threw the stuff into a canvas carryall. I could never remember if those instructions about how to pack for a trip said to put your guns under or on top of your clothes. I must ask the newspaper's travel consultant about that.

I looked around to see if there was anything else I should take, and the phone rang. I looked at it, trying to decide if I should answer it or not. I had turned off my machine, so that was no help. It rang some more. It might be the crooks or it might be the cops.

I picked it up. It was both. It was Ratchitt.

"Hunter, I've got some bad news for you." He was gloating.

"What's that?"

"Your good pal, Charlie Watkins. He couldn't take it anymore. He killed himself."

It wasn't possible for Ratchitt to have heard yet. That meant he knew. It could mean he did it. Stupid of him to call me. They were so confident of themselves that they were getting careless. They didn't care what I knew or what I didn't know.

"How'd he do it?" I said.

"Bullet in the mouth. Messy."

"But effective."

"Very."

"You wouldn't have any idea why he did it, would you?"

"How could I know?" Ratchitt laughed. He couldn't even be bothered to put up a good act. "But I have a feeling some people might be asking you that."

"What would I know?"

He laughed again. "Nothing, Hunter. Absolutely nothing. That's what's so funny." He laughed some more and then continued. "People are getting real concerned about you, Hunter. Hear you've been depressed lately."

"Me? No. I'm not depressed. I take great interest in the many curious occurrences of life."

"No, Hunter. You've been depressed. Everything that's been happening is taking its toll. It's getting to be too much for you. You'd better watch it. You never know, but you might get one of those suicidal urges too, and before you change your mind, it'll be too late."

"You really think that might happen?"

"I'm afraid I do. But you know, a nice long rest away from all this stress and strain, away from the mysteries of life, might do you a world of good."

"As much good as, say, thirty years in San Quentin would do you?"

His voice grew hard. "Some people just don't know what's in their best interests. Think about it, sucker." He hung up.

The anger came over me again. I drifted off for a second, thinking how much pleasure it would give me to bring Ratchitt down. But first things first.

I looked out the corner of the window. I had told what's-her-name to keep the cops busy for about ten minutes and then to work really hard because I'd be coming down. She played her part well. I heard her ask for some help applying her suntan oil, and both cops were out of the car in a flash. If they responded to their police calls that quickly, they'd have an enviable arrest record. They fought over the bottle of oil and then both set to work on her body like a pair of kneading machines in a bakery.

As I strolled down the driveway, I noticed that the bikini bottom had become untied. Everybody involved seemed to be enjoying themselves. Ah, Hunter, you spread pleasure wherever you go.

I reached my car and drove it to where I thought it wouldn't be found. I caught a bus and got off at a car rental agency where I got myself a new, inconspicuous set of wheels. That took care of one problem.

I rode along Ventura and pulled in at the Love Nest Adult Motel. The walls of the motel lobby were covered with centerfold pinups. From the number of magazines it took to accomplish that bit of decorating, it was obvious that someone was a lover of literature.

In answer to my shout, the manager emerged from the rear. He was a scrawny, bald-headed little guy with only a couple of yellow teeth in his head and a bad squint. He had a three-day growth of beard that made his face look dirty. He wore a discolored sleeveless undershirt, and suspenders held up an overly large pair of pants that looked more like hip waders than anything else.

He popped a breath mint into his mouth and pushed the register across to me. This seemed to be the favored accommodation of a lot of different members of the Smith family. Not wanting to break with tradition, I signed the same way.

"How many hours you want the room for, Mr. Smith?"

Amazing. He didn't look at the register, but he knew my name just the same. I noticed he had a faint southern accent.

"I might be here for a couple of days."

"Suit yourself. Most of the guests only stay a couple of hours, but maybe you got more going on. You want a regular or an X-rated one?"

"Regular."

"The X-rated are real nice. Eight-foot water beds. Mirrors on three walls and the ceiling. Special video tapes. Giant sunken bathtubs. Real nice. Our guests have a lot of fun there. How about it?"

"No. I'm alone."

"Alone?" He acted as if he'd never heard anything like it. Given the motel he ran, he probably hadn't. "Alone? Then I

got just the thing for you. Anna Mae, come here," he called
into the back. "I got a few guests who come here alone, just
because of Anna Mae."

A girl came out of the back room. She was dressed in a
transparent pink shortie nightgown and nothing else. Her
body was so perfectly, completely voluptuous it was almost
unreal. She looked to be eighteen, but the blank, vacant stare
in her eyes told me her mental age was about six. She was
clutching an old, ragged teddy bear. One of the doll's legs was
being squeezed between her thighs.

"Look at her," the manager wheezed. "This is my daughter, Anna Mae. Isn't she something. Bet you've never seen
anything like that. Now, Anna Mae ain't very bright, and she
don't know many things, but she sure does know how to give
and get pleasure. A regular pleasure machine, you might say.
How about it? We'll just charge it up to room service."

I told him I wasn't interested, and he got suspicious.

"Say, what's the matter with you? You're not planning to
do anything funny are you? Can't have any of that. We've got
our reputation to uphold."

I almost asked him what he considered to be "funny," but I
couldn't be bothered. I got my key and took my bag to my
room.

I called Harold Ace.

"It's no go, Sam."

"What do you mean?"

"The word came down this morning. They're not interested."

"How can they not be interested? You're a fucking newspaper. This is news."

"That's what I said, but they think it's a con, that it's
bullshit. They want no part of it."

"Who's they?"

"I think it went all the way up to the publisher. It looked so
hot that everyone wanted higher approval. The publisher
nixed it. Cold. I'm sorry."

"What's the publisher's name?"

Ace told me. It sounded familiar. I got out the Black
Knight's membership list. There it was. I told that to Ace.

"No shit! That son of a bitch! I'll be damned!"

He might have gone on like that indefinitely, but I cut him
off. "So that's it."

"Wait a second," he said. "This is a great story. If you can get me solid proof, like you said, I'll go private with this. There won't be any money up front, but we'll split whatever we get, and it could be a bundle. There might even be a book in this."

"Okay," I said, "if I can get it together, I'll get back to you."

It was a good idea, but somehow I didn't think it would come off. It all depended upon Faro, and whether they were on to him. He was all I had left.

I dialed his number. I got one of those recordings saying the line was out of order.

I didn't like it. Lately, whenever I tried to reach someone and couldn't, it meant just one thing.

TWENTY-ONE

I was right. I made the short drive into the hills to Faro's place. Or rather where Faro's place used to be. All that was there now was a pile of smouldering ashes. A couple of firemen were still around doing mop-up work, not that there was anything left to mop up.

I asked one of the fireman what had happened. He told me it had burned down. Instead of putting his fire hose where it would do the most good, I remained cool and asked for some more information.

"Looks like it started in the darkroom." He clucked a few times like a mournful chicken. "Some people just don't know how to take care of chemicals."

I clucked along with him. Some people don't, but others sure do. I asked about survivors.

"You gotta be kidding. Once the fire started, the whole place went up like a ball of paper. Whoosh. That was it. You see that box over there?" He pointed to a plastic container, a little bigger than a cubic foot in size. "We got what's left of the occupant in that. Never had a chance."

Faro's kind never do. They want a piece of the sky, but they always end up with a piece of dirt. I probably speeded Faro to his piece of dirt, but this was one death that didn't bother me. He was scum, and if it hadn't been me, it would have been somebody else. Or Faro would have done it on his own.

What did bother me was that I was now left with nothing. Nothing tangible. Nothing to use to apply pressure. Nothing to go on. I couldn't go to my office. I couldn't go to my apartment. And I had nothing to give the cops to buy myself some room to move.

Somebody'd had a busy day. Three up and three down. Everybody I talked to seemed to get their contracts canceled. Maybe I should get new cards printed up: Sam Hunter—Kiss of Death. I was left alone with only my smile and a worn-out line of patter which, along with a quarter, would get me a cup of coffee.

. . . Jesus Christ! I was really starting to get freaked. Faro and Stubby and Watkins and Maria. I was feeling responsible for them all, and that wasn't right. Faro I didn't care about. I might have helped prevent the deaths of Argyll and Watkins, but they never gave me the chance, and they supposedly knew what they were doing—whatever that was. It was Maria that was getting to me, and only Maria. She was on my head. Aw, fuck that shit. I didn't kill her, but I was going to nail the assholes that did. Right! Fuck guilt and get moving, I told myself, and I believed it. I was still on the loose and that was enough.

There was one avenue left that I hadn't yet explored. Medco Pharmaceuticals. It looked like both Stubby and Watkins had been poking around there. The fact that they both bought it must mean they'd found something. Now I'd give it a try. It was either that or leave town. And I don't run.

Since I wasn't about to go there during working hours, I had a lot of time to kill until it was late enough and dark enough to pay my visit. I picked up a bottle of gin and half a dozen chilli dogs and went back to the motel.

By the time I had finished the dogs—which weren't at all bad—and washed them down with the better part of the gin, I was feeling more myself. I had a long shower, drew the shades to darken the room, and lay down on the bed. The air conditioner in the window made a lot of noise, but it worked, and I felt pretty comfortable.

I must have fallen asleep because I was awakened by something moving next to me on the bed. It was Anna Mae.

"Oh, goody," she chirped happily when she saw me open my eyes. "Papa tell me to come and play with the nice man."

Good old Papa. I told her I didn't want to play. Her eyes got all puffy, like she was about to cry.

"Oh, please play. Please play with me. I like to play."

She grabbed both my hands and placed them on her breasts. Yes, she was completely naked, an impossible combination of mounds and curves and fleshy dimples. Her skin felt smooth as custard and as resilient as marshmallows. At my touch her nipples expanded and grew hard and hot, red diamonds drilling into the palms of my hands. Her breath came in quick gasps as she arched her back to press her breasts more completely into my grip.

Suddenly she took one of my hands and placed it at the juncture of her legs. Immediately she was steaming and moist. She moved her hips up and down several times and tensed for orgasm. "Goody," she said. Twice more she pushed herself into my fingers and tensed. "Goody. Goody," she said.

She gently took my hard penis in both her hands. "Now I play with you," she said.

I felt like the traveling salesman with the farmer's daughter. Fuck it. Who cared?

Some time during the course of the evening, I vaguely wondered what my room service charges would be. The thought passed.

TWENTY-TWO

It was about midnight when I approached the Medco building. I was tired, but I had that empty feeling I liked so much
because it gave me a really hard edge. There was nothing left
in me to get in the way. Everything was clear and clean and
immediate.

The first thing I noticed as I came up to the place was that
lights were on in the ground level. Blackout curtains masked
the windows high on the wall, but there was a tiny rim of light
that showed in the darkness. Not enough to notice unless you
were looking for something. Okay, somebody was home.

I started to go around the building, looking for a way to get
in. In an alley that ran along one side of the building, a giant
black limousine was parked in such a way that it would not be
seen from the street. Interesting.

The limo was unlocked and I checked the registration. It
was made out to a leasing agency. I made a note of the name
and also the car's licence number in case I needed to check it
out later.

I went into the immense backseat area. It was big enough
to hold a bridge table with room left over for kibitzers. I
opened a walnut cabinet that was built into the back of the
front seat. Along with a variety of heavy crystal glasses there
was a bottle of very expensive single-malt Scotch and a bottle
of fifty-year-old Cognac. There was a fancy humidor that held
some large cigars. They were the same kind as the one that
Ratchitt left on my floor. More and more interesting.

The car revealed nothing else, but I had a pretty good idea
who it belonged to.

I continued around the building and found a door that
looked promising. I had a ring full of skeleton keys, and I
hoped one of them would work. The third one I tried opened

155

the door as easily as if it had been made for it. No alarms. A
quick move and I was inside. Christ! And people are amazed
that burglary is the country's biggest growth industry. They
might just as well pile their belongings on the sidewalk for all
takers.

I was in a side corridor, and I started moving in the
direction where I saw the light. At the end of another
corridor, at the side of the building where I thought the light
was, there was a set of double doors. The sign on them said
Research Lab—Authorized Personnel Only. Light showed
under the doors, and a soft push told me they were locked.
Just as well. What was I going to do, walk in there and ask
directions to Hollywood and Vine?

When I had been in the building the time before, I had
noticed that the office walls were not structural. Each floor
was simply a large area, completely open except for support-
ing columns. Any differentiation of space was achieved
through the use of partitions. It's not unusual for interior
partitions not to reach the ceiling, and I was hoping that was
the case here.

I went back down the corridor. Another key easily opened
the first door I came to. It was a kind of storeroom that didn't
seem to be in use. I got lucky. The ceiling was ten feet and the
interior partitions were about a foot short. Down at the far
end of the storeroom, I saw light coming through the gap.

I was careful not to make a sound as I carried a couple of
boxes over to the wall. These gave me the height I needed to
see into the next room. I placed the boxes next to a pillar so
that I would be shielded. I stood up.

The lab was about forty feet by thirty. Work benches went
around the outside of the room, and several tables took up
the center of it. Some equipment was scattered around at
various places, but even from my position I could see that it
hadn't been used for a long time.

The far corner of the room was the source of the light,
provided by several high intensity lamps. Here there was
more equipment set up, and it was in use. Three men in lab
coats were working. I had seen enough of it in Saigon to guess
that the white powder the men were processing was heroin.
Off to one side, looking like the ogre in a dark fairy tale,
stood the bulk of Mountain Cyclone.

All of a sudden, a lot of things made a lot of sense.

I didn't need to see anymore. I got down from my perch. I crossed to the door. I listened to make sure no one was in the corridor outside, went out, and left through the door I'd come in. I looked at my watch. Not even five minutes had gone by, and most of the pieces had fallen into place.

I went to move my car. I wanted it close by when the limo started to move. If I could follow it home, that would just about complete the puzzle.

I positioned myself where I could watch the car without being seen, and waited.

No wonder people got upset when I started to look at Acker. And if Stubby and Watkins had discovered the secret, I wasn't surprised that they were killed. A heroin plant in the middle of L.A. was an operation that was worth protecting at virtually any price.

I shook my head. It was a beautiful setup, and you couldn't help but admire it. The French connection was gone, or at least severely curtailed. With the end of the Viet Nam war, Southeast Asian supplies were getting harder to come by. Even in Mexico, things were starting to clamp down, and anyway, Mexican brown was at best considered to be second-class goods.

The problem with heroin is never the manufacture or distribution of it, but its importation. That's the weakest, most vulnerable part of the chain, and the place the authorities attack the hardest and where they have their greatest successes. The scheme in effect at Medco entirely eliminated that link, and it was no wonder Watkins and his Narco buddies were having such a hard time getting a line on it. Even if they managed to crack part of the distribution scheme, they'd always run up against a blank wall.

The idea of using an established pharmaceutical supplier for the processing plant was so beautiful it was almost laughable. You might look for a backroom kitchen somewhere in the desert or the mountains, but you'd never look at a well-known drug company in the city. Not only that, but Medco could easily and legally obtain all the supplies of morphine they wanted. A simple chemical process converted the morphine into H., and because they were using good morphine, they would end up with a dynamite product. It wouldn't be difficult to juggle the company's accounts and records to make a pretty sizeable quantity of morphine disappear. Acker, having been general manager, would know how to do that.

By the same token, a lot of the profits from the heroin could be funneled through Medco's legitimate books—a slightly bigger sale here, a nonexistent order there, and pretty soon you've got the means to justify a considerable improvement in life-style; whatever is not declared that way is gravy, and the existence of that extra money would not be very obvious. As long as Medco's books looked good and they paid their taxes like a good corporate citizen, nobody would look very closely at them. If somebody did get curious, it would be a lengthy, difficult process to discover what was wrong, and the participants could be clear long before the whistle was blown.

Given all that, it was hardly surprising that things at the factory felt funny. The whole place was just a front, and the legitimate business wasn't enough to justify their existence.

If my reasoning was right, and I was sure it was, it was easy to see how the whole thing had come about. Through the Black Knight Club, Domingo had gotten something on Acker. I had no idea what it could be, but it had to be something pretty heavy because Acker didn't seem to be the type to be bothered by anything comparatively mild. In any event, pressure was applied, and they came up with this scheme. I didn't know for sure, but Acker must have been pretty agreeable to it, since he'd end up with more money than he could ever hope to get any other way.

There had been the problem of the proposed take-over, but that was easy to deal with. Sweet caved in without a struggle. It only remained to give Acker the money to buy out the owner, and the boys had their private chemical company to do with as they pleased, complete with protection, happily provided by their old pal detective Ratchitt. Nice, nice, nice.

It all held together, but, after thinking it through, I was still bothered by the fact that they reacted so strongly to my appearance on the scene. They were pretty secure, and it was unlikely I would have come upon the Medco setup unless I had been pushed into it. Even the coincidence of my poking around Venus Films asking about Linda Perdue didn't seem enough to account for their overreaction. Of course it could be that they were really stupid, but they couldn't have come up with this beautiful operation if they were that dumb. No, there were some things I didn't know. . . . Even beyond the identity of Domingo.

Clarissa Acker's face popped into my head, and I began to wonder what all this would mean to her. Not anything good, that was for sure. She had no involvement in her husband's dirt, but she would be affected just the same. Badly.

Shit. What was happening to me? Ordinarily, I wouldn't have given it a thought—I'd just let things fall where they would. And they were going to fall. Hard. Too much had gone on, and I was owed too much. I didn't have any choice. I had to take it all the way, no matter what, no matter who got buried. The damn thing was, I knew she would understand that, even if she was one of those who got buried. Well, I'd just have to try to pull her out. "How" was another of those things I didn't know.

Shit.

My deliberations were cut short by the appearance of Mountain around the corner of the building. He was carrying a couple of shopping bags, and they didn't contain his groceries.

He put the parcels in the back seat of the car and squeezed into the space behind the wheel like a giant hand going into a glove that's too small.

The limo moved out, a silent black shadow.

After a pause, I fell in behind.

TWENTY-THREE

It wasn't hard to follow the limousine. It was the biggest thing this side of the yacht harbor, and I was able to keep it in sight from a couple of blocks back.

Mountain made a lot of detours and circular maneuvers to see if there was a tail on, but I anticipated his moves and was so far behind anyway that he never picked me up. Finally he settled down and continued in a fairly straight line. He was heading toward Beverly Hills.

He left Sunset and turned up into the hills. A couple of more turns and he was onto one of the pricier streets. Suddenly I realized I knew where he was heading, and I knew what it was about Domingo that had been scratching away at the back of my skull.

When I had been staking out George Lansing's house to see what his idiot son was up to, I spent a lot of hours sitting in my car. This disturbed some of the residents and the cops came around to check me out. They would have liked to roust me, but there was nothing they could do. Just to make things look better, I moved around a bit—parking up the hill one day, down it the next. I spent two days in front of an elegant house that was three up from Lansing's. There was nothing special about the place, but there was a small ivy-covered sign at the bottom of the drive. I had just remembered that the sign said Casa Domingo.

It was fucking incredible. No, on second thought, it wasn't. I had stopped being surprised by anything a long time before. Now I knew what had started it all. In combination with everything else, my spending two days in front of his house had got him pretty nervous. He didn't know I was watching a different house and that the cops were trying to chase me away. What he thought he saw was cause for alarm . . . and for action.

160

I didn't need to follow the limo any more. I turned off at the first opportunity and raced up a street that ran roughly parallel to the one where Domingo lived. From the time I spent on the Lansing case, I knew the neighborhood pretty well, and I knew how to get into the backyard from the next street over. I figured it was better to approach the house that way than from the front.

I studied the houses I was going past and parked in front of the one I thought was likeliest. It was completely dark, so I didn't have to worry about being seen and having some half-wit hero defend his household by firing a shotgun into the night.

I went up the driveway and into the backyard. I skirted the swimming pool built in the shape of a giant star—very classy—and made it to the rear fence. I hoisted myself up and looked around. I could just see Lansing's house from where I was, and counted three. Dead on. I was looking into the backyard of Casa Domingo.

As I was letting myself over the fence, I saw the lights come on in the big room that looked out on the rear gardens. The drapes were open and it was like I was looking at a brightly illuminated stage. I moved as close as I could safely go and hid myself behind a large clump of spiky desert plants.

As soon as I was in place, Mountain trundled into the room carrying the two bags. He stood motionless for a few moments, and then a man crossed to him. The new arrival was of medium height but was grossly obese. He wore a dressing gown that was thickly embroidered with red and gold Chinese dragons. He had thick black hair, a prominent hawk-like nose, and droopy sensual lips. Without the excess weight he would have had the dark, striking good looks that one associates with Mediterranean gigolos, and he looked familiar to me. I concentrated.

Son of a bitch! Charlie Watkins was right after all. Take off fifteen or twenty years and more than 150 pounds and it was the guy that played that half-baked television detective Domingo. The critics had said his acting was criminal, and I guess he took it to heart. I realized then that his was the voice that had called me about Stubby Argyll.

Not much was happening on the stage. Domingo took the bags from Mountain and carried them off past where I could see. He returned in a minute, lit one of those special cigars, and opened a magnum of champagne that was icing in a bucket. He didn't bother to offer any to Mountain, who was pulling candy bars from his bulging pockets and stuffing them into his mouth. I couldn't tell if he troubled to remove the wrapping first.

The rest of the scene was about as interesting as Domingo's long-dead TV series, with about as much action. Domingo said a few words to Mountain, and Mountain left. The fat former actor continued to pour out glasses of champagne and toss them back in one swallow. The wine probably never even hit his tongue. I knew his kind. He'd buy only the most expensive stuff and then drink it like it was rotgut because he was too big a man to bother with niceties like tasting it.

After he had drained the magnum he tried to get out of his armchair. His fat ass was too heavy and sunk too low in the deep cushions, and he just rolled around like a beached walrus. On his fourth attempt he had built up enough momentum to propel himself from the chair. He staggered a few steps before he achieved equilibrium. With a shake of his head he adjusted his dressing gown and waddled over to the window. There he was, the big enchilada, and he looked out with a satisfied, master-of-all-he-surveys expression that made me want to flatten his face. I contented myself with the thought that he would not be nearly so pleased with things if he knew about the snake lurking in his garden. Domingo puffed on his cigar a few more times. He turned a little unsteadily, walked into the corner of a table, said something that was probably not very polite, and left the room. The lights went off as he did so. The stage was dark.

I waited a few minutes to make sure everything was quiet and went back over the fence. I got into my car and went over the hill into the Valley.

On the way back to the motel I stopped at Hamburger Haven, a burger joint with pretentions. I had no use for their dim attempts to be stylish. I mean, it was a fucking hamburger shop, and who cared if they had fake Tiffany lamps all over the place? However, they were open all night, and their burgers were okay.

I had a couple of half-pounders with a good half inch of Roquefort cheese melted on top and capped with slices of a very young dill pickle, still almost a cucumber. With it I had a double order of onion rings dipped in beer batter and deep fried. Three Amstel beers went down very easily.

I was sucking in my second Gitane, and feeling pretty good.

I now knew who I was up against, and I knew what was going on. I didn't know what I was going to do with this knowledge, but I'd think of something.

I always did.

TWENTY-FOUR

In the morning when I woke up I knew what I was going to do. I didn't have to think about it, it was just there. I realized I wouldn't be able to do it on my own. To do the job right was too big for me, especially since I was such a hot property at the moment. I looked at my idea from every angle and saw there wasn't any way around it. It didn't make me very happy, but I knew I'd have to use the cops if I was going to wrap up this thing.

But first I needed a little more info. Shit. I didn't even know that son of a bitch Domingo's real name.

I had some coffee and doughnuts at a place next to the motel. It was part of a large chain of dumps that ran from coast to coast and catered to people who lacked the sense to eat elsewhere. My doughnuts came on a small disposable plastic plate. I would have been better off eating the plate.

If I needed information about anything or anyone in Hollywood, there was only one person to go to—Cora Cardiff. She had been a syndicated gossip columnist for longer than anyone could remember, and if there was anything to be known about anyone, she knew it. She was a vicious, predatory old dyke with about as much warmth as a lizard in the Arctic, but I had helped her out a couple of times, and she seemed to like me.

She lived in a three-bedroom bungalow on the spacious grounds of an old Beverly Hills hotel. She had a staff of secretaries and a bank of telephones manned round the clock, and she never left the bungalow except for periodic excursions for cosmetic surgery. The days of her greatest glory were gone, but she still had significant power and an even more significant income.

I went through the massive oak door of the Spanish-style

bungalow, past the clutch of secretaries, typists, researchers, and telephone operators who were spreading the tendrils of Cora's web, and into the woman's bedroom, popularly known as the Lavender Lair. Everything in the room was in shades of purple—the drapes, the carpet, the furniture. Even the walls were done in padded, upholstered, lavender satin. It was like being inside a grape. The woman herself was propped up in her giant round bed covered in purple silk, the small, dry, hard seed at the center of the grape.

"Dear boy!" she said as I came in, her voice a harsh rasp like sandpaper on stone. "Here. Sit next to me on the bed." I sat. "How good of you to come. Especially since you're now a celebrity."

Huh? "What do you mean?" I said.

"You mean you haven't seen the morning paper?—Now where have I heard that line before?—Here. Take a look. You're famous."

She turned to an inside page of the paper and pushed it across to me. The headline said, "Private Eye Wanted for Questioning in Connection with Homicide." The story was about Maria and didn't say very much, but the impression was that I was suspect number one. The short article concluded with the ominous line, "Police wish to question Hunter about several other matters as well." Christ, I was hotter than I thought. There was even a picture of me. Fortunately, it was an old one, not very good, and could have been of almost anyone.

"They say that one day everyone will get to be famous for twenty minutes. This must be your time, dear boy. Enjoy it."

"I'll try," I said.

"But why are you here? I hope it's not to confess to me. I wouldn't mind getting the story, but I've been hearing so many messy confessions lately that I'm feeling positively soiled. Dear boy, you simply wouldn't believe some of the things that people do."

Just then a woman came in one door, slowly walked across the room, and went out another door. She was over six-four, large-limbed, with good muscle definition and a wild mane of brown hair that reached the middle of her back. She wore shiny black leather shorts and nothing else. Her breasts were a pair of large, firm cones protruding proudly in front of her.

Cora's eyes followed the Amazon until the door closed behind her.

"Do you like her, dear boy? That's Magda the Marauder, the queen of the roller derby. She's delightful, isn't she?"

"Delightful," I said, "but I don't think I'd want to go two out of three falls with her."

"But I do, dear boy. I do." Cora looked almost wistful for a second, and then asked me what I wanted.

I said I wanted some information, and she said if she didn't have it, she would make some up.

"Do you remember a guy—about fifteen or twenty years ago—played a detective on television called Domingo?"

I thought I detected a momentary twinge of uneasiness, but she recovered smoothly. "You mean Harvey Millicent. Of course I remember, dear boy. Only the body's going, not the mind."

"Harvey Millicent?"

"Yes, dear boy. Isn't it a scream that the actor they tried to promote as the New Valentino was called that? Somebody figured that there were so many Rocks and Biffs and Lances at the time that it would be a good idea to use his real name, which was Harvey Millicent. Except that as soon as the series started, everyone began calling him Domingo after the character he played, and the name stuck. I think he liked it. Wouldn't you, if you were named Harvey Millicent?"

"What happened?"

"The same old story, dear boy. So boring. The series was an instant hit. Overnight, as they say, Harvey went from being a nobody—people claim he was a not very successful pimp before he was discovered, but that may be just maliciousness—to being a star. He bought a house in Beverly Hills. I think he even named it after the TV show. Tacky, tacky. He had lots of money and he started spending it. Acquired quite a taste for *la dolce vita,* and it began to show. He started gaining weight and getting sloppy. In the second year of the series, you might say he became a gigantic shadow of his former self. He also became unmanageable, developed an ugly temper. That's fine if you have the talent to back it up, but old Harvey couldn't play dead if you shot him through the heart. Midway through the third year, the series was canceled. Good-bye, Domingo."

"And then?"

THE BIG ENCHILADA   167

"What 'then'? Dear boy, in this town there is no then. If you're canceled you cease to exist. You disappear."

"Except that Domingo didn't disappear. Come on, there's more."

She didn't look very happy. "If you know that, then you already know more than is good for you, dear boy. Domingo is one of those people it is not healthy to talk about in this town. If somebody tries to tell me something, I don't listen." I looked steadily at her, and she heaved a dry, scraping sigh. "You know, a taste for the good life can be habit forming. Domingo had the habit."

"How did he maintain it?"

"Not from carefully investing his earnings as an actor, I can assure you. Those were spent before the checks came in. No, Domingo became a supplier."

". . . Of?"

"Of anything. Of other people's habits. He would find out what people wanted—things that were difficult to get—and he would give it to them . . . for a price. Girls, boys, dope, protection, silence, whatever. A dream merchant in the land where dreams are made. There's money to be made doing that, and they say he made a lot of it. But the more money he made, the more invisible he became. People even stopped whispering about him. If his name came up, there would be a sudden silence, and people would look embarrassed or uncomfortable . . . or scared. He became—he is—a very powerful man. He's supposed to have more dirt on people than I do, and they say he uses it. He is a nasty man. I wouldn't take him on, and you know I take on anyone."

"Is that it? You can't give me anything else?"

"Like I said, he's invisible. No one ever sees him anymore. He values his privacy. He doesn't like people talking about him, and so people don't. Take some advice. Don't tangle with him. You're such a gorgeous hunk, it'd be a shame if something happened to you." She tried to leer at me and stretched out a bony hand in the direction of my crotch. I moved away from the old lizard.

"Come on," I said, "you're not interested in men."

"Not ordinarily, dear boy, but I might make an exception for you. It might be interesting. You never know, I may make it with you one of these days."

"Is that a threat?" I said, standing up.

"Dear boy." She looked appraisingly at me. "Perhaps we'll have a quiet tête-à-tête after I have my face lifted next month."

Her rasping, cackling laugh followed me out of the room.

"Don't forget, dear boy, to pass along anything juicy you might get," she called as I closed the door.

None of the staff paid any attention to me as I went through the front room. One of the girls was on the phone, looking very frustrated. "Look, sweetheart," she was saying, "I don't care if she eats hummingbirds and champagne for breakfast. I want to know who she's fucking this week. *Capisce?*"

That's what we like to see: investigative reporting.

I strolled across the expansive hotel grounds, which were being manicured by scores of wetback gardeners. At the swimming pool there were some pot-bellied men from Iowa who looked disappointed because there were no buxom starlets frolicking in the pool, only a pair of pot-bellied women from Kansas.

If Cora Cardiff knew nothing more about Domingo than she told me, he was a man with a lot of juice. You didn't need very many friends if your enemies were scared shitless of you, and Domingo's were that.

Cora had at least given me a little background. The gossip was probably right, and Domingo had been a low-level crook before his rise to stardom. When that went bust, he reverted to type. He saw his opportunity to play his same old game, only this time he was going to be in the big leagues. He started supplying goods and services. This brought him good money, but more important, it brought him knowledge. Knowledge of things people didn't want known. Knowledge meant power. Power meant more money. And more money in turn meant more power. Once he got started, it must have been easy, and the easier it got, the more he wanted. It didn't make any difference if he needed it, it was enough that he wanted it. And so it went. Until he brought me into it. Then he went too far.

I had reached the bank of phone booths off the hotel lobby. I took a deep breath. I didn't want to do this, but I had no choice. I dialed the police and asked to be connected with Burroughs, Watkins's partner.

"Yeah. Burroughs here." He sounded harried.

"This is Hunter. I—"

"Jesus Christ! This is all I needed. Hunter, do you realize that half the cops in the city are looking for you? I'd like to see you myself, but if you've called in to surrender, do me a favor and call someone else. Things are coming apart here, and I don't need any more grief."

"Maybe I can help you."

"Only by hanging up."

"Is Watkins's death part of the problem?"

"Naw. Things are always cool around here when a cop offs himself."

"Do you think he did?"

"It seems cut and dried. Why? What do you know?"

"I know he didn't. He was killed."

"How do you know? You do it?"

"Charlie was a friend of mine."

"So he said. Friends like you he didn't need. You know, someone called in here a while back. Said you had gotten Charlie involved in something dirty. He wanted out. You wouldn't let him. So he killed himself."

"Who told you this?"

"That information's confidential."

"Ah, the good old anonymous phone call. Right?"

"Maybe," he said grudgingly.

"Do you believe it?"

"Why shouldn't I?"

"Because it's not true. Charlie was murdered because he found out something. It was made to look like suicide. That phone call was to implicate me to get me out of the way. I know what Charlie found out."

"Yeah? What's that?"

"No. Not on the phone."

"Well, come on in, Hunter. I'll be here all day."

"No good. Look. Neither of us knows the other one. I don't think much of cops, but Charlie said you were okay. Charlie wasn't very bright, but you still might be okay. Are you enough of a cop to get some information about your partner's murder, or are you as dirty as some of your buddies down there?"

"All right, you asshole, I'll meet you someplace." He was genuinely angry. I thought that was a good sign. "But only because Watkins also said that you were okay. . . . But you're right—Watkins was stupid. Where do you want to meet?"

I told him the name of a small park. I told him to come alone in half an hour. I knew the place, and I would be able to tell in advance if he was playing straight.

"All right, Hunter, I'll go along with you. But if you're being cute, if you're playing games with me, I'm going to come down hard on you, and you'll see just what kind of a cop I am."

"That's what I wanted to hear. See you in half an hour."

TWENTY-FIVE

From my secluded vantage point on a small hill, I saw Burroughs approach. At least I assumed it was Burroughs since the guy exuded "cop" from a hundred yards. He was short and stocky, and his brown suit was creased and rumpled. He was starting to lose his hair, and what was left was wiry and turning gray. He reminded me of an especially pugnacious watchdog who might be a little slow in reacting, but would never let go once he got hold of you.

I let Burroughs pace around impatiently for a few minutes, just to make sure he was alone. Then I left my hiding place and walked down the hill to him.

"Burroughs, I presume," I said cheerfully.

"Hunter." He made it sound like a bad word. Neither of us extended a hand to the other.

"Where's the basket?" I said.

"What?"

"You were supposed to bring the picnic basket, and I was to bring the drinks. Or was it the other way around?"

"Hunter, don't be more of an asshole than is necessary, okay?"

"Lighten up, Burroughs. I was just trying to ease the tension."

"Let's just leave the tension alone."

We glared at one another, sizing up each other. There was no question that Burroughs was tough, and he probably was a bastard, but in a funny way I began to have confidence in him. I also realized that he had no confidence in me, and he'd have to if we were going to work together. I did something I didn't much want to do. I took a piece of paper out of my pocket and handed it to him.

"What's this?"

"That's the suicide note that Watkins was supposed to have left."

"Where'd you get this?"

"I obviously found Watkins's body before anyone else."

"What the fuck, Hunter, don't you know it's against—"

"Yeah," I cut him off, "I know it's a whole bunch of stuff. But I'm giving it to you now. If you decide to, you can use it against me in a couple of different ways."

"So why give it to me?" He was being very cautious.

"Because I want your help, and to get it I know I'm going to have to get you to trust me—at least partway."

I explained to him why the note was a phony. He didn't seem particularly responsive to my reasoning, and I began to wonder if I had made a mistake in opening up to him.

"Why should I believe you?" he said when I had finished.

"Because it's true, but even more because of the phone call."

"What do you mean?"

"Didn't it strike you as funny, getting that kind of call? Doesn't it seem even funnier, now that you see the note? You wouldn't have gotten the call if the note had been found."

"A case could be made that the call and the note support each other."

"Come on, Burroughs. You're a better cop than that."

"You're right. It is funny, except for one thing."

"What's that?"

He thought for a minute. "I shouldn't tell you, but what the hell. It can't make any difference. . . . We found a pound of pure heroin in the trunk of Watkins's car."

Nice touch. If I hadn't found the note first, it would have looked very suggestive.

"Then that should cinch it that it's a frame."

"Or that Watkins was involved."

"You don't really believe that, do you?"

"A week ago, no. But Watkins had been acting funny, and then he disappeared, so now I'm not so sure."

"Look, you knew Watkins for a long time. What feels better to you? That he was involved in heroin traffic? Or that to make up for some mistakes, he stupidly started investigating on his own, found out something, and was killed before he could do anything about it?"

He gave a big sigh. "I'll go along with you, Hunter, though I'm damned if I know why. What do you have?"

"I've got a line on an operation that's bigger than you could imagine."

"So tell me."

"Now don't take this the wrong way, but I think we should be dealing with a D.A."

His face grew red. He was taking it the wrong way. "I'm getting tired of you, Hunter. What's all your talk about trust? You'll tell me now or you'll tell me down at the station. What the hell do you think I'm going to do?"

"Take it easy, Burroughs. It's not you. This thing is really big, and if we're going to do it right, it's going to take someone who can move hard, fast, and secretly."

"You think I'm going to announce it on the radio?"

"I know you don't have the authority to set it up on your own, and the more people you involve, the more chance there is that the wrong person will hear about it, and that'll fuck it all up."

"Who are you afraid might hear about it?"

"Ratchitt."

"Is he in this?"

"With both hands up to his shoulders. He may even have done Charlie."

Burroughs's face grew dark. "That scumbag. He makes me want to puke. He's as dirty as they come and he thinks it's a joke. I'd love to get him."

Burroughs meant it. He might be an S.O.B., but he was straight.

"I can take him down," I said quietly.

Burroughs looked at me, and as he did so, the expression in his eyes changed. He still didn't like me, but the hard antagonism was gone.

"What do you want?" he said after a long pause.

"Can you get a D.A. with the authority—and the ability— to act quickly and quietly? And he'd better be squeaky clean. The bunch we're up against has a lot of juice where it does the most good."

Burroughs thought a minute and then nodded. "Jim Green."

I knew who he was. He was an assistant district attorney

who was young, tough, and ambitious. I told Burroughs he
would do.

"But you've got to give me something to take to him. He's
not going to agree to see you unless he knows what it's
about."

"Okay. It's about a heroin factory in full operation. It's
about a private club that's a brothel for kinky sex. It's about
prostitution—male, female, and children. It's about blackmail of some of the wealthiest and most powerful men in the
city. It's about bribery and protection. It's about a big
producer of child pornography. It's about the dirtiest cop of
them all."

"You can deliver all that?"

"I can. It's also about the murder of four people—Watkins,
my secretary, a P.I. named Stubby Argyll, and a cheap punk
called Faro. My secretary is the only one that's down as a
homicide."

"Jesus Christ, Hunter! You don't want to tell me about any
of this now?"

"Nope."

"Okay," he said reluctantly. "I'll get you your D.A. . . . .
Shit! I don't know why I'm doing this. If this gets fucked up,
we're all in for it, and it won't give me any satisfaction to
know that you'll get it worst of all."

I told him it wouldn't give me any satisfaction either, but
that I thought we could bring it off so that everyone smelled
like roses—or at least like cheap after shave. Burroughs
didn't find that very funny. The man has no sense of humor.

Burroughs left me after I cautioned him about a dozen
times to be sure he talked to no one except the D.A., and to
make sure the D.A. also said nothing to anyone.

I was surprised to find that I was so nervous about this. I
suppose that's what comes from having to rely on other
people. I didn't like the feeling.

Burroughs worked fast, and in a couple of hours I was
sitting in the back of a crummy bar with him and James "Mad
Dog" Green, the Young Turk of the District Attorney's
office. His nickname came from the way he played linebacker
in college football, but I gathered it was not inappropriate for
the way he did his job as D.A. He had a reputation for

single-minded ferocity that was most distressing to some of his less energetic colleagues. We disliked each other on sight, but we both realized that each of us could be very useful to the other.

I talked for a long time. I told them about Mound of Venus Films and how that enterprise was a major supplier of the child porn films that everyone was getting so bothered about, and how it also provided young talent to the club. I told them about the Black Knight Club—what went on in the club and what happened to the members after they made use of the facilities. I told them about the heroin factory at Medco and how that setup tied in with the club. I told them about the part Ratchitt played. I told them that one man was behind all of it. I told them everything except who that one man was.

When I started my story, they didn't believe me, but as I went on, explained connections, examined coincidences, they became less skeptical, and by the time I finished they were believers. Thank Christ for that!

As their incredulity changed to belief, anger turned to red-eyed fury. Green was jumping around, ready to call out the dogs, sound the alarms, order all hands on deck, and descend like an avenging angel. That was just about the worst way to handle things, and it took me a long time to calm him down and explain that a little subtlety was called for if he really wanted to close things up. I finally got him to agree that the more noise he made, the more likely it was that somebody would be tipped off and his net would come up empty.

Then Green started in on me about the identity of the man behind it all. I kept quiet.

"Damn it, Hunter," he said, "I need to know the name. I can't proceed without it."

"Come off it. I've given you enough stuff to act a dozen times over. You don't need the name right now."

"But he's the one I want," Green said, hitting the table with his fist.

"He's the one I want as well. The only one I want. I don't suffer from moral outrage, and all that other stuff doesn't bother me too much—except as it relates to the big man. And I intend to see him brought down. But it won't happen unless we do it my way. He's too well insulated, and he'll get off. He might be slowed down, but he won't be hurt. He should be hurt."

"Scum like that should be exterminated," Burroughs muttered.

"I didn't hear that," Green said quickly.

"I did," I said, and grinned at Burroughs.

From that point on, I had an ally in the cop, and together we talked Green around to leaving the big man to me, at least to begin with. Nobody talked about what I intended to do to him, but the unspoken idea hung over the table like a heavy shadow.

I outlined the way I thought Green should handle things. He was to get the necessary warrants as quietly as possible, from a judge in whom he had absolute confidence. He couldn't be too careful about this because the big man had connections all over the place. The same applied to the cops who would be chosen for the assignment. Only a small group was needed, but they should be handpicked and absolutely trustworthy. If possible, they should be from outside the immediate area, and they should be assembled with the least possible fuss in order to minimize the chance of anything being noticed or leaked. Up until the time they went into action, no one except Burroughs and Green would know what was going down. Then, if there was a leak, we'd all know where to look.

I asked Green if he could manage all that, and how long it would take. He thought it would be no problem and that he and Burroughs could have the strike force ready in a couple of hours. It's amazing how the red tape just falls apart if you use the right scissors.

Their first target would be Venus Films. They would hit it in the late afternoon when work would be proceeding as usual. They shouldn't run into any resistance there, and they should find enough material to keep them busy for quite a while. The important thing was that anyone they netted should be kept on ice until the rest of the operation was done. They should be kept incommunicado, out of sight and seeing no one. I told Green that if that wasn't done, he could forget about the rest of the evening. Just to be on the safe side, the cops should all be kept together as well. Green figured he could manage that.

That night they would split up. Burroughs would hit

Medco, and Green would take the rest of the men and raid the Black Knight, pulling in everyone on the premises. If possible, they'd be kept on ice until the morning. That wasn't too essential, but it would ensure me of a good night's sleep. After the second set of raids, Green would call off the search for me. That would let me return to my apartment. I wanted to be there in the morning. I figured Domingo might want to see me when he heard the news. I wanted to be available.

I had thought out the plan while I was waiting to see Burroughs and Green, and I got surprisingly little resistance from them when I explained it.

"That only leaves Ratchitt," Burroughs growled into his watery beer.

"Yeah," I said, "that's something of a messy problem, but I've got an idea of how to deal with it."

"Which is?" Green sounded stiff and cautious.

"You don't want to know," I said. "Let's just say it will take care of Ratchitt without embarrassing the department."

"That's not good enough, Hunter. I insist upon knowing what you have in mind."

"Don't insist, Green. You'll lose—what do you call it?—deniability."

"I can't have you going around doing God knows what. If you don't tell me, I'll pull the string on you."

"That wouldn't be a good idea. Do you know how bad the department would look if the story about Ratchitt got out? The smell would stick for years to come."

"You'd do that?"

"I don't want to," I shrugged.

Burroughs cut in. "Give Hunter some rope. If he fucks up, we can always yank him back." He smiled at me. I couldn't tell if the idea appealed to him.

Green sighed and reluctantly agreed to let me have my way.

"Don't look so bothered," I said to Green. "I've given you the best present you'll ever get. If you pull this off, you'll be a shoo-in for governor—or at least mayor."

"And what will you get out of this?"

"I'll look after myself."

"I think that's what worries me."

I grinned at him. It didn't seem to make him less worried.

I asked him if he wanted to discuss this all afternoon, or did he want to start getting things moving.

I parted from Burroughs and Green. We made arrangements to coordinate activities when the fireworks started.

TWENTY-SIX

I drove around a while just to make sure I wasn't being followed, but Burroughs and Green seemed to be playing straight. I went back to the motel, called somebody I knew at the phone company, and got a number that was otherwise unlisted. I then made a call I had been looking forward to for some time.

The voice that answered the phone was the same one that had called me about Stubby Argyll.

"Harve?" I said. "Is this Harvey Millicent?"

"Who is this?" The voice sounded annoyed.

"This is Sam Hunter, Domingo."

"Yeah? So?"

"So I want to talk."

"You got nothing to say to me."

"I want out. You win." I tried to sound scared and beaten.

He laughed. "Of course I've won. I'd won before it even started, but you were too stupid to know that, so I had to show you." His voice grew hard. "Why are you calling?"

"Like I said, I want out. Things are too hot for me here. I want to get away."

"So? Go."

"I need some money."

He laughed again. "And you think I'm going to give it to you? Why should I?"

"I've been beaten. I admit it. But I can still be a nuisance. I don't want to get picked up by the cops—we're not on very good terms—but if I am, I'll talk. I'll talk loud enough and long enough, and maybe somebody'll listen. You don't own everybody. In the long run it probably won't make any difference, but you never know, it might be awkward for you. You don't need that, especially since the Medco thing is

179

coming along so nicely. Give me some money and I'll disappear. I want to."

There was silence for a moment.

"How much are you thinking about?"

"Ten K and I'm gone."

"You overestimate your nuisance value. I'll give you five."

"Come on, I need more than that." I tried to sound desperate.

"Five. And be glad I'm feeling generous."

"Okay. But I want it now. I want to get away tomorrow."

"You're fucking right you'll go tomorrow. Come up in half an hour. I want to see if you look as dumb as you act."

"No tricks?"

He laughed and hung up.

I had wondered how I was going to get into his house, but he had made it easy. Overconfidence will do it every time.

I dug out the gun I had taken from Faro and taped it to the side of my leg just above my ankle. I had to figure they wouldn't frisk me too carefully, and even if they found the gun, I hoped it wouldn't make much difference to what I had in mind. To increase my chances, I put my own weapon in a holster that attached to my belt in the back. I pulled my shirt out so it covered the gun, and put on a jacket.

I went over one of the canyons, took some back roads, and pulled up in front of Casa Domingo in just over half an hour. I sat in the car a minute to get myself into the part I was going to play. It wasn't going to be easy to resist the temptation to blow a hole through the guy, but it was necessary if my plan was going to work.

I shambled up the long curving drive, trying to look like I was busted and beaten. I was coiled tight inside, not from nervousness, but from anticipation, and I had to keep it from showing so that Domingo wouldn't get tipped off that his house was about to come tumbling down.

I pressed the door bell and heard the chimes play what I recognized as the first few notes of the theme song of his old television show. He probably thought that was really nifty.

The door was pulled open wide, and the space was entirely filled with the towering bulk of Mountain Cyclone. He looked even uglier than before.

He looked at me with his little pig eyes for a long time and then turned sideways to let me in. Even that didn't leave much space, but I squeezed by.

We stood in the entry hall looking at one another. The monster gurgled something that sounded like "Hold out your arms." I obliged, and he ran two hands that were the size of Smithfield hams over my chest and under my arms.

"Watch it, I'm ticklish," I said.

He made a sound like a hippo wallowing in the mud, and ran his hands around my waist. He snorted derisively when he found the gun, and roughly pulled it from the holster, nearly lifting me off the floor. He made another gurgling sound that I took to signify amusement and dropped my gun in his pocket. And that was that. Frisk over. They'll do it every time. I loved it.

He motioned with a thumb like a large zucchini squash that I was to precede him. We walked to the back of the house to the large room I had seen the night before. In the doorway, Mountain gave me a gentle push that sent me flying into the room.

I whirled around, but Mountain was gone and I was alone. They couldn't have made it easier for me. I looked around the room and sat down on the large overstuffed sofa. I was still alone. A couple of quick movements and I had gotten the gun off my leg and buried under the thick cushions. I didn't know what I was going to do with it, if anything, but I figured I could use all the edge I could get when the final scene was played.

It was a comfortable room and a large one, taking up most of the width of the house. It was done in shades of rich brown and deep red. The furnishings were not new, but were of the kind of high quality that mellows and improves with use. Antique Persian rugs covered the pegged wooden floor and even older Peruvian weavings hung on the walls. An odd feature was that part of the wall opposite the glass back wall was covered with floor to ceiling drapes. I wondered what was behind the covering, but I didn't want to be caught snooping around, and I remained seated.

In one of the side walls there was a door that was half open. Originally it would have been a closet, but the opening was blocked with a huge steel door that must have led to a walk-in vault. It looked to be too elaborate an arrangement for storing his expensive cigars, so it must be where Domingo kept his "sensitive" materials.

Domingo kept me waiting a long time, obviously trying to rattle me, but I just relaxed and thought about what was going to happen in a couple of hours.

Finally Domingo strolled in, his fat cigar preceding him by eight inches. He was wearing a greenish brown terry jump suit which, with his plump body, made him resemble a furry New Zealand kiwi fruit. He stood in front of me, legs apart, heavy lips curled in a sneer around his cigar, and looked me over. I tried to appear uneasy.

"You're a fucking, cheap, stupid bum," he said.

"I'm pleased to meet you as well," I said.

"You were expecting an embrace and a kiss on both cheeks, punk? I leave that to Mountain. Shall I call Mountain?"

I hastily waved off the suggestion with what I hoped was suitable anxiety.

"Good choice," he sneered. "Mountain's embraces tend to flatten things, and his kisses might very well tear off both your ears."

"I've seen samples of his work."

"Yeah, I guess you have." He laughed. "Must have been real pretty. Sorry I missed it."

"I can understand the others, but why was my secretary killed?"

"It was a lesson. I guess you learned it. Besides, I have to let Mountain have some fun every once in a while. He's hard to handle if I don't. He just loves to tear apart pretty girls. I find it a wasteful habit, but what is one to do?" He shrugged.

My hand slipped under the seat and touched the gun. It was all I could do to keep from opening up on him.

"Did Mountain also do the others?" I tried to keep my voice even.

"Why do you want to know?"

"It's not important," I shrugged. "Some of them were my friends."

"It figures you'd have friends like that." He stared at me for a while. "No, Mountain didn't do them all. Only your girl and that old guy."

"Stubby Argyll."

"Yeah, him. I don't know what a guy that old was doing

still working. He shoulda been in some retirement home."
The fat man laughed briefly. "I guess you can say he is
now. . . . Mountain spotted him coming out of Medco late at
night and figured he must have seen the late shift at work.
There was no choice but to take care of him. Mountain
wanted to do it his own way, but I made him fix it like an
accident. Mountain wasn't happy about that. He likes the
personal touch."

"An old-fashioned craftsman," I said.

"He likes his work."

"What about Watkins?"

"Christ, that dummy! Tried to bust Medco singlehanded,
like he was in the movies. But Ratchitt was onto him and took
him out. He gets enough of the profits, he has to do some of
the work. Besides, I don't much care about offing cops."

"So you let a cop do it."

"He didn't mind."

"What'd he do, drug Watkins so he'd write the note?"

"Oh, so *you* found it?"

"Yeah."

"I wondered what happened to it. I thought Ratchitt had
screwed up. He's been nervous lately."

"He's got a lot of financial responsibilities."

"He is fond of spending money," Domingo chuckled. "I
give him plenty, but he earns it."

"Then who did Faro? You or Lascar?"

"Lascar? That turkey. He's a big disappointment to me.
Thinks he's Mr. Sophisticated. He doesn't know it, but he's
through. . . . No, when my people doublecross me, I like to
take them out myself. Of course, Mountain helped a little. It
was something to see, Hunter. Faro was still alive when I
soaked him with gasoline and tossed the match. I usually
don't care that much for bonfires, but this one was nice.
There's a lesson in that for you, punk. You try to burn me,
and that's exactly what'll happen to you."

I shifted uneasily in my seat and tried to sound nervous.
"Thanks for the advice. Now, if you'll just give me my
money, I'll go."

"In a minute, punk. Mountain likes breaking things; I like
seeing punks like you squirm. Come here. I want to show you
something."

He walked across to the closed drapes and I followed. He

pulled something and the drapes opened, revealing a wall of glass behind which was a terrarium. At first I saw only a lush tangle of tropical plants, but then I started to pick out the black and green and speckled shapes that were coiled around the branches and hidden under leaves.

"Snakes," Domingo said.

"I noticed."

"But not just any snakes. Poisonous snakes. Some of the most deadly in the world. See those large gray ones there? They're black mambas, some of the largest poisonous snakes in the world, and the quickest. Their bite is nearly always fatal unless treated immediately. One of the specimens I have is probably the largest one in captivity, and it has enough venom in it to kill several men. And that little brown one under the leaf. That's a saw-scaled viper. It causes massive hemorrhaging. Death can follow quickly. I've got snakes from all over the world, and I've gotten them to live together without destroying each other. It's kind of a hobby of mine."

"They make nice pets. Do they curl up at the foot of your bed? Or do you take them for walks in the park?"

He continued as though I hadn't spoken. "They're fascinating creatures. They're just about the most deadly animals on earth, but they're not really vicious. They're quite passive, in fact. All they want is to be left alone, and if they're not disturbed, they don't care what goes on. But as soon as they are bothered, as soon as something intrudes upon their privacy, they strike immediately and with total force until the intruder bothers them no more. . . . Hunter, punks like you could learn about the world from observing these snakes."

"I don't get many reptiles for clients."

He sadly shook his head. "I mean there are people like these snakes, Hunter, and if you step too close to them, you are made to regret it. If you are to survive, you must learn to recognize them and stay as far away from them as you can. You and your friends did not do this, Hunter, and you have paid the price."

He reached into his breast pocket and pulled out a packet of money. He was about to hand it to me when he hesitated.

"You know, Hunter, I'm still wondering why I'm giving you this money instead of killing you. I do not think the black mamba would understand."

"You're giving me the money because I may have left a

letter behind telling everything I know about you. That letter combined with my death would be far more trouble for you than me alive and out of town."

"Did you leave such a letter, Hunter?"

"I did. And if I don't personally pick it up in one hour, it'll be opened. Then somebody else will know about you. . . . Look, I told you and I meant it. I don't want any more trouble. All I want is to get out of town, out of your life, away from all this. Give me the money, and I'll be gone tomorrow."

"I know you'll be gone tomorrow. Because if you're not, you'll be dead tomorrow, letter or no letter."

He handed me the money. There were fifty one-hundred-dollar bills. I put them in my pocket.

"Okay, that's that," I said as though I was relieved.

Domingo blew some smoke in my face. "You really are a cheap punk, Hunter, settling for five Gs. It would have been worth a hell of a lot more to get you out of my hair, but you're just a nickel-and-dime wise guy who comes on strong but scares easy. You want to play with the big boys, but you'll always be small time. Now get out of here."

I walked across the room and stopped at the door. "Your man took my gun. Can I get it back?"

He snorted disgustedly. "Outside."

Mountain was waiting for me and trailed me down the hall. I opened the door, stepped outside, and held out my hand. Mountain motioned that I should keep walking. He threw the gun about thirty yards over my head.

I was grinning to myself as I picked it up. The next eighteen hours or so would be a positive pleasure.

TWENTY-SEVEN

I called Green. He said everything was going perfectly and they were going to hit Venus Films in two hours. He sounded like a hound on the scent of a fox. I urged him not to fuck it up. He didn't appreciate the advice and told me that I should keep far away from the action. I didn't appreciate that advice. I had no intention of following it, but I told him not to worry.

I had some time to kill so I went to the Krakatoa restaurant. It's one of the few Indonesian places in town, and while it's not great, when you feel like Indonesian-style noodles it can be pretty good. Honoring its name, they served a huge cone-shaped pile of noodles that was volcanically hot. The side dish of chile sambal that I poured onto the noodles was nearly strong enough to dissolve the bowl it was in. The delicate, sarong-clad girl who served me couldn't believe what I was doing. She called the rest of the staff out and they stood a discreet distance away as I worked through the heap. They politely applauded when I finished and returned to their respective jobs. After I finished my third Oranjeboom Dutch beer and a couple of smokes, it was time for me to go.

I parked across the street and a little down from Mound of Venus Films. I wasn't there very long before four unmarked cars and a panel truck pulled up, and Burroughs and Green got out, leading more than a dozen cops, half uniformed, half plain clothes. A couple went around the back and the rest burst into the front entrance.

I didn't think it would be a good idea to stick my nose into the operation, but I wanted to know how it would come out. I was sort of dozing in the stifling heat of late afternoon, feeling uncomfortable because I was sticking to the car seat, when I saw somebody coming down the alley next to the building. It was one of the uniformed cops, and he was looking nervously over his shoulder.

He reached the sidewalk, looked both ways, and started walking quickly in my direction. I waited until he passed me. I got out of my car and followed him on my side of the street. He didn't even look around. He reached the gas station on the corner, and when he went toward the phone booth there, I hurried across the street. Shit! I was pretty sure he wasn't ordering in pizza. Fucking incompetents. I told them to make sure the cops they picked were clean and to keep everybody together. Jesus Christ!

He was still dialing when I got to the booth. I yanked open the door, grabbed the receiver from his hand, and pulled the cable out of the box.

"Sorry. This phone's out of service," I said.

"Wha—" he said.

"Who were you calling?"

He didn't answer but started to reach for his gun. The cramped quarters of the phone booth made it awkward for him to unsnap his holster, and I had plenty of opportunity to swing the receiver back and smash it into his mouth. Fragments of teeth and a spray of blood spattered the walls of the booth. He groaned and tipped his head back. I clubbed him in the forehead with all my force, and a couple of times on the back of his head as he sank down. He wasn't moving as he settled into the pile of dog shit that adorned the floor of the phone booth.

I didn't know what it was, but beating the shit out of a dirty cop sure made me feel good. I just hoped that Green hadn't sent him to make the phone call. Fuck it. It was a little late to worry about that.

I took his handcuffs off his belt and secured his wrists behind his back with the chain of the cuffs running around one of the phone booth's metal supports. He'd stay there for a while.

The gas station attendant, an overweight adolescent with "Bob" written above his heart, looked on with mild interest. He shrugged and went back to work.

I went into Venus Films. The outer office was empty except for Green, who was looking through the desk. He wasn't pleased to see me.

"Before you say anything," I said, "did you send one of your men down to the corner to make a phone call?"

"Of course not. No one except Burroughs and myself was to have any outside contact."

"Then one of L.A.'s finest is in a phone booth with his nose buried in a mound of dog shit. He must have slipped or something, because he's all cut and bruised. Funny thing was, as he was falling he managed to handcuff himself to the booth. Damnedest thing I ever saw."

"Is this one of your jokes, Hunter?"

"No. He was about to make a call when he had his accident."

"Lucky accident."

"Wasn't it?" I said sourly. "Shit, Green, what are you doing? Didn't you check out any of these guys?"

"I thought I did. Who was it?"

"Gryffin."

"He was a last-minute replacement."

"Nice going."

"Leave it alone, Hunter." He opened the door to the studio and called out a name that sounded like Purble. In a minute a very young, pink-cheeked, uniformed cop came out and snapped to attention.

"Yes, Chief?" he said.

I looked at Green and rolled my eyes. He rolled his back.

"What do you know about Gryffin?" Green asked.

"Gryffin, Chief?"

"Gryffin. He's in your division."

"I know that, Chief."

"What do you know about him?"

"Nothing, Chief." The cop looked bewildered, but then he probably always looked that way.

"Do you know where he was before?"

"Northern Valley Division, Chief."

"And before that?"

"I don't know, Chief. I think he once said he was down-town. He worked with Ratchitt of Vice, I think he said."

"Nice going, Green," I said, somewhat unnecessarily because Green looked disgusted with himself.

"At least that explains it." Green told the young cop he could go.

"Right, Chief," he said, bringing himself up so straight it

looked like he was trying to propel himself through the ceiling. He did a military turn and went to the door.

Green called after him. "In the future, Purble, please don't call me Chief. I'm not, you know."

"Okay, Chief," the kid said cheerfully as he went out of the room.

"That's good material you got there," I said.

"At least he's clean."

"Only because no one's tried to bribe him with bubble gum."

Green shook his head. "Don't worry. He'll be all right."

"Sure, he's just the kind of sophisticated cop you want to bust prostitution and dope rings. How'd it go?"

"Great so far. We caught them in the middle of filming a scene using four underage girls. You wouldn't believe what they were doing."

"Yeah, I would."

He looked at me. "You probably would. We were lucky to catch them in the act, but even without that, we're finding enough stuff here to put the bosses away for a good long time . . . unless, of course, they cooperate."

"How does that look?"

"Not bad. At least that Monroe guy went pretty limp. There's no fight in him. His mother's another story. Shit. What a nasty old broad. She almost took out one of my men, and she hasn't stopped yelling since we got here. We've had to restrain her. If we keep her away from Monroe, he'll talk pretty quick. We should get enough stuff to break up a big distribution outfit, and the feds will be interested in the out-of-state stuff. This was a good tip, Hunter."

"There's still more to do, you know."

"I know. We'll bring it home." He looked at me for a minute. "Uh, Hunter, thanks for sticking around. If you want, come along tonight."

I went to the door and turned around. "Okay, Chief."

He laughed. "Where are you going?"

"Outside—to make sure no other birds decide to fly."

None did.

It took another two hours for them to wrap up things at the studio. They filled up the truck with boxes of material, and everyone was hustled off to a quiet precinct house where it was hoped everything would remain quiet.

This was one of those operations where the cops watched each other more closely than they watched the prisoners. No one was to use the telephone or to leave the room alone. They even went to piss in pairs.

Green talked to the girls they had picked up. They were twelve to fourteen years old, runaways who had all been on the street for a while. They gave him some good info on the connection between Venus Films and the Black Knight. Promising talent got the chance to move over to the club where the hours were shorter, the work easier, and they were taken care of better. None of the girls seemed to be getting much money for what they were doing, and they were unaware how valuable a commodity they were. When they got older—if they got older—they would probably regret the missed opportunity they had had to score big when they were more than just another piece of twenty-year-old meat on the block. I looked at one of the twelve-year-olds who seemed about as wasted as a thirty-five-year-old hooker-junkie. Her life was essentially finished. That's the way it goes in the big city, folks.

The hours passed slowly until it was time to begin the second phase of the operation. About eleven-thirty the troops started to assemble. More than half were to go with Green to the Black Knight. The rest would go with Burroughs to take out the smack factory. It was planned that the hits would go down simultaneously, and since Medco looked to be a piece of cake, I decided to go with Green.

As usual the house that contained the Black Knight looked deserted, but the Lincolns, Caddies, and assorted expensive sports cars scattered along the street indicated that things were in full swing.

Two cops went to cover the rear door, and the rest moved silently up the walk and stood close to the door out of sight of the spy hole. I knocked on the door.

"This is Sam Hunter," I called. "I've got to see Lascar right away."

The door flew open. Bulldogs I and II had been replaced by III and IV, though it looked like they were wearing the same dinner jackets.

"We been told what to do with—" one of them barked, but he never finished because the side of my hand rammed him in the Adam's apple. He made a noise like "Quah, quah" before he fell over and was grabbed and cuffed by one of the cops.

As soon as Bulldog IV saw what was happening, he started to reach under his jacket, but one of the uniformed cops—Purble, remarkably enough—was through the door and brought his nightstick down hard on the bulldog's elbow. There was a sound of crackling kindling, and the fight kind of went out of the guy. Purble giggled, blushed, and then giggled again.

The cops descended on the lounge, abruptly terminating that evening's performance—"The Rape of the Vestal Virgins." Unfortunately they were not in time to preserve the virtue of the girls in question. But ten minutes wouldn't have made any difference. Ten years, maybe.

The audience was shocked that they were being busted, except for one fat, old, bald bastard seated in a dark corner. A girl was on her knees in front of him with her head buried between his legs. "Just a minute! Just a minute!" he shouted. "I'm almost there. Give me a break, will you? It's the first time in years I've had it up."

I didn't wait around to see if they gave him a break. I led Green and a few cops down the corridor to Lascar's office. We went in without knocking.

Lascar was behind his desk, engrossed in watching a television that was built into a wall cabinet. It wasn't the movie of the week that held his attention, not unless one of the networks had been taken over by an S-M leather freak. A barely pubescent girl, clad only in thigh-high boots complete with spurs, was busily swatting the flabby bare ass of a guy wearing a baseball cap. There was no sound, but he seemed to be shouting encouragement. Abruptly he turned on the girl, pulled her over his knee, and began spanking her. As she squirmed in his lap, a rapturous expression came over his face. The plot wasn't very good, but the performances were strong.

Lascar swiveled in his chair. His look of annoyance changed to incredulity and then fear when he saw the uniforms.

"What the fuck is going on?" he managed to squawk.

"Police," Green said. "You're busted."

"Hey, you're making a big mistake. That's all taken care of."

"Not anymore," Green said.

Lascar's head was twisting around so much he couldn't speak. It looked like he was trying to shake it off his neck. I was standing in the background, but he finally noticed me when his spasm subsided. "Hunter! You're in this? You're a dead man."

I grinned at Lascar, and, following Green's order, he was cuffed and removed. He started to weep like a girl as he was dragged from the room. Tough guy.

I walked over to the TV.

"Shall we see what else is on? This is getting boring."

I turned the dial. The next channel on the closed-circuit television showed an unoccupied room decorated with lots of frills and stuffed animals, like a little girl's room. I turned again, and a couple humping in the missionary position appeared on the screen.

"Hmm. How dull. Must be a rerun," I said, and switched the channel.

A dark-complected man with a hairy, muscular chest appeared.

"Say, that's Rick Stallion!"

That exclamation of surprise came from Purble, who was still in the room. It was, indeed, Rick Stallion, a pop singer whose sexy, super-macho, stud image made middle-aged ladies dampen their drawers. The intricate posture in which he was entangled with a slender young man would not have helped his image.

"What's he doing?" Purble said, open mouthed, and his expression changed from puzzlement to horror as the couple shifted their position. "That's disgusting!" Purble said just before he threw up on the carpet.

"Hardened crew you've got here, Green," I said, but Green was busy issuing orders for his men to grab the occupants of the private rooms.

I watched the action on the TV. It was the funniest show I'd ever seen on the tube.

The net haul included a pair of corporation presidents, a prominent banker, and a municipal judge who had made a name for himself by being tough on pornography and prostitution. He'd probably try to explain that he was in the club doing field research, the asshole.

Everything was under control, but Green had a lot of

tidying up to do. I wanted to get over to Medco and see how things had gone there. Before I left, Green assured me that he'd hold everyone as long as he could. I told him it didn't matter anymore, now that the operation had gone down smoothly, but that Lascar had to be kept on ice for at least twelve hours. He was the only one that could tie me to the raid, and if he did, it would fuck up my plans for the morning. I reminded him about what he was to do if I called him, and he impatiently nodded. He was anxious to start bargaining with the fat asses he'd caught.

Green was humming happily to himself as I left. I was sure he was already seeing beyond the governor's mansion to Washington. He could have it. He wouldn't get my vote, but nobody else would either.

I drove across to Medco. For a change, there was hardly any traffic and I made good time. If everything went as well there as it did at the club, friend Domingo would have a nice surprise in the morning.

I hadn't told Burroughs about Mountain. I wasn't sure why I didn't warn him, but I thought it might tip him to Domingo, and I wanted the man to myself. If Burroughs had run into Mountain, he would really be pissed at me, so I had to hope that the giant hadn't shown up.

Medco was dark and quiet. I saw the unmarked cars parked at the back of the building, and there were no ambulances around, so I figured Mountain hadn't been there.

I went to the side door off the alley. It was being guarded by a cop who recognized me. He said that everything had gone well. I went in and found Burroughs in the lab. The chemists were across the room, cuffed, guarded, and not looking terribly pleased with developments.

Burroughs seemed pretty happy, or as happy as that sour son of a bitch ever got.

"Good tip, Hunter," he said reluctantly.

"These the only ones you found here?" I said, gesturing at the three prisoners.

"Yeah."

"You couldn't have overlooked a guy about seven feet tall? Weighs five hundred pounds and looks like he escaped from a Japanese monster flick?"

"Who's that? You didn't tell me anything about that. What're you trying to pull?"

"Take it easy. He wasn't here. And you could have handled him anyway. He's not nearly as tough as he looks. Cut off his arms and his legs and he's nearly defenseless."

"Hunter!" he growled at me.

I had mixed feelings about Mountain. If the cops had got him, I would have felt more comfortable. On the other hand, he owed me a lot, and I wanted to collect so badly it made my fingers ache.

"How'd it go?" I said.

"Perfect. We caught them making the junk. Quite a setup they had here. There's no question this is the source of all the shit that's been floating around. Christ, they must have processed twenty kilos a week. In a little while there are going to be some mighty unhappy people on the street. Looks like a long, dry summer ahead."

"Have you gone through the company records yet to see how all that extra money was accounted for?"

"Not yet, but we have lots of time. There's only one thing I want to know."

"What's that?"

"Where Acker is."

"Why?"

"He's not at home. I called."

"You called?" I said. Shit.

"Don't worry. I just asked if he was there. Some woman answered. Said she didn't know where he was and she didn't care. She sounded like she meant it."

"She did. That was his wife."

"Oh. I just hope the bastard hasn't skipped."

"Why should he?"

"How the hell should I know? I just want that scumbag." He looked at me curiously. "You wouldn't by any chance know where he is, would you?"

"I might have an idea."

"Well?"

"I'll check it out and let you know."

"Hunter!"

"Stay calm, Burroughs. I haven't let you down yet." If I could manage it, I wanted to see Acker before the cops got him. There were still some loose ends, and I thought I might tie them up easier than the cops. I was also thinking about

Clarissa Acker. If I was going to pull her out, I had to get going.

"All right, Hunter. But remember, you still got a rope attached to you. If you fuck up, it's your ass."

"Your confidence in me is really encouraging," I said as I left the lab.

Christ, I gave Burroughs the biggest score of his life, and he still treated me like I was the enemy. Fuck it. He was right. I was the enemy. I just happened to be on his side for this one.

TWENTY-EIGHT

I figured that there was a good chance that Acker had gone to his private apartment, a rodent returning to his hole. I drove into West L.A. and parked in front of the ten-story building that had about as much architectural interest as a freeway off ramp.

I went into the underground garage, spotted Acker's car, and took the elevator up to the sixth floor. Using the key that had gotten me into the apartment once before, I silently opened the door and went inside.

There were no lights on, and at first I thought that Acker must be asleep. As I became accustomed to the darkness, I noticed there was an odd glow coming from the living room, and I heard a strange giggling sound, a metallic hee-hee-hee from a robot's voice box.

I crossed the small entry hall and looked into the living room. The glow originated from a large TV screen. The giggle came from Simon Acker. He was seated on the couch about five feet from the television. He was leaning forward, his eyes fixed on the screen. He was naked. He was vigorously masturbating, and his penis was large and swollen. Okay.

I turned my attention to the television, which I saw was connected to a video recorder. This was apparently my night for kinky viewing. I saw a man wearing a long cloak that hung open in the front. He was naked underneath the cloak and in a state of arousal. He crossed the room to a young blond girl who was chained to the wall, her arms and legs spread wide. She was naked and looked afraid. The man looked steadily at her and then ran his hands slowly over her body. The girl tried to twist away from his touch, but she was too securely fastened to the wall. He then started to grab and squeeze her with increasing force, pinching her nipples and twisting her breasts. The girl protested, and, even though there was no

196

sound coming from the television, it was obvious that she was pleading with the man. He slapped her hard across the face several times and then dipped his head. The girl screamed in pain as he bit the soft flesh of her breast. At the same time his hand went between her legs and viciously tore at the inside of her thighs. The man was frenzied now, and his hands flew over the girl's body, scratching, digging, pulling at her skin. The girl was screaming frantically, and the man punched at her to quiet her, but she continued to scream. His face contorted with passion and anger. To silence the girl he put his hands around the girl's slender throat and applied pressure. The girl stopped screaming and her eyes grew wide with fear. The man continued to choke her, pressing his penis against her belly as he did so. The girl's eyes turned up in her head and her body sagged. The man continued to throttle her long after she was dead. Finally he ejaculated, his mouth open wide in a triumphant yell. He released his hold on the girl and fell to the floor. There was no doubt this was a snuff film. The real thing.

The quality of the picture was poor, but I recognized the room as one at the Black Knight. I recognized the man as Simon Acker. And I recognized the girl as Linda Perdue, the missing daughter of my friend.

The final piece of the puzzle had fallen into place.

The screen went white as the videotape ran out. Acker's breathing grew harsh and labored. His eyes were tightly shut. His whole body was straining. Finally a gasp of relief escaped from his throat, and his body relaxed as he brought himself to climax.

I felt cold and hard. I was going to enjoy this.

I flicked on the overhead light, revealing the black walls hung with medieval weapons. "What's the second feature?" I said.

Acker whirled around, startled, a frightened weasel in the chicken coop. As soon as he recognized me, though, his composure instantly returned, and he glared at me with those soulless blue eyes.

"I didn't hear you knock," he said, pulling on the heavy, black dressing gown that was next to him on the couch.

"You probably wouldn't have, even if I had knocked. You were too wrapped up in the late show. Interesting bit of tape, that."

"What do you want?"

"You may not believe this, but I'm here to help you."

"I don't, but go ahead."

"About two hours ago Medco was busted. They found the smack factory." I waited for some reaction. There was none. The son of a bitch was hard as ice. "Every cop in the city is looking for you now. By morning, it'll be every cop in the country. You've had it. But I can get you out."

"How and why?"

"The how is easy. False papers. A little bread in the right place. And you're out. Mexico, Brazil, the Caribbean. Wherever looks best. The why is obvious."

"How much?"

"A lot."

"What makes you think I have anything?"

"Anybody producing heroin will have more cash than he could possibly spend. Even after a lot is funneled through the company's books, there'll be buckets of the stuff left over. You've got it stashed somewhere. That's why you can get away. That's why I'll get you away."

"How much?"

"How much you got?"

He stared at me for a minute. "About three hundred grand."

"Is that all?"

He shrugged. "Domingo took a lot, and a lot went into the house and things. I like expensive things. They suit me."

"Where is it?"

"Safe deposit." He named a bank.

"I won't be too hard on you. I want a hundred."

"Too much."

"You've got no choice. I won't bargain."

"All right. A hundred."

"How much cash have you got here?"

"Why?"

"I need money to get things moving, man. Arrangements take dough."

"I've got a couple of thousand."

"Not enough."

He sighed, which was the extent of the emotion he displayed. "Okay. There's about ten thousand."

"Give it to me."

He looked at me with his cold eyes and then went to a cabinet and unlocked it. He took out a thick envelope. He hesitated before he handed it to me. "How do I know I can trust you?"

"You have no choice. Besides, one phone call and I cancel your ticket. I haven't made that call. With a hundred K coming, I won't."

He handed me the envelope and I put it in my pocket.

"Now some information," I said.

"Why?"

"Call it professional curiosity. I'm tired of chasing shadows. . . . Who was the girl?"

"How do I know? Just some tramp. She was nothing. A whore. She only existed to provide me with pleasure."

"And you killed her?"

"So what? Her death was the only significant thing in her life. It provided me with pleasure, and thus her existence had meaning."

"That's a tough way to get meaning."

"It is more than most people get. Most people are only robots, things, machines. They exist only to serve those of us who are set apart." His eyes were staring at some unseen thing far away. "We can do with them whatever we want. We have that privilege by right of our superiority, by right of our power, by right of our needs. They understood that in the Middle Ages. That girl only existed to serve my needs. I have The Power."

"Did you get off on it?" I sneered at him.

He looked at me with contempt. "You can never understand. You are one of them. You try to pull me down to your level, but you cannot. Because I am set apart. She gave me pleasure. And she continues to give me pleasure. She still lives—there, on the tape—and in my mind. The experience is still there. She will never die. By using her, I have made her immortal. I have The Power."

The man was fucking crazy, but he would pay. I owed my friend at least that much.

"Unfortunately," I said, "this is not the Middle Ages, you're not a feudal lord, and murder's a crime."

"We who have The Power can commit no crimes."

"The police may not agree. You did kill someone, and there was a tape of it."

"That is so." He appeared to have returned to normal—whatever that meant with someone like Acker.

"Domingo blackmailed you?"

"In a manner of speaking. He said he had no wish to turn me in to the police, but if he was to do me a favor, I would have to do something for him in return. He asked me what I could do. I had long thought about the potential that existed in the company for the manufacture of illegal drugs, but I was not in a position to implement my ideas. I mentioned my ideas to Domingo, and he was much taken with them."

"I imagine he would be. A licensed drug company producing smack is like having a key to the mint."

"I, too, was sensitive to the financial implications. Too long had I worked for people who were my inferiors. It was not fair. I was being stifled. Great wealth was my right. I needed it to develop my potential."

His eyes were beginning to glaze over, and I didn't want him to get started again on that subject. "But the company wasn't yours at that time. It was about to be taken over by Megaplex."

"That's right. I told Domingo about that. He did not seem too concerned. He's a most remarkable man. He understands power . . . and the needs of power. He said he would investigate. I don't know how he did it, but he stopped the take-over."

"And gave you the money to buy the company?"

"That's right. He wanted it kept in my name. He also made the necessary preparations to begin operations. It took longest to set up a distribution system. He ran the heroin side. I ran the company and fixed the books to absorb the profits. We went into production about a year ago."

"Why do you have a copy of the tape?"

He looked surprised at the question. "I insisted upon it, of course."

"Of course. How nice to have a partner who understands you."

"It has been a most successful arrangement."

"Until tonight."

"Until tonight. Now I must leave." He paused and stared off into the distance before he continued. "That is all right. It will be good to go. It feels right. I would have liked to leave with more, but I will have enough for my purposes. . . . I will go to some Latin American country, I think. They understand there that some men are set apart from others—that power must be exercised. Yes, it will be fine. . . . You will help me, won't you?" He smiled confidently at me.

I smiled back at him. "I'll help you—right into the slammer."

His smile faded. "What do you mean? You agreed—"

"Too bad. You see, I don't really give a shit about the heroin operation. I think it's a dirty way to make money, but I'm used to dirt."

"Then what—"

"It's the girl. The girl you killed. The girl whose death gave you pleasure. The girl whose name you don't know. Her name is Linda Perdue. She's the daughter of a friend of mine. She's the reason I'm going to bring you down."

"I do not understand. She was nothing. She was a tramp. She probably would have been dead now anyway."

"She was the daughter of my friend."

"Do you want more money—money to give to your friend?"

"I should take all of your money, and then still turn you in, but I won't. I'll just turn you in. And I'll feel good doing it."

Acker's mask of icy control cracked. His face contorted into a grimace of anger and ferocious hatred. Foaming saliva appeared at the edges of his mouth. "You're all the same," he screamed, his pale blue eyes rolling in their sockets. "All the same! You try to bring me down because I am too great. But you cannot do it. I have The Power, and The Power is supreme." He ran to the wall and pulled the four-foot-long broadsword from its cradle. Oh, shit. Holding the heavy weapon overhead with both hands, he ran at me. "You will pay the price! All my enemies will pay, and you will be first."

I could have pulled my gun and plugged him cold, but I didn't. It would have been too easy, too impersonal. I wanted Acker's blood, but I wanted to taste it. I wanted to hurt him in a way that he would feel the pain for the rest of his life. This was for Linda . . . and for me.

The sword came down toward me with enough force to split me in half, but it was slow and I easily stepped aside. The sword hit an end table, splintering it. The weapon was sharp, all right.

I looked around and spotted something. I grinned. It was a

weapon amusingly called a morning star. Before Acker could
make another charge at me, I removed it from where it hung
on the wall. It was heavy in my hand. The steel ball weighed
about five pounds with two dozen sharp spikes sticking out of
it. It was attached to the wooden handle by a short heavy
chain. Fuck! Acker had gone back seven hundred years and
taken me with him.

I swung the ball in a slow circle, backing Acker away from
me. His eyes gleamed feverishly and his lips were pulled back
in a snarling smile. The goddamn maniac looked pleased that
I too had a weapon.

He circled me cautiously, but the small room did not
provide much space to maneuver in. He feinted once and
then slashed at me. I backed up, but tripped over a footstool,
and the blade caught me on the arm, tearing the sleeve of my
jacket but only grazing my skin. At the same time I swung the
mace and it hit him on the side of the upper leg, cutting
through his robe, pulling it open, and digging into his flesh. A
long gash appeared that soon welled up with blood. Acker
looked surprised and put his hand on the wound. His fingers
came up red. He uttered that same metallic giggle I heard
when I entered the apartment.

"Blood. Purifying blood," he said, and giggled again.

Suddenly he ran at me, catching me off guard. His leg shot
up and kicked me in the ribs, knocking me off balance. As I
stumbled to the side he closed in on me, preparing to bring
the blade down on my neck. In desperation I yanked the ball
from the floor in an upward arc. It caught him square between
the legs, crushing his testicles and ripping them from his
body. Dark red blood spattered the floor. An animal groan
rose up in his throat. He clutched what was left of his
bleeding balls.

He advanced toward me with the sword held straight out in
front of him, the sharp tip gleaming dully as it approached
me. I tried to back him off by swinging the mace, but he no
longer seemed concerned and moved steadily forward. He
backed me into a corner and was able to keep me there with
quick thrusts of the sword. One thrust caught me in the right
shoulder and sent a shock of pain down my arm, almost
causing me to drop my weapon. I could tell it was not very
deep, but my jacket started to darken with absorbed blood.
Acker's pale eyes narrowed and he giggled again.

"I am The Power," he hissed through labored breaths.

He moved back for a small step and drew in his arms. I could see he was preparing for a final thrust. The point of the blade was aimed at my stomach. The chain on my weapon was not long enough to reach him, and I knew I'd have to time my swing with his lunge if I was to avoid being run through.

Just like a boxer, I kept my eyes fixed on his, hoping they would reveal his intentions a split second before he moved. His eyes darted to the side, I fell to the left just as he came forward, swinging the steel ball with all the force in my arm. The ball went over the out-thrust sword and rose above his head. His forward movement brought him into contact with the ball as it descended. The steel spikes cut into the left side of his head, tearing off the skin from his forehead, the side of his nose, his eye, and most of his cheek. The sword buried itself two inches into the wall as he fell to the floor.

Taking deep breaths, I knelt over him. Half his face was gone, but my blow had not been strong enough to break the bones. He would live, but no amount of surgery would ever make him resemble anything human again. I was satisfied.

I took off my jacket and shirt and examined my shoulder. The cut was not bad and the bleeding had nearly stopped. It should have been looked at, but I didn't want to bother. I went into the bathroom, found some iodine, and poured half a bottle into the wound. That hurt a lot worse than the cut itself.

I got dressed and went back into the living room. Acker was still motionless and would be for a long time to come, but he was is no danger of dying. The blood was still oozing weakly from his groin, and his skull showed whitely through the ragged flesh of his face.

I called and got Green at the Black Knight. He had nothing new to report, but it sounded like he was having a hell of a good time. I told him about the money in Acker's safe deposit box. I told him where he could pick up Acker. I told him he better send an ambulance.

"He's not dead, is he?"

"Hell, no. He'll only wish that he was."

"Hunter, do you intend to go on leaving broken bodies scattered around the city?"

"Not for much longer. But I can't help it if people accidentally do themselves an injury, can I?" There was no reply. "Don't complain. I'm even giving you a bonus with Acker."

"Yeah? What's that?"

"Just about two years ago you had a Jane Doe murder victim. I don't know where the body was found. A fourteen-year-old blond girl. Death by strangulation. The girl's name was Linda Perdue. Her family lives in Eugene, Oregon. If your photos are any good, they'll give you an I.D. If not, the dental records will. Acker killed her at the Black Knight."

"How do you know this?"

"There's a videotape of him doing it. It's in the apartment where you'll find Acker."

"You're shitting me."

"Would I do that?" I tried to sound offended.

"Probably."

"You might be right, but this is on the level. You can see for yourself."

"I intend to. What are you doing now?"

"I thought I'd go home. Have you taken off the pickup order that's out on me?"

"Done."

"And you remember what I want you to say if I call you in the morning?"

"I do. I just wish I knew what you had in mind."

"I wish I did as well. If things go right, though, I'll put the bow on your package, and all your troubles will be over."

He made a skeptical noise as I hung up.

I was starting to feel tired. I took a last, long look at Simon Acker. I felt better.

And then I thought of Clarissa Acker.

I had one more stop to make before I could go home. Time was running out.

I left the lights on and unlocked the door before I shut it behind me. That would save the police the trouble of breaking it down. I shook my head. I must be going soft.

TWENTY-NINE

Considering the total success of the evening, I should have been feeling better as I drove up to the Ackers' Bel Air house, but I wasn't.

Clarissa Acker had wanted me to get her even, and then to get her out. Well, I guessed she was more than even, and, in a way, she was out. But it was hardly done in the way she had expected, and there were going to be repercussions she hadn't counted on. I had no idea how she would react; what continued to surprise me was that it made a difference to me. A big difference. Shit.

I had to ring the doorbell about a dozen times before I heard footsteps coming to the door.

The door opened a crack, and I saw Clarissa Acker looking kind of tousled.

"Hunter!" she said, and let me in.

She wore a loose robe that she held closed at the waist, succeeding in covering very little of what she had. Even half asleep she looked pretty good to me. My throat felt tight, and I didn't know how I was going to do what I had to do.

"What is it? Why are you here?" She sounded puzzled and confused.

Before I could answer, a slender young Mexican padded into the entry hall, clad only in a towel that he held around his waist.

A bitter feeling rose up from my belly and I tasted it in my mouth. Disappointment? Anger? Jealousy? I didn't know what it was, but the strength of the feeling confirmed what I had tried to avoid facing for the last few days: this woman mattered to me.

"Is everything all right? Who is this?" The Mexican tried to sound like he belonged there. He didn't make it.

"It's okay. This is a friend. Go back to the bedroom," she said.

He didn't look too happy about that. He moved out of hearing, but he kept us in sight.

"Gardener?" I said, and she nodded. "Congratulations. You've just joined the beautiful people of Bel Air." It was supposed to be a joke, but even in my ears it sounded all wrong.

She looked at me for a long minute. "Hunter, you're making me feel like I should be apologizing."

Was that what I wanted? Probably, but as soon as she said it, I knew I was wrong. "No, not at all," I said, and I meant it. Fuck the double standard.

She continued to study my face, but I didn't know what she saw there. "Hunter, I think you might be human after all." She smiled. "I'm glad." Her smile faded, however, when she noticed my torn and bloody jacket. "What happened?"

Here it comes.

"Your husband did that. We had a fight."

"What! What happened? You look okay. How does he look?"

Was there any point in trying to be delicate? No. "Half his face is gone and his balls have been ripped off."

Her face went pale beneath her dark tan, and she took a step backward. The news hit her almost like a physical blow, but she struggled to deal with it. "Why?"

"By now the police have arrested your husband for the sex murder of a fourteen-year-old girl. It happened two years ago. Your husband gave me no choice. He tried to kill me."

She looked at me, but didn't say anything. I read a question in her eyes.

I nodded. "Maybe *I* gave *him* no choice. The girl was the daughter of a friend of mine."

"Oh, Hunter!" There was pain and sadness and understanding in her voice. I watched as she thought about what I had told her. She was still shocked, but the shock was no longer at what I had done to her husband, but rather at what he had done. Finally, she looked up at me.

"It's funny," she said. "I can't believe that Simon is a murderer, but at the same time there's something—a part of me—that's not really surprised. I guess I always knew he was sick, but I never wanted to think he could be that sick. I wonder how much I'm responsible for? Probably a lot."

"No! He did it himself, all by himself. He did it because he chose to do it. He wanted to do it. The evil son of a bitch got off on it." I spoke harshly because I wanted her to see it the right way, and fast.

"Oh, Hunter," she said. She came over to me and held me. Her robe opened and I felt her body against mine and her strong fingers digging into my back. The Mexican kid flinched, but he did not move otherwise.

After a moment she stepped back. "Well, I guess I got what I wanted. I won."

"I guess you did."

"Does victory always feel so shitty?"

"Not always, but it always has its price."

"Yeah." She thought for a minute, and then nodded. "I can live with it." She waved her hand at the house. "All this stuff was so important to him, and now he's got nothing, and I've got it all. That's what'll kill him. I guess that's what's known as revenge."

"Not quite."

"What do you mean?"

"Besides being busted for murder, your husband was arrested for manufacturing and selling heroin out of Medco."

"What? Is that true?"

"It's true. They raided Medco tonight. How do you think this house was paid for? Not from a bankrupt pharmaceutical supply company, that's for sure."

"Heroin! Jesus! Hunter, do you have any more surprises for me?"

"One more, I'm afraid. You have to pack your bags and get out of here."

"Why?"

"I figure any minute now this place is going to be crawling with cops. Local narcs, state narcs, federal narcs, the IRS, and maybe a couple of other government agencies."

"What?"

"Don't keep saying 'what.' Get your ass moving. And take

all the money you have around here. And all your jewelry. And anything else that's portable and valuable."

"What for?"

"All this property's going to be seized. Without much trouble the cops'll be able to show Acker's entire income came from the sale of illegal drugs. Beyond the income he declared, there's a large undeclared income for which be owes taxes. The factory, property, bank accounts, and everything else of your husband's will be confiscated or frozen. Maybe one day you'll get some of it back, but it'll be a long time, and there won't be much left."

She looked at me with disbelief. At first I thought she was upset, but then she shrugged and her mouth broadened into a smile. "No more Bel Air rich bitch?"

"No more."

"What a relief!" She laughed. "But why should I go, and why should I take anything?"

"Just because you're no longer a rich bitch is no reason to become stupid. If you're around, you're going to be hassled, and you don't need that, at least not right away. Let things cool down a little. And if you don't take anything, you won't have anything, and, lady, you've got a big bill to settle with me."

She laughed again. It sounded pretty good. "You've really got a lot of class, don't you, Hunter?"

"That's me. And your little friend had better get out of here unless his immigration papers are in order." I called to the kid. "You got your green card?"

He looked at me, and then at her, and then without a word he dropped his towel and ran in the direction of the bedroom. Thirty seconds later I heard a door open and slam shut.

"So much for romance," I said. "He was pretty cute, though."

"Fuck off, Hunter."

She went to pack her things. With the cash in the house, and the jewelry, and the stuff that was easily convertible to cash, it turned out that she'd have a pretty good stake. Not enough to last forever, but enough to set her up fairly well if she was smart, and I figured she'd be smart.

I kept telling myself I wouldn't let her know about the ten thousand I got from Acker, but I knew I'd give it to her in the end. Stubby Argyll would never have understood, but fuck it. If I was going to be stupid, I was going to be stupid.

She didn't even look back as we drove away from the house. It was behind her, and over, and that was that. That was a tough lady.

On the way down the hill, we passed four official-looking government cars going up. Each car was filled with official-looking men.

"It's all yours," Clarissa Acker said quietly.

Tough.

I still had my room at the Love Nest Adult Motel, and I figured that was as good a place as any for her for the night.

"Oh, Hunter, how charming!" she said as I pulled her into the parking space in front of the room. "From Bel Air to the Love Nest in one night. You really did a good job for me."

Yeah, didn't I?

I got her stuff inside and started to leave.

"You're not going to stay?"

I looked at her for a long time. "I can't. I'm expecting somebody to come to my place in the morning." That was true, but was that the real reason?

"Okay," she said.

I went to my car, opened the door, and stopped. All the way to the motel I had been thinking about something, but I hadn't said anything about it. Now was the time, but did I want to do it? Yes? No? Maybe? What if?

Fuck it.

I went back and knocked on the door.

"Look," I said when she opened it, "if everything goes right in the morning, I'm taking off for Mexico for a while. It might be a good idea if you came along."

"What about the authorities? Won't they need to talk to me?"

"Probably . . ." I hesitated. Shit. "But I think I'll need you more."

She looked at me and then smiled. "Okay. I think I'd like that."

"Okay. I'll call you." I turned and then stopped. "Oh, by the way. Don't ask for room service."

"What?"

"Nothing," I laughed.

It was after 4 A.M. With luck I could get a couple hours' sleep before I received an angry visit.

It had been a pretty good night.

I hoped.

THIRTY

I didn't get to sleep very long, and I also didn't sleep very well. Usually there's nothing like giving it good to some assholes to guarantee that you have sweet dreams, but mine were troubled. For the first time in years I saw the face of the Vietnamese girl in Saigon, soft, quiet, and gentle. Then she faded into Maria, happy and laughing and shaking her long dark hair. And then both those faces melded, and they became that of Clarissa Acker, and that face stayed. The eyes showed warmth and strength, understanding and humor, and they scared me.

I woke up wondering what the hell I was doing. I kept trying to tell myself that taking her to Mexico was a mistake, but somehow I wasn't very convincing. Fuck it.

Mexico was a long way away, and I had a lot of other problems to deal with before that one. Who knows? Maybe the decision would be made for me.

I got up earlier than I probably had to, but I wasn't going to face those dreams again, and I wanted to be sure I was ready for what I thought would come down.

It was still quite early, but it was already fucking hot. The radio that was blasting away in the next apartment said the heat wave would continue for at least ten more days and maybe longer. Brown- and black-outs could be expected to continue from the over-use of air conditioners, and acute water shortages were inevitable. Forest fires were engulfing half the state. A crackpot mystical group said the weather was due to L.A.'s bad karma, and would not improve until everyone ate only green leafy vegetables and stopped using underarm deodorants. And that was the news.

I saw that I was covered with sweat. I didn't know if it was from the heat or from anticipation . . . or from something else. Whatever the reason, a cold shower took care of it. In the interests of water conservation, I held it to a quick ten minutes.

In the shower I thought about what I was doing. I mean, I had over fifteen thousand in cash. I could just take off, either by myself or with Clarissa Acker. Why didn't I? I didn't have a good answer, but I knew I had to see things through to the end. I thought maybe it was for Maria and Stubby and Watkins, but I knew it was mainly for myself. Fuck it. I was going to do it, and that was that.

I dried off and pulled on an old pair of pants. I was about to put on a shirt when I got an idea. I got out my gun and checked the load. I was about to snap the barrel shut, but I reconsidered and emptied out the bullets. I reached in the back of my dresser drawer and found the box of ammo with the cut points. I could almost hear my friend in the D.A.'s office groaning to himself. My gun was already strong enough to go through steel, but I figured if I had to use it, I wanted to be sure I made a really big hole. Using dum-dums, you didn't have to be very accurate to do a lot of damage.

I pulled up my trouser leg and taped the gun to my shin. Shit, it worked once. It should work again. A .357 is a bulky weapon, but my pants had wide legs and it didn't show. I didn't bother with a shirt and went to fix breakfast.

I fried up four eggs and smothered them in jalapeño salsa. I used some San Francisco sourdough to soak up all the juices. I was sitting at the table, drinking coffee and waiting.

I was on my third cup and thinking that I might have figured wrong when suddenly an incredibly loud cracking sound shot into the room. This was followed by the hinges of my front door being ripped from the wall and the door itself falling flat into the apartment. Mountain Cyclone walked in over the door, making one of his typical entrances. I dropped my hand to my leg and touched the gun. Just in case.

"You should have knocked," I said.

He made a gurgling noise that sounded like "I did."

"Would you like some coffee," I said, "or would you just like to chew on a cup?"

"We go to Domingo."

"I was just getting ready to leave town. Isn't that what Domingo wanted? Why does he want to see me?" I tried to make it sound good.

"Domingo! Now!" he gurgled. The guy sure had a way with words.

"But what about my plane reservation?"

"Now!" Mountain brought a fist down on an end table, causing the legs to buckle and fly off.

"Hey! Take it easy. That was antique Formica."

He made an impatient growling sound, and his hand went into his pocket and came out pointing a gun at me.

"Okay, okay. I'm coming. Can I put my shirt on first?"

He watched me closely as I took the shirt from the back of a chair where it was hanging and put it on. As far as the big ape was concerned I was unarmed. Slick, Hunter, very slick.

On the way out I propped up the door as best I could, not that I thought it would do any good. With the piranhas that lived in my neighborhood, the apartment would probably be stripped bare by the time I reached the bottom of the stairs. I didn't care. Anything important of mine was well hidden, and the furniture belonged to the apartment, not to me. I was planning on moving anyway, and besides, unless things went right, I might not even be coming back.

We went down to the limo, which seemed to require three parking spaces. Mountain made me drive, keeping his gun fixed on me the whole time. The only sound in the car was the wet, bubbling noise of Mountain breathing.

I parked in Domingo's driveway and was escorted into the big back room. The vault door was open and there were two suitcases sitting on a table. The fat man was in the process of taking things from the vault and putting them in the cases. One case held plastic bags that were full of white powder. The other was filling up with envelopes and folders that appeared to contain documents and photographs.

"Packing a few things for a weekend in the country?" I said.

Domingo looked up at me, his features contorted with an expression of contempt, anger, and hatred. His heavy lips were wrapped around the large cigar stuck in the center of his mouth. It had gone out.

"You stupid schmuck," he said, his heavy jowls shaking. "You thought you were going to be real cute. You thought you would fuck with me. Well, asshole, you can't."

"What are you talking about? I was just about to leave

town when your gorilla here came in my apartment without bothering to open the door. What's going on?"

"Don't try to come on dumber than you are, Hunter. It won't work. As though you didn't know, I was hit last night."

"Yeah, I heard this morning. Too bad." I paused for a second and then looked surprised. "You don't think I had anything to do with that?"

"Nice try, schmuck."

"Hey, you've got it wrong. I swear to you I had nothing to do with it. Man, I wouldn't cross you. No way." At this point Domingo was supposed to ask who would cross him.

"You know, of course, you're dead." He said this as though he were announcing that the tonic water was flat. This interview didn't seem to be going quite the way I had intended, and I started to get genuinely nervous. Mountain was only about two steps away from me, watching closely, and there was no way I could get the gun off my leg. Shit.

"I could have had Mountain finish you in your apartment," he continued, "but I wanted to see it. I guess I'm just a sentimentalist, but I wanted to be there when you were torn limb from limb and spread out thin around the room. You've caused me a lot of trouble, Hunter, but no more."

"You're making a mistake. I—"

"My mistake was in not doing this long ago. Waste him!"

Before I could even react, Mountain had closed the short distance between us. His giant arms went around me, pinning mine to my sides. He pulled me to him in a bear hug, lifting me off the ground. His immense stomach pressed into my rib cage, forcing the air from my lungs. The pressure continued to mount as he applied more force than I thought a human being was capable of. I wouldn't be able to hold out much longer, and desperation must have given me extra strength. I started to squirm in his grasp and managed to pull an arm free. That didn't help any. On the contrary, it served to increase the pressure on my chest. Pain shot through me as I felt several ribs crack. I started to club at his head with overhand blows. I did no damage, but I distracted him enough to get my other arm free. I grabbed and scratched at his face, but he squeezed me all the tighter. I couldn't draw breath. The pain in my chest was incredible. I knew I was very close to passing out or to having my ribs snap completely and pierce my lungs. I summoned my last remaining strength and spread my arms wide. With all my force I brought an open hand down on each of his ears. He bellowed like a wounded buffalo and released me. I fell to the floor and would have liked to lie there for about a year, but I forced myself to scramble away from him. From the way he clutched at his ears and rolled his head, I knew I had succeeded in bursting his eardrums.

I tried to suck in air, but every breath felt like I was taking in fire. My vision was badly blurred and I was seeing double or triple. My whole body was weak and trembling and I was unable to stand up.

Mountain tilted back his head and roared, a cry of pain and rage. He started advancing toward me. I pulled at my pant leg, trying to clear my gun. My fingers would hardly do my bidding. Mountain approached. I got the gun exposed, but I couldn't get the tape free. He was almost upon me when I finally tore it off my shin. He aimed a kick at the gun, but I managed to half fall, half roll away in time. He was a step away from me. I still couldn't see clearly and my hand was shaking so badly I could hardly hold the gun, but I pointed it in his direction and pulled the trigger. The loudness of the explosion and the strong recoil caused the gun to fly from my hand.

I had been trying to hit him in the body but only succeeded in catching his upper arm. The soft bullet hit him. The head opened like a flower. It tore through muscle and cartilage and bone, continually expanding as it traveled. The bullet completely severed the arm above the elbow, and the torn limb was thrown five feet before it hit the floor, still twitching spasmodically like a giant worm.

Mountain looked down, saw the blood streaming out of the wound, saw the shreds of muscle hanging loosely, saw the ragged edge of bone protruding. He didn't scream in pain. He didn't collapse on the floor. He didn't even slow down. The unnatural son of a bitch just grunted as if to say "So that's that," and continued toward me.

I tried to scramble for the gun, but he got to me before I got to it. He bent down and grabbed me around the throat with his remaining hand. The fingers closed below my jaw like a vise. With no more effort than if I had been a rag doll, he picked me up. Blood was still pouring from the stump of his arm, but he lifted me off my feet, straightened his arm, and raised me above the level of his head. I didn't know how long he could hold me there before he was weakened by loss of blood, but I knew I didn't have much longer to go before I was choked to death. I was seeing things through a red haze that was quickly turning to black. My windpipe felt like it was about to collapse.

I made a sudden thrust and jammed my thumbs into the corner of each of his tiny pig eyes. He started to growl. I would have as well, but I couldn't make a sound. He increased the pressure on my throat and jaw. I continued to press as hard as I could on his eyes, even as I was about to pass out. Finally I felt something give beneath my fingers. Warm blood ran over my thumbs and down my wrists. He screamed, and I was dropped to the floor.

He rubbed his one hand over his eyes, smearing blood across his face. He tried to clear his vision, but there was nothing there to clear. One eye was closed tight in pain. The other was only a bright red socket.

He turned his head from side to side, trying to locate me. He roared once again and ran in the direction he thought I was. His aim was pretty good, but I managed to pull myself to one side. As he stepped over me, I stuck a leg up, tripping him. He staggered forward, flailing his arms, trying to regain his balance. His great weight and his momentum carried him forward until he hit the glass wall of the terrarium. The glass was thick, but not thick enough to withstand the force of 500 pounds of madman. Mountain gurgled in panic as the glass broke, cutting him deeply in his thick neck, and he fell into the snake pit. There were lightning flashes of moving color, black and green and striped. The snakes struck repeatedly at the intruder who had shattered their peace. Mountain made several convulsive movements and then lay still. Domingo looked on, unmoving, an expression of mild curiosity on his face.

I crawled over, picked up the gun, and struggled to my feet. Using both hands, I pointed it at him. We stood like that for several minutes. My lungs started to function properly. Strength returned to my muscles and the trembling diminished.

Domingo looked unruffled. He broke the silence. "Very impressive, Hunter. Very impressive. I didn't think anyone could take Mountain, but I guess that none of us are invulnerable. I had thought that I was invulnerable, but I suppose I'm not." He gave a philosophical shrug.

"Look, Domingo," I said and then paused. My voice sounded raspy and harsh, and it hurt when I spoke. I swallowed hard several times to lubricate my throat, and it felt better. "Now that I've got the gun on you, maybe you'll believe me. I didn't set you up." I thought I would give it another try.

"Under the circumstances I have to believe you. But if you weren't the one, who was?" Finally.

"Ratchitt."

"Why would he do that? He stood to lose as much as I. Maybe more, because my resources are greater."

"There was pressure on him. The department was about to come down on him. He had to bargain. He sold you out."

"Possibly. But I don't think it's true."

"We can find out."

"How?"

"I know Green, the assistant D.A. who was behind the raids. We'll call him and I'll ask."

Domingo looked skeptical but finally nodded. "All right. But I'll place the call. Just to be sure I'm talking to the D.A. and not to some friend of yours."

"Go ahead."

He called information and got the number of the District Attorney's office. He had to ask for Green several times as he was transferred. When he got the right connection he handed the phone to me. I held it so Domingo could hear what Green said.

Green and I exchanged a few pleasantries, just like we had arranged, and then he asked me what I wanted.

"I heard about your busy night. Congratulations. That won't hurt your career."

"No, it won't. Things went pretty well."

"How'd you get the information to set it up?"

"It was the result of a long investigation by the police department."

Domingo inhaled sharply.

"Who did it?" I said.

"A lot of people were involved, but it was mainly Detective Thomas Ratchitt of Vice. He set it up. He'll get a commendation and maybe a promotion out of this."

Domingo's face grew dark, his jaws clenched, and he bit through his cigar. He didn't seem to notice that it dropped to the floor. He bought it. But then why shouldn't he? It was coming from the D.A.

I thanked Green, congratulated him again, and told him I'd be in touch as he hung up.

"Convinced?" I said.

"That double-crossing son of a bitch."

"What now?"

"Nothing's changed."

"You were leaving?"

"Yeah. It seemed like a good idea."

"And you were taking your blackmail material and your dope with you?"

"To help me get established again."

"Forty pounds of smack and a suitcase full of incriminating photos should be enough to do that."

"Should be. But I don't see what difference it makes to you. Why bother to convince me about Ratchitt? What's your interest?"

"Couple of things. I'll feel more comfortable if you know that I didn't cross you." He thought about that and nodded. "I'm still hot—too hot. I want to get away. You can help me." He looked steadily at me. "Also, as things have turned out, you've lost your bodyguard. The kind of life you live, you could use one. I might consider taking over, but only if the price was right."

"How much?"

"A piece of the action. I'd want to be partners with you. I'm willing to forget past differences, and I could make an active contribution to the business. . . . It could work out well for both of us."

"It might. It might, indeed. Perhaps I underestimated you." He thought for a minute. "If you were my partner, what do you think is the first thing we should do?"

I didn't hesitate. "Wipe Ratchitt."

"At least we see things the same way, Hunter. The question is, how to do it. He'll be very careful."

"I'll get him up here."

"Do that, if you can. After we deal with that dirty prick, we'll discuss a more permanent arrangement."

I said that was fine with me and went to the telephone. It took a couple of calls before I got Ratchitt. He didn't sound good when he came on.

"This is Hunter. You'd better get up to Domingo's right away. He's about to take off with all the assets of the partnership."

"What!"

"He's making a deal with the D.A. He's turning you in for Watkins's murder and he's going to disappear . . . with lots of stuff that belongs to you."

"How do you know this?"

"I just know it. If you're interested you'd better get up to his house." I hung up.

"Shit, Hunter, was that smart?" the fat man said.

"You want him up here, don't you? How do you expect to get him? 'Mr. Harvey Millicent requests the company of Detective Thomas Ratchitt because he wants to off him?' He'll be up here in no time."

"Yeah, but—"

"Don't worry. I'll take care of him."

I was a little too confident.

Domingo went to pack some clothes and things for his immediate departure. Everything was going according to plan, and I had succeeded in pitting Ratchitt and Domingo against one another. When thieves fall out . . .

A wave of exhaustion washed over me, and I realized how wiped out I was from the fight with Mountain. My legs started to shake again, and I sank heavily into one of the deep armchairs. It felt pretty good. Too good, in fact, because I must have dozed off. The next thing I knew, Ratchitt was standing next to me, his gun pressed against my temple. Shit. This wasn't supposed to happen. My first assignment as Domingo's bodyguard, and I blew it.

I cautiously looked around. One of the glass doors out to the rear yard was open. At least I knew how he came in.

"Don't make any quick moves, Hunter," Ratchitt said. "Nice and easy, pick up your gun by the barrel and hand it to me."

My gun was lying on the arm of the chair. I did as he said.
He looked at the weapon.

"It's a fucking cannon. What are you after? Elephants?"

"Mostly rodents and other vermin."

"Don't get funny." He put his own gun back in his shoulder
holster and kept my .357 trained on me. "Stand up slowly and
spread. I want to see if you've got any surprises hidden on
you."

He frisked me thoroughly, and, when he was through, he
motioned me into the center of the room. This was getting
awkward.

"Hey, Ratchitt, I'm not feeling very good. I've got a few
busted ribs, courtesy of Mountain Cyclone, and maybe some
other broken stuff. Can I sit down, or do you want me to pass
out in the middle of the floor?"

"You can pass out anywhere you fucking well want. But go
ahead, sit down."

I sank gratefully onto the couch. More gratefully than
Ratchitt could realize, because, as I pressed my hand onto a
cushion, I felt the hard shape that told me the gun was still
there. And a good thing, too, the way events were going.

Ratchitt glanced at the body of Mountain but said nothing.
He was far more interested in the two suitcases Domingo had
filled from the vault.

"So he was leaving, the fat bastard," he said to himself.

"He thinks you sold him out."

"Why should he think that? Was that your cute idea?"

"He heard it from Green, the D.A."

"It's not true. I didn't know anything about it until this
morning."

"Then it looks like you're being squeezed from two sides.
The D.A.'s pressing and Domingo's taking off."

"Yeah. He was going to leave me bare, the cocksucker.
Half that stuff should be mine, and I need it. I got a lot of
heavy payments to make."

"Well, you seem to be in a position to get your share," I
said.

"Yeah. But I don't understand why you tipped me."

"Simple. I need help. The cops want to talk to me, but I
don't want to talk to them. I figured if I did you a favor, you
might do one for me."

He considered that and smiled in an unpleasant way. "Hunter, I think I just might do you a big favor," he said in a way that made me think he had a very permanent favor in mind.

Just then Domingo walked in. If he was surprised to see Ratchitt pointing a gun at him, he didn't show it. He nodded his head slightly in greeting.

"Nice of you to stop by," Domingo said.

"It would have been nicer to be invited. It looks like you're going away."

"It seemed like the wise thing to do at this point."

"And it must have looked even better to get away with the whole bundle?"

"You would have gotten your share."

"Naturally." Ratchitt laughed in an ugly way.

"But since you're here, you can take your share now."

"I will. I think I'll take your share as well. What do you say to that?"

"There's not much I can say except that it would be a serious error on your part."

"Well, we all make mistakes. You made your last one. Good-bye, Domingo."

The room was filled with the sound of the gun exploding. The bullet hit Domingo in the middle of his large belly. The entry hole was small, but the exit wound was about the size of a basketball. Most of Domingo's internal organs were propelled out of that hole, splattering obscenely on the wall behind him. The fat man fell to the floor, a thick, red puddle immediately forming around him.

Ratchitt looked at the mess without much interest. "My, my. Dum-dums. Don't you know that's illegal?"

"So are lots of things. You going to bust me?"

"No, Hunter, I'm going to kill you."

"That'll be messy."

"For you, perhaps. Not for me. In fact, it will solve my troubles. You see, I happened to come in here just as you blasted Domingo. I ordered you to drop your gun. You took a shot at me, fortunately missing. I had no choice but to shoot you. I aimed to wound, but in the heat of battle, my aim was off and I killed you. That's the way things go. I'll leave a few bags of heroin around to show what the fight was about. I'll take the rest of the stuff and hide it. I should be a big hero. I got a killer and I broke up a dope ring. In a few months, I'll retire from the force. Between the dope and the blackmail, my retirement should be most pleasant. Perhaps the South of France. What do you think?''

While he had been talking I had worked my hand under the cushion in what I hoped looked like a nervous gesture. I got my hand on the stock and my finger on the trigger. I sure as hell hoped the safety was off.

"The South of France is okay," I said. "I guess this means you won't do me a favor?"

"I'm doing you a big favor, Hunter. I'm ending all your difficulties. . . . Now, I'm afraid I have a lot to do, and we won't be able to talk any longer. I would enjoy using your own gun on you—it makes such a nice large hole—but I'm afraid I will have to use my own."

He transferred my gun to his other hand and reached inside his jacket to his shoulder holster. It was now or never, as they say. I threw myself off the couch, bringing up the gun and firing at the same time. I caught him right beside his nose and saw his face fall apart. He was dead before he dropped.

That was that. And that was a little closer than I liked. The end result was just what I had planned. The way we got there was not quite as smooth as I had intended.

I got up and looked the scene over. Just about perfect. Ratchitt had the right idea; I was only going to change the combination of the players.

I wiped my prints off the gun I held and put it in Domingo's hand. Ratchitt held my gun, which became his weapon when I took the gun from his holster. What we now had was one of those terrible tragedies—a shoot-out with each participant simultaneously killing the other. Mountain was an early casualty of the episode. It wouldn't hold up to a lot of scrutiny, but I was counting on Green to make sure it was accepted at face value.

I called Green. I told him the police department had a new hero. Thomas Ratchitt had single-handedly broken up a heroin ring, killing the big boss in the process. Unfortunately, he, too, had met his death, felled in the line of duty. I gave him the address of Casa Domingo.

"So you've left another two bodies for me to clean up? Is that what you're saying, Hunter?"

"Actually, there's a third body, but I wouldn't worry about it."

"I know you're not worrying. Maybe you should start."

"Look, Green, you couldn't want anything better. A big porno-sex-dope operation has been smashed, a crooked cop has been taken care of, everything holds together, and no one's going to ask embarrassing questions. You're a hero. Enjoy it."

"And what about you?"

"I'll leave your jurisdiction until this settles down. See you around." He started to sputter protests, but I hung up.

I wasn't worried about him. He'd keep me out of it. He had to, or he knew I'd be talking. And if I talked he wouldn't look very good, being an accessory to a whole string of felonies. Yeah, it was okay.

I looked at the two suitcases. I thought about taking some of the heroin but decided against it. Too complicated. Why fuck up a good thing?

Now the suitcase with the blackmail material, that was a different story. You never knew when the assistance of influential friends might be helpful. I snapped the suitcase closed and was about to leave when I remembered something.

I called Adrian Sweet.

"This is Hunter. You remember our deal?"

"Yes?" He sounded hopeful.

"You're off the hook—for good. The club is shut down and the guy blackmailing you is dead."

"Do you mean that?"

"I do. You owe me six grand."

"It'll be a pleasure to pay it. When do you want it?"

"Right now. Bring it to the airport in two hours."

"The airport?"

"Yeah, I'm going to Mexico. I was going to go with a friend, but she can't make it. So I'm going with somebody else. I owe it to both of them." I told him where to meet me and hung up.

I called up Clarissa Acker and told her to get to the airport. That was that.

I picked up the suitcase and started out. I looked back at the room. Yeah, it would play. It would play just fine.

I noticed several of the snakes had found their way out of

the broken cage and were headed toward the open back door. Black mambas loose in Beverly Hills. That should liven things up a bit. I thought about calling somebody to let them know.

I grinned.

Fuck it. I had a plane to catch.